THOMAS W. TALLEY'S
Negro Folk Rhymes

THOMAS W. TALLEY'S
Negro Folk Rhymes

A New, Expanded Edition, with Music

Edited, with an Introduction
and Notes, by Charles K. Wolfe

Music Transcriptions by Bill Ferreira

The University of Tennessee Press   KNOXVILLE

Original edition published and copyrighted in 1922 by The Macmillan Company.
Copyright © 1949 by Thomas W. Talley
New edition copyright © 1991 by Thomasina T. Greene
Introduction, notes, and music transcriptions copyright © 1991
by The University of Tennessee Press / Knoxville.
All Rights Reserved. Manufactured in the United States of America.
First Tennessee Press Edition.

Frontispiece: Thomas W. Talley. Portrait by Wright Studios, Jefferson City, Missouri.
Courtesy of Thomasina Talley Greene.

The paper in this book meets the minimum requirements of the
American National Standard for Permanence of Paper for Printed
Library Materials.   ∞   The binding materials have been chosen
for strength and durability.

Library of Congress Cataloging in Publication Data

Talley, Thomas Washington.
  [Negro folk rhymes]
  Thomas W. Talley's Negro folk rhymes. — A new, expanded ed., with
music / edited, with an introduction and notes by Charles K. Wolfe:
music transcriptions by Bill Ferreira, 1st Tennessee Press ed.
      p.   cm.
  Rev. ed. of: Negro folk rhymes, wise and otherwise. New York:
Macmillan, 1922.
  Includes bibliographical references (p.   ) and indexes.
  ISBN 0-87049-673-5 (cloth: alk. paper)
    1. Folk poetry, American — Afro-American authors.
2. Folk-songs, English — United States.   3. Afro-Americans — Song and music.
4. Afro-Americans — Poetry.   I. Wolfe, Charles K.
II. Ferreira, Bill.   III. Talley, Thomas Washington.
Negro folk rhymes, wise and otherwise.   IV. Title.
PS595.N3T3   1990
782.42162'96073 — dc20   90-12561   CIP

Contents

Introduction to New Edition

by Charles K. Wolfe

In January 1922, Thomas Washington Talley, a black chemistry professor at Fisk University in Nashville, published a book entitled *Negro Folk Rhymes (Wise and Otherwise)*. It contained the lyrics to some 349 folksongs, a handful of musical notations, a 100-page essay by the compiler explaining various aspects of the collection, and a short introduction by Vanderbilt University literature professor Walter Clyde Curry. Most of the rhymes were short, from four to eight lines, and were presented as poetry, with no musical notation. A press release issued with the book claimed, "It is a curious fact that until this very day there has been no publication of any considerable number of the folk rhythms and rhymes of the American Negro. This great lack in the world literature is now supplied in part by a book by Thomas W. Talley." The present volume is a new edition of that work, an edition incorporating additional songs and musical transcriptions not included in the 1922 edition, and featuring headnote annotations for many of the songs and poems.

The first edition of *Negro Folk Rhymes* was published by Macmillan, then and now a major commercial press, and was a success with both scholars and the public. It was widely discussed in the national press, and reviewed even in England and Europe. It was generally hailed as a masterpiece of sorts, the first substantial collection of black non-religious folk music. Both black and white publications praised the book; famed black scholar W. E. B. DuBois lauded it; national magazines showered Talley with offers and compliments. "It seems that this collection of yours is one of the finest contributions not only to folklore but to American literature," wrote the editor of *The World Tomorrow* to Talley.[1] Up until this point, most writing about black folk music had reflected the opinion of Talley's fellow folklorist at Fisk, John Work II, who had said, "Negro folk music is wholly religious." Talley showed that this was nonsense, and that there was a rich, complex folksong culture among blacks, a culture that had little to do with spirituals, jubilee songs, or even the blues.

Suddenly, however, all the excitement about the book died down. A planned companion volume entitled "Negro Folk Myths" never reached publication. Other pioneer collections of black traditional music, such as Dorothy Scarborough's *On the Trail of Negro Folksongs* (1925) and Howard W. Odum and Guy B. Johnson's *Negro Workaday Songs* (1925), appeared on the scene and overshadowed *Negro Folk Rhymes*. The great cultural and commercial fad for the blues developed and began to dominate the way people looked at black secular music. Talley himself seemed to turn his energy to research in chemistry. As a result, his work and his reputation as a folksong collector languished. In recent years, seminal books on blues history by major scholars like Paul Oliver and Bruce Bastin mention Talley only in passing, while Harold Courlander does not mention his name even once in his 1963 book *Negro Folk Music, U.S.A.* Talley does not rate an entry in the prestigious *Grove Dictionary of American Music*, nor does his name appear in the assertive *Encyclopedia of Southern Culture*. *The Journal of American Folklore* mentions his work only once in the centennial index to its first hundred years of publication. Even a 1940s brochure entitled *Music at Fisk*, which was designed as a catalog of the school's accomplishments in that area, fails to mention Talley and his work. In the last twenty years, original editions of *Negro Folk Rhymes* have become expensive collector's items, known and respected by a relative few.

In spite of this neglect, *Negro Folk Rhymes* has considerable significance to students of American music. It was the first attempt to assemble a substantial cross-section of black secular folksong. Modern folk music scholarship is only now beginning to acknowledge an entire body of black rural music, since eclipsed by faddish fascination with blues and spirituals, a body of music that had far-reaching ties to

---

1. Personal correspondence to Talley from Ridgley Torrence, 6 March 1923, in the Talley papers at Fisk University.

vaudeville, minstrel music, white folk and country music, popular music, and even nineteenth-century formal music. Talley's book documents, better than any other effort, this "lost" tradition of rural black music and song.

Negro Folk Rhymes was also the first collection of secular folksongs by a black scholar, and the first by a black scholar born into and raised in the traditional culture he studied. Talley was born near Shelbyville, just south of Nashville, in Middle Tennessee, and he maintained close ties there as he was collecting his material. In fact, the book was one of the first to utilize such a network of informants, and Talley was one of the first to go into the field to seek out material from a cohesive geographical group, and to supplement his collection with his own memories of folksongs he had heard in his childhood from 1870 to 1880. In a more narrow sense, Talley was probably the first scholar, white or black, to do any serious collecting of folksongs in Tennessee. Aside from a few scattered items from East Tennessee published by E. C. Perrow in *The Journal of American Folklore*, the tentative inroads made in the eastern mountains by Cecil Sharp, the handful of blues tunes W. C. Handy was collecting and adapting in Memphis, and the samples included by Emma Bell Miles in her *The Spirit of the Mountains*, little had been done to document the folksong culture of the state that would eventually become the center for southern music.

These facts alone would be sufficient cause for a new edition of *Negro Folk Rhymes*, but there are even more immediate ones. Foremost is our discovery, among Talley's uncataloged papers at Fisk, of a substantial body of material not included in the original edition. This material is of two types. One is a collection of numerous loose sheets of paper that contain handwritten lyrics for some fifty songs, texts that were in some cases sent to Talley by informants. The second is a manuscript notebook entitled "Leading Themes Used in Singing Negro Folk Rhymes." This contains musical transcriptions for some 106 tunes, about 50 of which correspond to texts appearing in the printed volume. Also, recent advances in the study and discography of commercial recordings made in the South in the 1920s and 1930s of traditional songs by both black and white artists have opened up a vast new area of study, and for comparison to Talley texts. By utilizing these advances, as well as the many collections of southern folksong that came after Talley's, one can put many of the Talley songs into broader perspec-

tive and provide headnote annotations for many key items. By adding
to the original edition the new texts and songs found in manuscript,
and by reuniting the musical scores with their original texts, one can
reconstruct, at least partially, the full dimension of Talley's achieve-
ment. Thus the rationale for this new, expanded edition of a classic
collection, and the nature of the expansion; we can but hope that Talley would have approved our decision to make available almost every
item found in his manuscript collection.

What inspired a middle-aged teacher of chemistry to plunge so
wholeheartedly and with such enthusiasm into a subject so novel and
so complex as the study of black folksong? Part of the answer lies in
Talley's own background and his own life history. In a 1942 article for
the distinguished journal *Phylon*, Talley wrote: "I was born and reared
among the Negro masses whose educational equipment consisted
largely of traditions. They planted, cultivated, cooked, ate, and drank
in the traditional way. All men born among such people inherit a love
for the past. . . . Born with such a love, I could not help longing to
see and to know the dim prehistoric past."[2] For Talley, this tradition
started on October 9, 1870, when he was born at Shelbyville, Tennessee,
a town some forty miles south of Nashville which has since become
noted as the center for the Tennessee Walking Horse industry. Thomas
Talley was one of nine surviving children born to Charles Washington
Talley and Lucinda Talley, former slaves in Mississippi who had moved
to Bedford County, near Shelbyville, and bought a hundred acres of
land shortly after the Civil War.

Charles Washington Talley had been a "house servant" during slavery
times and had been educated with his master's children by a private
tutor. During the war, he had served in the Union army, occasionally
dressing in a Confederate uniform to slip back across the lines to visit
Lucinda. Such exploits formed some of the family lore that Thomas
Talley grew up with. So did his family's experiences with the "Night
Riders" after they moved to Tennessee; these terrorists rode through
the Middle Tennessee countryside at night in an effort to intimidate

---

2. Thomas Talley, "The Origin of Negro Traditions," *Phylon* (4th quarter, 1942), 371.

the newly freed blacks who were settling in the area. Charles Washington Talley and his brother protected their homes by sitting in trees at night with shotguns; young Thomas, while only a boy, was assigned the job of sitting under these trees and running home to warn the others if anything happened to his father or uncle.[3]

Though the Talley family was soon well established in Middle Tennessee — several of his father's relatives had bought adjoining farms in Bedford County — they did not have the kind of money to send all their children to school. They zealously encouraged it, though, and about 1882, when Thomas had completed six years of public school, he managed to get a teaching job himself to earn enough money to attend high school at Fisk University. He began matriculating as an undergraduate in 1886. Soon he was drawn into the famous Fisk music program, probably more for recreation than formal study, and by 1888 was performing vocal solos at various university functions.[4] By 1900 he had graduated and had begun a tenure of several years as a teacher in the Shelbyville public school system.

His love of singing and his interest in continuing his formal education soon led him back to Fisk. By all accounts, he was quickly establishing his reputation as a singer; years later, historian W. E. B. DuBois would compare Thomas Talley to singers like Paul Robeson, Marian Anderson, and Roland Hayes and lament that in an earlier generation "great voices such as those belonging to Sissy Dorsey, Alice Mayton and Tom Talley went unnoticed in the world at large."[5] On October 16, 1890, he left Nashville to go on tour with a Fisk group called The New Jubilee Singers, in which he sang bass. The idea behind the tour was to raise money to build a new theological seminary at the school; for three months the singers traveled around New England, appearing (among other places) at the annual meeting of the American Missionary Association in Connecticut. Unlike earlier tours of Fisk

---

3. Sonoma Talley, "Thomas Washington Talley," unpublished manuscript, in the Talley papers at Fisk University.

4. Much of this early detail comes from the files of Nashville's black newspaper, *The Globe*, and I am indebted to researcher Doug Seroff for providing me with key citations.

5. *Amsterdam News*, 13 July 1940.

singers, though, this one was not entirely successful; at least, it was not repeated the following year. Talley had received his A.B. from the school in 1890 and almost at once began work on a Master's degree.

In August 1891 he began a series of moves to various black colleges in the South. In August 1981 he took a job at Alcorn A & M College in Mississippi and two years later moved to Florida A & M in Tallahassee; here he taught chemistry, but continued his interest in black folk culture. With each change in venue, the young scholar was able to compare the folk culture he had grown up in with similar folk cultures in other parts of the South. In 1900, when he was thirty, he made yet another move, this time to Tuskegee Institute in southeastern Alabama. His reputation as a teacher was by now obviously rising, and his folklore interest continued as well; during this time he writes of making "a Sociological Investigation for Tuskegee Institute, which carried me into a remote district in the Black Belt of Alabama." In 1903 he was able to finally return to Fisk on a full-time basis and was hailed by then-President Merrill as "a genius at teaching." His apprenticeship was complete; he was a skilled and experienced teacher, and he had started to understand the problems blacks were experiencing and the techniques they were acquiring as they began to make tentative inroads into the study of their own traditional culture.

Throughout his peregrinations, Talley had maintained close ties with Fisk and with his jubilee singing mentor, the famous Ella Sheppard Moore. In August 1893, just before the start of the fall college term, he joined a Fisk mixed quartet which performed at the African Congress meeting in Chicago, and in October he returned to Nashville to take part in a concert given at Fisk. He would have had to come from Talahassee, where he was then teaching, for the concert — a testimony to his interest in music. Of more personal import was his meeting, while at Florida A & M, a young woman named Ellen Eunice Roberts, from nearby Jacksonville. After a courtship, the pair were married on August 28, 1899 — a union that would last until her death in 1939.

From 1905 until 1920 Talley settled into a routine of teaching chemistry, biology, and science at Fisk. He and Ellen started their family; their first daughter, Sonoma Carolyn, was born in 1904; their second, Thomasina, came along in 1914. Talley continued his involvement in the university's music activities and with the Fisk Union Church. During this time, though, he came into contact with several people who were, like him, interested in the roots of the music he sang with various Fisk groups. Having finished his doctorate at Walden University (then associated with Nashville's Meharry Medical College), he spent two postgraduate summers, 1914 and 1916, at Harvard. He went there to further his knowledge of science, but the Harvard of this era was the Harvard of Child, Kittredge, and Lomax, the Harvard that had, in the words of D. K. Wilgus, become "the unofficial center of folksong study."[6] It is hard to imagine that Talley was not in some ways impressed by the pioneering work in folksong collection that was going on there and by the fact that the nation's most prestigious university saw nothing wrong with its faculty studying and publishing information about the same kinds of songs Talley had heard as a youth.

Other influences were closer to home. One was his colleague at Fisk, John Work II. Work was at Fisk from 1897 to 1923, and while there assisted his brother Frederick in compiling a number of paperback collections of jubilee and gospel songs. In 1915, Work published a hardback collection and study, *Folk Songs of the American Negro*. In this latter work, he asserted that the only black folk music of worth was religious music—the kind of jubilee songs and spirituals featured by the Fisk Jubilee Singers. He emphasized "the paucity and utter worthlessness of . . . secular songs," and concluded that "we may justly state that the Negro folk music is wholly religious."[7] It is easy to imagine Talley, recalling his own childhood in rural Tennessee, responding to such statements as a challenge. He knew first hand dozens of the secular songs from the rural black tradition—and knew that many could rival religious songs in their history and complexity. Yet he also sensed that his interest in these songs was unusual for the time. "I have felt for some time that I have seen outlines of the past unrecognized by my fellow travellers," he would write twenty years later.[8] By the end of World War I, he was starting to collect the songs and rhymes that his colleague thought of such dubious value.

---

6. *Anglo-American Folksong Scholarship Since 1898* (New Brunswick, N.J.: Rutgers University Press, 1959), 174.

7. Work II, 27.

8. *Phylon* (1942), 371.

Talley went about his collecting in a variety of ways. His daughter Thomasina recalls that he went into the countryside actively seeking texts, much in the same way Cecil Sharp was doing three hundred miles to the east. There is also evidence that he could recall many songs from his own childhood, and from the singing of his father, mother, and his considerable extended family in the Bedford County area. He was around fifty when be began to compile these songs and rhymes in earnest—an impressive time span from which to draw. He also had behind him some twenty-five years' teaching experience, fifteen of it in Middle Tennessee, and this provided him with a network of former students and colleagues, many in ideal positions to help him find material. Typical of these contacts was a former student named Joe H. Bishop, teacher in a rural school in Belfast, Marshall County, south of Shelbyville. In a 1920 letter preserved in the Talley files, Bishop wrote: "I have enclosed a few lines, I think, of what you want. If these are all right, I will send you more at an early day. Excuse the writing; you know how it is in a rural school where children are talking." Other correspondents sent Talley more texts; some are on the lined paper of children's tablets, written in the wavering, infirm hand of older informants; others are written on good stationery in a handwriting that reflects classes in formal penmanship. Other correspondents, unsure of what exactly Talley was seeking, sent in riddles, proverbs, superstitions, and autograph album verses. He even collected from his colleagues at Fisk; a couple of songs, he noted in his manuscripts, came from Mrs. John Work—the wife of the man who had so disparaged secular songs. Working in the late teens and early 1920s, Talley was able to, in theory, tap the memories of people who grew up before the Civil War and who recalled an entire era of black culture that later scholars could only explore at second or third hand. At least one of the Talley songs, "Master Is Six Feet One Way," may well date from as far back as colonial times.

Unfortunately, songs Talley received from his network of former students and friends did not come with music, and in many cases his busy teaching schedule prevented him from traveling around to collect the music. When he could, though, he eagerly transcribed the music to songs he found, writing them in a small music notebook which he labeled "Leading Themes of Negro Folk Rhymes." Over one hundred songs eventually made their way into this notebook. In some cases, when he already had the texts written down, he simply sketched the melody and identified it by title; in other cases, he sketched in words under the melody lines. He was a careful musician, occasionally changing the key of a song, occasionally crossing out a transcription and redoing it on another page. His time and meter were invariably accurate, and only his lack of tempo indication for tunes renders his transcription work inferior to others of the day. In one perceptive note, not included in the 1922 edition, he apologized for a transcription by saying: "I have written this note as G# through the song because that is the best of which the Caucasian scale will admit. In the melody as sung by the antebellum Negro, the technically scientific G♭ was the note used—a note lower in pitch and giving an impression of sorrow. The other Negro intervals were also just a little different but it cannot be shown on our musical scale." This awareness of the difficulty of transcribing African-American traditional or vernacular music with standard European notation was decades ahead of its time. Only now are musicologists and historians widely accepting this view.

The song texts themselves Talley eventually copied into two 8½-by-11 looseleaf notebook binders. He grouped them into categories—the same ones that would be used in the later published edition—added explanatory footnotes to some, and regularized the dialectical spelling. According to the family, Talley was quite defensive about this latter point; he felt it was very important to maintain a "true record of the language" used by the ex-slaves who sang the songs and recited the poems in the collection. In using the strong phonetic reproduction of dialect, Talley was setting the stage for later collectors of black folksongs, including Scarborough, Odum and Johnson, and Newman I. White. When he submitted the manuscript to Macmillan, Talley made a special point of addressing the issue of the orthography; "the rhymes may need critical examination to determine the accuracy and consistency in the dialect and spelling," he wrote. Yet a comparison of the handwritten manuscript with the printed version reveals that the editors at Macmillan were impressed enough—or intimidated enough—to make very few changes.

Talley also created his own titles for the poems and songs, since very few of the pieces had any well-entrenched traditional titles. Some readers, noting the stilted formality of the titles, which often ignored the dialectical spelling of the text, have surmised that Talley submitted only texts to his editor at Macmillan, and that some effete eastern copyeditor provided the titles. This was not so, however; the titles were indeed Talley's and were part of the original manuscript. Some were oddly inappropriate or even misleading; the title "A Day's Happiness" is used for a rollicking version of "Turkey in the Straw"; the familiar "Look Down That Lonesome Road" is disguised under the title "Mourning Slave Fiancees." Later published collections of similar songs would adopt a first-line index for their work, but, again, since Talley was one of the first to create such a collection, he had no models to follow. (A first-line index has been added to the present edition.)

Talley had less luck with his musical notations. In the final published edition, he was able to include the music for only four of the songs ("Jaybird," "An Opossum Hunt," "Baa Baa Black Sheep," and "Frog Went A-Courting"). These melodies were taken from his music notebook, the "Leading Themes" notebook. In his concluding essay, "A Study in Negro Folk Rhymes," he included seven other musical examples, four of them for wordless songs; none of these was taken from the notebook. Yet his notebook included music for some 106 songs, about half of which match texts in the printed edition. Others not in the printed edition but in the notebook have full or partial texts written in under the music. Certainly Talley was ahead of his time in recognizing the importance of collecting music as well as texts, as the very existence of the notebook proves. There is also little doubt that he saw his collection as actually one of songs rather than of spoken rhymes. He wrote at the start of his "Study": "A few of the Rhymes bear the mark of a somewhat recent date of composition. The majority of them, however, were sung by Negro fathers and mothers in the dark days of American slavery to their children. . . . The little songs were similar in structure to the Jubilee Songs, also of Negro Folk origin." Even Walter Clyde Curry, the Vanderbilt Shakespeare scholar who penned the introduction to the first edition of *Negro Folk Rhymes*, and who might be expected to emphasize the texts, repeatedly refers to the pieces as "folk-songs." Most of the reviewers of the book saw it as a collection of songs.

Why, then, did not Talley include more of his music in the original edition? Did his publisher feel it was too expensive? Did Talley feel it would be a more acceptable volume if it was presented as folk poetry? We do not have clear answers to these questions. If Talley took as a precedent John Work's 1915 book *Folk Songs of the American Negro*, the product of a senior Fisk colleague, he would have found rather little music. Nor is there a great amount of musical notation in Odum and Johnson's *Negro Workaday Songs*, published three years after Talley's book. Yet the earlier collections of religious songs by the Work Brothers, the series of folk music books done by Schirmer, and the emerging publications of Cecil Sharp all were on the scene, and all contained musical notation. The fact that Talley included no music in the manuscript notebooks of the texts—apparently the acutal notebooks he sent off to Macmillan—suggests that he himself made the decision not to include the music. His teaching load at Fisk was not light, and he was here working outside his formal teaching discipline of chemistry and science; perhaps he simply did not have enough time to deal with the musical notation.

In late 1921, Talley submitted his final copy to Macmillan. He had earlier sent a draft of the manuscript, which included most of the rhymes but only the first half of the "Study." Macmillan had encouraged him to finish the essay and accepted the final product with very little editing or change. With some fanfare, the book was issued in January 1922. The rhymes, said Macmillan's publicity department, "taken as a body are the record of the Negro slave told by the slave himself; they "sparkle with pure, clean wit and humor." The *Nashville Globe*, the community's black newspaper, announced the publication with a headline that read: "Nashville man forges to front as author—Gets big send off from populace." "Professor Talley's book and magnificent volume is the first of its kind," concluded the story.

During the next six months, *Negro Folk Rhymes* was reviewed widely, both in the United States and abroad. Reviewers for southern magazines and newspapers lauded the book for its nostalgic appeal. "Many who read this book will call to mind some song that was a part of his childhood," wrote the reviewer for the *Norfolk* [Virginia] *Ledger-Dispatch*; "Those in the South who were familiar with many of the songs and ballads from childhood will be delighted to see them in printed form," said the *Dallas Morning News*; "Every Southerner will find in the book rhymes and songs he has heard many times," said the *Southern Agriculturalist*.[9] The New York papers generally reviewed the volume as a book of poetry, sometimes including it under the "Poetry" column. "A gap in American literature has been filled," said the *New York Evening Post*. The *New York Evening Mail* saw it as "folk poetry" and spent most of its long review quoting excerpts. "A most valuable contribution to the history of rhythm," concluded *The Bookman*, "as well as a book of what should prove popular verse."

Other reviewers quite properly related the collection to music. A perceptive review in the *London Times Literary Supplement*, later reprinted in the *Fisk University News*, emphasized Talley's comments about banjo, fiddle, quill, and triangle music, and related the rhymes in the book to "the popularity of jazz music." An early review in the *Nashville Tennessean* described the pieces as "homely songs of the day's work" and "jilting dance tunes formed to the tune of a banjo"; the reviewer concluded that "Negro music is thought by certain critics to be the foundation of an ultimate school of American music." The music trade publication *Billboard* noted the book and concluded, "Composers, producers, etc. will find a wealth of suggestion within its covers." Some reviewers even managed to relate the book to the then-infant field of folklore studies. Virginia McCormick, "Literary Editor" of the *Norfolk* [Virginia] *Ledger-Dispatch*, placed Talley in the company of "Child, Kittredge, and Louise Pound" as a collector of songs; the *Nashville Banner* related him to Joel Chandler Harris; *The Crisis* asserted that the book was more important to sociologists than to students of literature; and *The Spectator* hailed it as "a distinct contribution to folklore."

As glowing reviews continued to appear in the national press, in England, even in the Netherlands, Talley, at age fifty-two, found himself becoming a national celebrity. A magazine called *The World Tomorrow*, planning a special issue on "economic problems of blacks," asked for some unpublished songs from Talley's collection. Robert Kerlin sought permission to reprint some of the *Folk Rhymes* in a book he was preparing called *An Anthology of Negro Poetry*. Florence Hudson Botsford invited Talley to contribute a song to her collection, *Folk Songs of Many Peoples*,

---

9. This and other reviews are quoted from scrapbooks in the Talley papers at Fisk.

and he sent her an original composition called "Behold That Star" (cf. below). Locally, the Fisk Club of Memphis staged a recitation program in which different members selected a poem from the book and "declaimed" it. (One of the pieces chosen was "How to Get to Glory Land," the famous stanza better known as "The Talking Blues.") During all the excitement, Talley selected a number of the songs in the "Leading Themes" notebook and sent them to his older daughter, Sonoma, then studying in New York at Julliard. Both he and Sonoma had met the noted composer and arranger Harry T. Burleigh, who was working in New York at the time as a music editor at Ricordi. Talley was hopeful that Sonoma might be able to use the songs in recitals, and that Burleigh might be able to arrange or publish some of them.

Almost at once, Talley set to work on a follow-up volume. This new book would collect black folk narratives—what Talley called in one place "Negro folk myths" and what he eventually came to call "Negro Traditions." According to the family, Talley did not go out and actively collect these tales to the extent that he did with the rhymes. "Many of them he remembered as stories told to him by his parents or relatives when he was a little boy," says daughter Thomasina Greene. In many of the stories, Talley took from his music notebook songs— music and words—and inserted them at appropriate places in the text. (Some of these songs appear in the "Additional Songs" section of this edition.) Throughout 1922 and 1923 he worked on this manuscript, which eventually grew to more than five hundred pages and included some fifteen lengthy stories. Had this manuscript reached the national market, it might well have solidified Talley's reputation as the nation's leading black folklorist and established his ideas on collecting and study, which were generations ahead of their time. Unfortunately, it did not; it languished in manuscript for another twenty years, until Talley's retirement, when he made another effort to publish it. That, too, failed, and only in the last year has the book been finally scheduled for publication (by the University of Tennessee Press).

In the meantime, in the late 1920s, Talley turned his attention to his other career, that of a senior professor in chemistry and science at Fisk, and of a distinguished educator. In 1926 he was selected by Governor Austin Peay as a delegate to a major national conference of black educators; in 1928 and 1929 he attended summer sessions at the University of Chicago, eventually finishing a degree at Chicago, and doing a dissertation entitled "Theories Relating to the Constitution of the Boron Hydrides" (1931). In 1929 he also published an article in *The Morehouse Journal of Science* entitled "A Systematic Chronology of Creation."

His personal and family life continued to be filled with music. He managed to send both of his daughters, Sonoma and Thomasina, to Julliard; both had careers on the concert stage, and both eventually won reputations as music teachers and performers. As a singer himself, Talley was active in the Mozart Society at Fisk and conducted the Fisk Choir for several seasons. He was a member of the Fisk Union Church and was for many years a deacon there. His rising reputation attracted other job offers, including the presidency at Florida A & M and the chairmanship of the chemistry department at Howard. These he rejected, out of devotion to Fisk. Disenchanted with the records of both major political parties on civil rights, he voted consistently for Eugene V. Debs and the Socialist Party ticket.

Talley was sixty-one years old in 1931, when he completed his dissertation at Chicago—a time when many teachers consider retirement. Talley was far from ready to quit, however; in fact, seven years later, when Fisk tried to force him to retire, he protested vigorously—both at the retirement in general and the amount of his retirement benefits. Famed educator W. E. B. DuBois, who had become a friend of the family, even intervened on Talley's behalf, asking Fisk to reconsider. In January 1939, Talley filed a lawsuit against Fisk in the matter and won a settlement. He returned to teaching during the 1940–41 school year. When he did retire the next year, he applied (unsuccessfully) for a Guggenheim fellowship, published a long article about his "Negro Traditions" in the distinguished journal *Phylon*, and by 1943 had moved to Jefferson City, Missouri. There his daughter Thomasina, who had established herself as a concert pianist, had married Lorenzo J. Greene, a Howard university graduate who became an early leader of the civil rights movement in the Midwest, and an authority on the history of blacks in America.

During the war, Talley did classified work for the War Department; he returned to Nashville during this time and began working on a book-length manuscript entitled "A New Concept of the Magnetic

Atom." During his latter years, he seemed to view this as his life's work and he produced several drafts of it. It had little to do with folklore. He continued to compose music and completed a mass which was never published. His song "Behold That Star" entered the Christmas music repertoire and was widely reprinted in anthologies. In the early 1970s, the piece was performed on a national broadcast by Leonard Bernstein and the New York Philharmonic, with Leontyne Price singing. By this time the song had become so pervasive that Talley's name had been detatched from it, and Bernstein announced that he regretted that he did not know who had composed the song.

Talley died on July 14, 1952. He had had a stroke in the mid-1940s and then developed cancer, for which he volunteered to be treated with an experimental process involving radioactive gold. In a eulogy for him at Fisk, Professor A. A. Taylor said, "Essentially a teacher, Professor Talley had the outlook and the native or acquired equipment of the sciences, and the humanistic qualities of the poet, or the singer and interpretator of song." He served Fisk "as a teacher, a scientist, a musician, as a folklorist, as a bulwark of the Fisk Union Church, and in carrying forward the banner of Fisk, he has contributed to the advancement of the human race." In the 1960s, Fisk recognized his achievements by naming their new science building after him.

Even if Talley had wanted to, it would have been almost impossible for him to have annotated his collection when he was assembling it in 1920 and 1921. Cecil Sharp's standard collection, *English Folk Songs from the Southern Appalachians*, was still being transcribed and was ten years away from publication. Frank C. Brown had been collecting materials in North Carolina since 1912, but in 1922 he was only beginning to approach publishers about it, not dreaming that its eventual publication was decades away. Dorothy Scarborough and Howard Odum had not published any of the material that would appear in their major books in 1925, though Odum had published two small collections of secular black songs in the *Journal of American Folklore* in 1911. No one as yet took the infant phonograph record industry seriously enough to compile even basic checklists of material being recorded, nor had the record industry yet begun to record traditional performers to any appreciable extent. About the only published collections of black folksongs Talley had at hand were various anthologies of religious songs; even the pioneering booklets by Natalie Curtis-Burlin (*Negro Folk-Songs*, 1918–19) were devoted primarily to religious songs.

To complicate matters further, Talley was collecting material from a bewildering variety of sources, including some that even modern folk scholarship has not yet come to grips with. There were familiar ballads and lyrics, such as "John Henry," "Frog Went A-Courtin,'" and "Old Section Boss." But there were also a large number of play-party songs and children's jump-rope rhymes. There were minstrel songs which had gone into tradition from the pre–Civil War era, when many were published in cheap "songsters" such as *The Negro Singer's Own Book* (1846) — songsters which have yet to be fully studied and indexed even today. There were songs from the late nineteenth-century popular stage, and old pop sheet music hits like "Carve Dat Possum" (1906) and "When I Had But Fifty Cents." There were fiddle and banjo tunes, full of floating verses and indeterminate form, which were in some cases only incidental to the instrumental music. There were parodies, autograph album verses, toasts, blessings, even riddles in verse. Among the most intriguing items were oral versions of nineteenth-century printed poems by formal dialect poets such as Irwin Russell, pieces which got into black traditions as oral recitations. It is to Talley's everlasting credit that he did not pass judgment on any of these categories, to determine that one type of material was "more suitable" as folksong than another. He might not have been able to identify every source, but he sensed the importance of fully representing the repertoire of his informants in all its richness and diversity. In the end, his most important legacy to us might be the way in which he revealed to us the full complexity of black secular folk music at the dawn of the twentieth century.

Most of Talley's songs apparently came from the rural Middle Tennessee area south of Nashville. Though this area today does not have a black population to compare with the one in the southwestern Tennessee counties, around Memphis and Jackson, things were somewhat different in Talley's day. The standard stereotyped view of Tennessee music sees Memphis and the western counties, with their large black population, as the home of the blues, while Middle Tennessee and Nashville are considered the center of white country music. Yet the 1910 census, the last census before the state's folk music felt the impact of mass media like radio and records, shows demographics somewhat different from today's. First of all, Memphis and Nashville were far closer in population in 1910: Memphis was 131,000 and Nashville was 110,000. Second, they were far closer to each other in the percentage of blacks in each city: Memphis was 39 percent black, Nashville was 36 percent black. Third, there were two rural regions of black concentration. One was the West Tennessee area long recognized as a population center where some counties had over 50 percent black population. But the other was an area not as well recognized: a crescent running roughly from northwest to southeast, directly bisecting Nashville's Davidson County and including Talley's home base of Bedford County. Within this broad basin of fertile flatlands and gentle rolling hills, black populations often ran as high as 25 to 37 percent — in contrast to less than 12 percent in counties to the east, and in counties west of Dickson County.

While this area certainly generated a number of blues musicians, it never saw anything approaching the huge blues flowering of Memphis and West Tennessee. Very few of the items Talley collected look or sound like blues. One reason was that he was mining the pre-blues era, before artists like W. C. Handy, Ma Raney, and Bessie Smith had made the form almost synonymous with black music. Much of the music from this region and this time was what black Grand Ole Opry star DeFord Bailey called "black hillbilly music."[10] Bailey, who grew up just a few miles from where Talley did, came from a family that played fiddle and banjo music, not blues; it was a music similar to, though not identical to, the kind of Anglo-American fiddle and banjo music that gave rise to country and bluegrass. There is a growing body of evidence to suggest that it was this music, not blues or gospel or jazz, that was the dominant form of nineteenth-century black secular music in Middle Tennessee. Dozens of early written accounts describe various forms of black string band music featuring fiddles and banjoes from the 1840s to the present,[11] and research by this writer has traced at least twenty black "hillbilly" bands active from the 1920s

10. Personal interview with DeFord Bailey at his home in Nashville, 13 July 1974.

11. For samples of early references, see Dena J. Epstein, *Sinful Tunes and Spirituals* (Urbana: The University of Illinois Press, 1977).

to the 1960s in this Middle Tennessee region. Just why there was such a concentration of this music in Middle Tennessee is beyond the scope of this introduction, but it is worth noting that the music has been shamefully neglected by historians and folklorists. One reason was that the big commercial record companies of the 1920s, almost from the very moment they began to record southern musicians, segregated the music into two artificial genres of "blues" and "old time music." Into the former category (and record release series) went all black performers; into the latter went all whites. Black fiddlers and banjo players and songsters violated these sterotypes, so the companies by and large ignored them. Only a handful of recordings — probably no more than seventy — were made in the 1920s of black string band music; young black musicians quickly learned that the way to get to the mass media was through one of the accepted forms of blues or gospel. The older purveyors of black string band music dropped further and further from public view, plying their trade at local community dances, at family reunions, and on the comfort of their own back porches.

Talley was very much aware of this tradition. In addition to the overwhelming evidence of the song texts themselves, there is Talley's long analytical essay which includes, among other things, a wealth of first-hand accounts of pre-blues music. These include detailed descriptions of dancing games he remembered as a child in the 1870s and observed in later settings at the turn of the century. He offers descriptions of dance steps, and of "patting," and even includes some musical notation. He writes vivid and detailed descriptions of quill and triangle playing, perhaps the best accounts of such in print, and presents careful drawings of quill sets and transcriptions of tunes. He examines field hollers and street calls, again adding musical notations. He explains the prevalence of black fiddle and banjo music, and how it is related to some of the lyrics he includes. He says of the song "Devilish Pigs," for instance: "It was the banjo and fiddle productions of this kind of rhyme that made the old time Negro banjo picker and fiddler famous. . . . The compositions were comparatively long. From one to four lines of a Negro folk rhyme were sung to the opening measures of the instrumental composition; then followed the longer and remaining part of the composition, instruments alone." Talley was never able to capture on phonograph record the kind of music he described and documented, but a year after he retired from Fisk, in

1942, his colleague John Work III managed to preserve on disc a sample of such music from two Middle Tennessee older black musicians, Nathan Frazier and Frank Patterson; their recordings, now preserved in the Library of Congress, contain music that almost exactly fits Talley's descriptions of "Devilish Pigs."[12]

The same Middle Tennessee area that gave Talley so many examples of "black hillbilly music" was also a fertile source for much early country music. Barely four years after Talley's book was published, WSM radio in Nashville announced it would be starting a regular Saturday night "barn dance" program—a program that a few years later would be redubbed "The Grand Ole Opry." Though the show would be filled with professional entertainers by the mid-1930s, for its first ten years it was staffed by performers who had their music roots in the rural Middle Tennessee countryside. The repertoires of these performers, such as Uncle Dave Macon, Obed Pickard, Sam and Kirk McGee, Jack Jackson, Dr. Humphrey Bate, and Robert Lunn, are fairly well preserved through phonograph records and songbooks. What is surprising is the number of their songs that also appear in Talley's collection. In the course of annotating individual songs in *Negro Folk Rhymes*, we found more than eighty-five items that appeared in the repertoires (i.e., in early commercial recordings or artists songbooks) of early country artists of the period 1925–35. More intensive research later may yield even more overlaps. Uncle Dave Macon, the banjo-playing songster from Rutherford County, adjoining Talley's Bedford County, used an especially high number of Talley songs. A possible reason for this may be that Macon was one of the older Opry and record stars from the 1920s; he was born in 1870, the same year as Talley, and drew on the same late-nineteenth-century music era for his songs.

What all this suggests is that there might have been a common repertoire shared by both rural whites and blacks in nineteenth-century rural Tennessee. It included banjo tunes, fiddle tunes, old play-party songs, minstrel songs, genuine folk ballads, old pop songs, and vaudeville songs. To be sure, each group probably performed this reper-

---

12. Some of the Frazier-Patterson recordings from 1942, as well as other samples of black Tennessee string bands, have been reissued on a Rounder LP entitled *Altamont: Black String Band Music from Tennessee* (1989).

toire in distinct styles, but in an age before "blues" and "hillbilly" music segregated it, the rural music of the upland South might have had much more in common than in difference. Talley's may well be one of our best, and earliest, glimpses of this phenomenon. We have only in the last decade begun to seriously compare the repertoires of early country music recordings and blues, as well as their commercial songbook counterparts, with the songs collected from oral tradition by folklorists and historians. As this develops, the true relationship between black and white traditions may become much clearer, and the significance of Talley's collection may loom even larger.

Unlike his white counterparts, who were collecting song texts that often had generic cohesiveness, Talley had to struggle with songs that had often rather vague lyrics and others that were comprised of floating stanzas. He often solved this by treating stanzas that were sometimes merged with other similar stanzas as individual elements. For instance, his two pieces called "Frightened Away from a Chicken-Roost" (No. 126) and "How to Get to Glory Land" (No. 128) were often combined in the well-known "Talking Blues" text. In annotating these stanzas, or groups of stanzas, we have followed the lead of the only other compiler of a large number of black secular folksong texts, Newman I. White (*American Negro Folk Songs*): we have offered analogues to individual stanzas rather than composite text as a whole.

There were similar problems with classification. Talley divided his rhymes into thirteen sections, the most important of which were "Dance Rhymes," "Play Rhymes," "Pastime Rhymes," "Nursery Rhymes," and a series centering on love, courtship, and marriage. In an index at the end of the volume, he offered a "Comparative Study Index" that used a slightly different set of categories. There were "Love Songs," "Dance Songs," "Animal and Nature Lore," "Nursery Rhymes," "Charms and Superstitions," "Hunting Songs," "Drinking Songs," "Wise and Gnomic Sayings," "Harvest Songs" (containing a single song), "Biblical and Religious Themes" (five items), "Play Songs," and a very large "Miscellaneous" section. Talley apparently based some of his classifications solely on texts, but he made others on the basis of the social contexts of the songs, using information that he remembered from youth or collected from informants. Since we have very little of this information for the "new," additional songs in this expanded edition, we have not attempted to fit any of them into these categories. Instead, we present them in their own separate section entitled "Additional Songs from Manuscripts."

One could make a lengthy list of highlights in the Talley collection: first publications of songs popular in both black and white traditions, such as "Bile'em Cabbage Down" ("Cooking Dinner") or "Big Ball in Town"; pre–Civil War charms and marriage ceremonies; rare examples of social protest, such as "I'd Rather Be a Nigger Than a Poor White Man" and "Hard Times in Shelbyville Rock Jail"; black antecedents of bluegrass favorites like "Hot Corn, Cold Corn" ("Bring on Your Hot Corn") and "Here, Rattler, Here"; rare black versions of well-known Anglo-American ballads such as "Misery in Arkansas" ("Old Section Boss") and "Frog Went A-Courtin'," as well as rare black songs such as "When I Was a Roustabout" and "Outrunning the Devil." Here are vital early texts of folksong favorites such as "Shortening Bread" ("Salt Rising Bread"), "Cotton Eyed Joe," "My Little Rooster," and "Raise a 'Rucus' Tonight." Then there are the songs that appear to have no folk analogues at all, that appear with virtually no annotation, and that may well be unique to Talley's collection.

The main purpose, however, of this new edition of Thomas Talley's work is not to present a definitive analysis of his collection or its exact role in American vernacular music. It is, rather, to make available to the public and to scholars an important body of traditional materials that has for too long been ignored, misunderstood, or unknown. Working virtually alone, with very little funding or university support, trusting to his own remarkable instincts about folksong and folk tradition, Thomas Talley preserved an almost lost heritage. To say that he was ahead of his time would not do him justice; in some respects, he was ahead of our own time, in his wide vision, his ebullient curiosity, and his unswerving dedication. He was America's first great black folklorist, but more than that, he was one of America's best folklorists. We hope this collection will bear that out.

CHARLES K. WOLFE
MIDDLE TENNESSEE STATE UNIVERSITY
MURFREESBORO, TENNESSEE

Acknowledgments

This book would not have been possible without the generous help and advice of many people. I would like especially to thank Doug Seroff for sharing his vast knowledge of Fisk and its musical heritage; Bill Ferreira for his patient and tireless work in editing and transcribing the music in the Talley notebooks; Bruce Nemerov for sharing his research into the life of Talley's colleague, John Work III; Gerald Davis, for discussing with me his own research into Talley's career; and, for various kindnesses, W. K. McNeil, Kip Lornell, Guthrie Meade, Paul Wells, Paul Oliver, Robert Cogswell, Norm Cohen, Samuel Floyd, and John Hartford. I am grateful to the family of Thomas Talley, especially Mrs. Thomasina Greene, for her permission to undertake this project and for sharing key information and documents about her father. I am grateful too to Ann Allen Shockley and Beth Howse of the Fisk University Library's Special Collections for their assistance in examining the Thomas Talley materials. I must thank Carol Orr of the University of Tennessee Press for her unwavering support of the project. Mrs. Betty Nokes oversaw the preparation of the first-line index and greatly assisted in matters secretarial. My colleagues and administrators of Middle Tennessee State University were, as ever, supportive, and a grant from the Faculty Research Committee allowed me to complete the work sooner than I had envisioned. Last, but by no means least, I am pleased to acknowledge the considerable help of my wife, Mary Dean, in producing and collating an extremely complicated manuscript and working through a vast amount of documents concerning Talley.

CKW

A Note on the Musical Transcriptions

Not a great deal of actual "editing" was required in the preparation of the Talley musical manuscript. Talley was quite meticulous in his transcriptions, and the bulk of the true editing work on my part occurred on those tunes in which the musical arrangements had not been finalized by Talley. In those cases, revisions by Talley himself made the score difficult to read (with notes and bar-lines crossed out, meter and key signatures changed, etc.). It is important to note, however, that this was the case in a small number of the musical examples; most of the musical arrangements were apparently in more "finished" form.

What was a factor in the re-copying of a *majority* of the musical examples was the *size* of the notes in Talley's manuscript. Talley's musical hand was characterized by rather small notes, and it often was hard to differentiate between a note on a line and its neighboring note in a space. In these instances, examination of the remainder of the musical example often clarified these discrepancies. (Often, the same musical phrase would occur elsewhere in the piece, and the notation would be more legible.)

Talley's extensive knowledge of music and musical notation resulted in an overall very understandable score, and what relatively few ambiguities exist are due to non-musical factors: running ink and the previously mentioned revisions.

BILL FERREIRA

Introduction to the Original Edition

by Walter Clyde Curry

Of the making of books by individual authors there is no end; but a cultivated literary taste among the exceptional few has rendered almost impossible the production of genuine folk-songs. The spectacle, therefore, of a homogeneous throng of partly civilized people dancing to the music of crude instruments and evolving out of dance-rhythm a lyrical or narrative utterance in poetic form is sufficiently rare in the nineteenth century to challenge immediate attention. In *Negro Folk Rhymes* is to be found no inconsiderable part of the musical and poetic life-records of a people; the compiler presents an arresting volume which, in addition to being a pioneer and practically unique in its field, is as nearly exhaustive as a sympathetic understanding of the Negro mind, careful research, and labor of love can make it. Professor Talley of Fisk University has spared himself no pains in collecting and piecing together every attainable scrap and fragment of secular rhyme which might help in adequately interpreting the inner life of his own people.

Being the expression of a race in, or just emerging from bondage, these songs may at first seem to some readers trivial and almost wholly devoid of literary merit. In phraseology they may appear crude, lacking in that elegance and finish ordinarily associated with poetic excellence; in imagery, they are at times exceedingly winter-starved, mediocre, common, drab, scarcely ever rising above the unhappy environment of the signers. The outlook upon life and nature is, for the most part, one of imaginative simplicity and child-like naïveté; superstitions crowd in upon a worldly wisdom that is elementary, practical, and obvious; and a warped and crooked human nature, developed and fostered by circumstances, shows frequently through the lines.

What else might be expected? At the time when these rhymes were in process of being created the conditions under which the American Negro lived and labored were not calculated to inspire him with a desire for the highest artistic expression. Restricted, cramped, bound in unwilling servitude, he looked about him in his miserable little world to see whatever of the beautiful or happy he might find; that which he discovered is pathetically slight, but, such as it is, it served to keep alive his stunted artist-soul under the most adverse circumstances. He saw the sweet pinks under a blue sky, or observed the fading violets and the roses that fall, as he passed to a tryst under the oak trees of a forest, and wrought these things into his songs of love and tenderness. Friendless and otherwise without companionship he lived in imagination with the beasts and birds of the great out-of-doors; he knew personally Mr. Coon, Brother Rabbit, Mr. 'Possum and their associates of the wild; Judge Buzzard and Sister Turkey appealed to his fancy as offering material for what he supposed to be poetic treatment. Wherever he might find anything in his lowly position which seemed to him truly useful or beautiful, he seized upon it and wove about it the sweetest song he could sing. The result is not so much poetry of a high order as a valuable illustration of the persistence of artist-impulses even in slavery.

In some of these folk-songs, however, may be found certain qualities which give them dignity and worth. They are, when properly presented, rhythmical to the point of perfection. I myself have heard many of them chanted with and without the accompaniment of clapping hands, stamping feet, and swaying bodies. Unfortunately a large part of their liquid melody and flexibility of movement is lost through confinement in cold print; but when they are heard from a distance on quiet summer nights or clear Southern mornings, even the most fastidious ear is satisfied with the rhythmic pulse of them. That pathos of the Negro character which can never be quite adequately caught in words or transcribed in music is then augmented and intensified by the peculiar quality of the Negro voice, rich in overtones, quavering, weird, cadenced, throbbing with the sufferings of a race. Or perhaps that well-developed sense of humor which has, for more than a century, made ancestral sorrows bearable finds fuller expression in the lilting turn of a note than in the flashes of wit which abundantly enliven the pages of this volume. There is one lyric in particular which, in evident sincerity of feeling, simple and unaffected grace, and regularity of form, appeals to me as having intrinsic literary value:

> She hug' me, an' she kiss' me,
> She wrung my han' an' cried.
> She said I wus de sweetes' thing
> Dat ever lived or died.
>
> She hug' me an' she kiss' me.
> Oh Heaben! De touch o' her han'!
> She said I wus de puttiest thing
> In de shape o' mortal man.
>
> I told her dat I love' her,
> Dat my love wus bed-cord strong;
> Den I axed her w'en she'd have me,
> An' she jes' say, "Go 'long!"

There is also a dramatic quality about many of these rhymes which must not be overlooked. It has long been my observation that the Negro is possessed by nature of considerable, though not as yet highly developed, histrionic ability; he takes delight in acting out in pantomime whatever he may be relating in song or story. It is not surprising, then, to find that the play-rhymes, originating from the "call" and "response," are really little dramas when presented in their proper settings. "Caught By The Witch" would not be ineffective if, on a dark night, it were acted in the vicinity of a graveyard! And one ballad — if I may be permitted to dignify it by that name — called "Promises of Freedom" is characterized by an unadorned narrative style and a dramatic ending which are associated with the best English folk-ballads. The singer tells simply and, one feels, with a grim impersonality of how his mistress promised to set him free; it seemed as if she would never die — but "she's somehow gone"! His master likewise made promises,

> Yes, my ole Mosser promise' me;
> But "his papers" didn't leave me free.
> A dose of pizen he'pped 'im along.
> May de Devil preach 'is funer'l song.

The manner of this conclusion is strikingly like that of the Scottish ballad, "Edward,"

The curse of hell frae me sall ye beir, Mither, Mither,
The curse of hell frae me sall ye beir,
Sic counseils ye gave to me O.

In both a story of cruelty is suggested in a single artistic line and ended with startling, dramatic abruptness.

In fact, these two songs probably had their ultimate origin in not widely dissimilar types of illiterate, unsophisticated human society. Professor Talley's "Study in Negro Folk Rhymes," appended to this volume of songs, is illuminating. One may not be disposed to accept without considerable modification his theories entire; still his account from personal, first-hand knowledge of the beginnings and possible evolution of certain rhymes in this collection is apparently authentic. Here we have again, in the nineteenth century, the record of a singing, dancing people creating by a process approximating communal authorship a mass of verse embodying tribal memories, ancestral superstitions, and racial wisdom handed down from generation to generation through oral tradition. These are genuine folk-songs — lyrics, ballads, rhymes — in which are crystallized the thought and feeling, the universally shared lore of a folk. Recent theorizers on poetic origins who would insist upon individual as opposed to community authorship of certain types of song-narrative might do well to consider Professor Talley's characteristic study. And students of comparative literature who love to recreate the life of a tribe or nation from its song and story will discover in this collection a mine of interesting material.

Fisk University, the center of Negro culture in America, is to be congratulated upon having initiated the gathering and preservation of these relics, a valuable hertiage from the past. Just how important for literature this heritage may prove to be will not appear until this institution — and others with like purposes — has fully developed by cultivation, training, and careful fostering the artistic impulses so abundantly a part of the Negro character. A race which has produced, under the most disheartening conditions, a mass of folk-poetry such as *Negro Folk Rhymes* may be expected to create, with unlimited opportunities for self-development, a literature and a distinctive music of superior quality.

WALTER CLYDE CURRY.
Vanderbilt University,
September 30, 1921.

A Note on Song Annotations

Talley offered annotations for a few songs in his original edition, and I have incorporated these into my headnotes without any editing whatsoever. The references to analogues in both print and on phonograph records are not intended to be exhaustive, but representative. Often other collections mentioned in the headnotes contain extensive histories of the song in question, and rather than repeat these, I have simply referred the reader to them. A list of the references used in the annotations appears at the end of this volume, as well as an explanation of the phonograph record citation system.

CKW

Negro Folk Rhymes

(Wise or Otherwise)

Dance Rhyme Section

I Jonah's Band Party

For other variations, see Courlander, *Negro Folk Music U.S.A.*, 161; White, *American Negro Folk-Songs*, 162–63; and, more recently, Jones and Hawes, *Step It Down*, 131. In the original edition, Talley added the asterisks, explaining: "These are dance steps. For explanation read the Study in Negro Folk Rhymes." (See below, this edition.)

> Setch a kickin' up san'! Jonah's Ban'!
> Setch a kickin' up san'! Jonah's Ban'!
> "Han's up sixteen! Circle to de right!
> We's gwine to git big eatin's here to-night."
>
> Setch a kickin' up san'! Jonah's Ban'!
> Setch a kickin' up san'! Jonah's Ban'!
> "Raise yo' right foot, kick it up high,
> Knock dat * Mobile buck in de eye."
>
> Setch a kickin' up san'! Jonah's Ban'!
> Setch a kickin' up san'! Jonah's Ban'!
> "Stan' up, flat foot, * Jump dem Bars!
> * Karo back'ards lak a train o' kyars."
>
> Setch a kickin' up san'! Jonah's Ban'!
> Setch a kickin' up san'! Jonah's Ban'!
> "Dance 'round, Mistiss, show 'em de p'int;
> Dat Nigger don't know how to * Coonjaint."

2   Love Is Just a Thing of Fancy

Love is jes a thing o' fancy,
Beauty's jes a blossom;
If you wants to git yō' finger bit,
Stick it at a 'possum.

Beauty, it's jes skin deep;
Ugly, it's to de bone.
Beauty, it'll jes fade 'way;
But Ugly'll hōl' 'er own.

3   Still Water Creek

The second stanza, especially, has been widely collected and even appears
in the undated nineteenth-century songster, *Christy's Nigga Songster.* See *Frank
C. Brown Collection* (3:541), White (138), Perrow (135), and others. Title often
given as "Cedar Street" or "Pumpkin Creek" in addition to "Still Water Creek."
See also, regarding the first stanza, popular commercial record by Middle
Tennessee singer Uncle Dave Macon, "Gray Cat on a Tennessee Farm"
(Vocalion 5152, 1927).

'Way down yon'er on Still Water Creek,
I got stalded an' stayed a week.
I see'd Injun Puddin and Punkin pie,
But de black cat stick 'em in de yaller cat's eye.

'Way down yon'er on Still Water Creek,
De Niggers grows up some ten or twelve feet.
Dey goes to bed but dere hain't no use,
Caze deir feet sticks out fer de chickens t' roost.

I got hongry on Still Water Creek,
De mud to de hub an' de hoss britchin weak.
I stewed bullfrog chitlins, baked polecat pie;
If I goes back dar, I shō's gwine to die.

4 'Possum up the Gum Stump

The first two stanzas of this song have been widely collected from both black and white sources. See, for example, Brown (3:207), White (236–38), Scarborough (173), Randolph (2:361), and Lomax and Lomax, *American Ballads and Folk Songs*, p. 238. Often sung to fiddle tunes; cf. the commercial recording by the East Tennessee string band The Hill Billies (Vocalion 5118, 1926). The latter two stanzas, on the other hand, are rather rare.

'Possum up de gum stump,
Dat raccoon in de holler;
Twis' 'im out, an' git 'im down,
An' I'll gin you a half a doller.

'Possum up de gum stump,
Yes, cooney in de holler;
A pretty gal down my house
Jes as fat as she can waller.

'Possum up de gum stump,
His jaws is black an' dirty;
To come an' kiss you, pretty gal,
I'd run lak a goobler tucky.

'Possum up de gum stump,
A good man's hard to fin';
You'd better love me, pretty gal,
You'll git de yudder kin'.

5 Joe and Malinda Jane

Ole Joe jes swore upon 'is life
He'd make Merlindy Jane 'is wife.
W'en she hear 'im up 'is love an' tell,
She jumped in a bar'l o' mussel shell.
She scrape 'er back till de skin come off.
Nex' day she die wid de Whoopin' Cough.

6   Walk, Talk, Chicken with Your Head Pecked!

Rooster fighting, though illegal, continues to be very popular in the Middle Tennessee area Talley came from. This song, seldom collected, appears to celebrate this pastime. The title is echoed in a popular commercial recording by Grand Ole Opry star Little Jimmy Dickens, "Walk, Chicken, Walk" (Columbia 20722, 1950).

> Walk, talk, chicken wid 'yō head pecked!
> You can crow w'en youse been dead.
> Walk, talk, chicken wid yō' head pecked!
> You can hōl' high yō' bloody head.
>
> You's whooped dat Blue Hen's Chicken,
> You's beat 'im at his game.
> If dere's some fedders on him,
> Fer dat you's not to blame.
>
> Walk, talk, chicken wid yō' head pecked!
> You beat ole Johnny Blue!
> Walk, talk, chicken wid yō' head pecked!
> Say: "Cock-a-doo-dle-doo!"

7   Tails

Brown (3:498–99) prints a variant under the title "Lynchburg Town"; see also "The Racoon" in this collection.

> De coon's got a long ringed bushy tail,
> De 'possum's tail is bare;
> Dat rabbit hain't got no tail 'tall,
> 'Cep' a liddle bunch o' hair.
>
> De gobbler's got a big fan tail,
> De pattridge's tail is small;
> Dat peacock's tail 's got great big eyes,
> But dey don't see nothin' 'tall.

8   Captain Dime

The first stanza, sans the "Captain Dime" detail, is common to many of the collected versions of "Old Dan Tucker"; the second stanza is rarer, and shows up in Brown (3:117) in versions from Kentucky and North Carolina.

> Cappun Dime is a fine w'ite man.
> He wash his face in a fry'n' pan,
> He comb his head wid a waggin wheel,
> An' he die wid de toothache in his heel.
>
> Cappun Dime is a mighty fine feller,
> An' he shō' play kyards wid de Niggers in de cellar,
> But he will git drunk, an' he won't smoke a pipe,
> Den he will pull de watermillions 'fore dey gits ripe.

9   Crossing the River

The first two lines of the third stanza are very common in the South and have been collected both in white and black traditions; for citations, see Brown (3:227). The entire third stanza, very similar to that given here, appears in White (297), collected from Alabama about 1916. The first two stanzas are much less common.

> I went down to de river an' I couldn' git 'cross.
> I jumped on er mule an' I thought 'e wus er hoss.
> Dat mule 'e wa'k in an' git mired up in de san';
> You'd oughter see'd dis Nigger make back fer de lan'!
>
> I want to cross de river but I caint git 'cross;
> So I mounted on a ram, fer I thought 'e wus er hoss.
> I plunged him in, but he sorter fail to swim;
> An' I give five dollars fer to git 'im out ag'in.
>
> Yes, I went down to de river an' I couldn' git 'cross,
> So I give a whole dollar fer a ole blin' hoss;
> Den I souzed him in an' he sink 'stead o' swim.
> Do you know I got wet clean to my ole hat brim?

10   T-U-Turkey

T-u, tucky, T-u, ti.
T-u, tucky, buzzard's eye.
T-u, tucky, T-u, ting.
T-u, tucky, buzzard's wing.
Oh, Mistah Washin'ton! Don't whoop me,
Whoop dat Nigger Back 'hind dat tree.

He stole tucky, I didn' steal none.
Go wuk him in de co'n field jes fer fun.

11   Chicken in the Bread Tray

Ira Ford, in his *Traditional Music of America* (36), lists this as a square dance
tune, with the lyrics as "occasional verses" fiddlers sang in calling sets. It
often appears under the title "Granny Will Your Dog Bite?" and has been
collected widely from Mississippi to California. A good sampling of references
appears in Brown (3:205). Ray Browne, in *The Alabama Folk Lyric* (445), notes
that he has heard it often as a banjo tune and that "it seems to be a greater
favorite with Negros than whites." The opening quatrain appears often in
white old-time music recordings of the 1920s.

"Auntie, will yō' dog bite?"—
   "No, Chile! No!"
Chicken in de bread tray
   A makin' up dough.

"Auntie, will yō' broom hit?"—
   "Yes, Chile!" Pop!
Chicken in de bread tray;
   "Flop! Flop! Flop!"

"Auntie, will yō' oven bake?"—
   "Yes. Jes fry!"—
"What's dat chicken good fer?"—
   "Pie! Pie! Pie!"

"Auntie, is yō' pie good?"—
   Good as you could 'spec.'"
Chicken in de bread tray;
   "Peck! Peck! Peck!"

12   Molly Cottontail, or, Graveyard Rabbit

This particular rabbit song — one of dozens in circulation — does not appear in any of the standard collections of black folksong. According to Talley, "leg bail" in line 4 meant "to run away"; "hants" in stanza four referred to "ghosts or spirits"; and the phrase "To give me yo' right hin' foot" (stanza 5) "embraces the old superstition that carrying in one's pocket the right hind foot of a rabbit, which has habitually lived about a cemetery, brings good luck to its possessor."

> Ole Molly Cottontail,
> At night, w'en de moon's pale;
> You don't fail to tu'n tail,
> You always gives me leg bail.
>
> Molly in de Bramble-brier,
> Let me git a little nigher;
> Prickly-pear, it sting lak fire!
> Do please come pick out de brier!
>
> Molly in de pale moonlight,
> Yō' tail is shō a pretty white;
> You takes it fer 'way out'n sight.
> "Molly! Molly! Molly Bright!"
>
> Ole Molly Cottontail,
> You sets up on a rotten rail!
> You tears through de graveyard!
> You makes dem ugly hants wail.
>
> Ole Molly Cottontail,
> Won't you be shore not to fail
> To give me yō' right hīn' foot?
> My luck, it won't be fer sale.

13   Juba

Among the many other citations to this song are: Courlander (192), Nathan (443–46), Scarborough (98–99), White (161–63), and Jones and Hawes (37). Talley also discusses this kind of dance rhyme in his "Study of Negro Folk

Rhymes" (below) and marks in the text the names of specific kind of dance steps. Sadly, no one today is at all clear about what these early steps were like.

> Juba dis, an' Juba dat,
> Juba skin dat Yaller Cat. Juba! Juba!
>
> Juba jump an' Juba sing.
> Juba, cut dat Pigeon's Wing. Juba! Juba!
>
> Juba, kick off Juba's shoe.
> Juba, dance dat Jubal Jew. Juba! Juba!
>
> Juba, whirl dat foot about.
> Juba, blow dat candle out. Juba! Juba!
>
> Juba circle, Raise de Latch.
> Juba do dat Long Dog Scratch. Juba! Juba!

14   On Top of the Pot

> Wild goose gallop an' gander trot;
> Walk about, Mistiss, on top o' de pot!
>
> Hog jowl bilin', an' tunnup greens hot,
> Walk about, Billie, on top o' de pot!
>
> Chitlins, hog years, all on de spot,
> Walk about, ladies, on top o' de pot!

15   Stand Back, Black Man

This piece does not appear in any of the standard collections. Talley appended the following note to it: "In a few places in the South, just following the Civil War, the Mulattoes organized themselves into a little guild known as 'The Blue Vein Circle,' from which those who were black were excluded. This is one of their rhymes."

> *Oh*!   Stan' back, black man,
>   You cain't shine;

Yō' lips is too thick,
An' you hain't my kīn'.

Aw! Git 'way, black man,
You jes haint fine;
I'se done quit foolin'
Wid de nappy-headed kind.

Say? Stan' back, black man!
Cain't you see
Dat a kinky-headed chap
Hain't nothin' side o' me?

16 Negroes Never Die

For songs similar in sentiment (though not variants of this), see White (376–86).

Nigger! Nigger never die!
He gits choked on Chicken pie.
Black face, white shiny eye. Nigger! Nigger!

Nigger! Nigger never knows!
Mashed nose, an' crooked toes;
Dat's de way de Nigger goes. Nigger! Nigger!

Nigger! Nigger always sing;
Jump up, cut de Pidgeon's wing;
Whirl, an' give his feet a fling. Nigger! Nigger!

17 Jawbone

While the jaw bone is a recognized instrument in nineteenth-century black traditional music, the "Jawbone" here probably refers to a stock character in old minstrel shows. Songs similar to this have appeared in sources like *The Negro Minstrel* (Glasgow, 1850), *The Negro Forget-Me-Not Songster* (ca. 1847), and *Christy's Negro Melodies No. 4* (Philadelphia, ca. 1854); headnotes to some of these indicate the song was associated with the "Colored Saboyard" Cool

White on the minstrel stage. See also White (305, 333), and Browne (311–13), who prints versions collected from whites in Alabama in the 1950s. Library of Congress files show pre-1942 recordings from Florida, Missouri, Washington, D.C., and Ohio, and at least one old-time string band, Pope's Arkansas Mountaineers, recorded the tune on commercial discs in the 1920s (Victor 21577, 1928).

> Samson, shout! Samson, moan!
> Samson, bring on yō' Jawbone.
>
> Jawbone, walk! Jawbone, talk!
> Jawbone, eat wid a knife an fo'k.
>
> Walk, Jawbone! Jinny, come alon'!
> Yon'er goes Sally wid de bootees on.
>
> Jawbone, ring! Jawbone, sing!
> Jawbone, kill dat wicked thing.

18   Indian Flea

Not found in most standard collections; possibly of minstrel origin.

> Injun flea, bit my knee;
> Kaze I wouldn' drink ginger tea.
>
> Flea bite hard, flea bite quick;
> Flea bite burn lak dat seed tick.
>
> Hit dat flea, flea not dere.
> I'se so mad I pulls my hair.
>
> I go wild an' fall in de creek.
> To wash 'im off, I'd stay a week.

19 As I Went to Shiloh

As I went down
To Shiloh Town;
I rolled my barrel of Sogrum down.
Dem lasses rolled;
An' de hoops, dey bust;
An' blowed dis Nigger clear to Thundergust!

20 Jump Jim Crow

For background on this well-known minstrel piece, see Lomax and Lomax, *Folk Song U.S.A.*, p. 78 and following. See also Nathan (50–52), White (162–63), Scarborough (127), and, for survival of the piece into the modern era, Jones and Hawes (55).

Git fus upon yō' heel,
An' den upon yō' toe;
An ebry time you tu'n 'round,
You jump Jim Crow.

Now fall upon yō' knees,
Jump up an' bow low;
An' ebry time you tu'n 'round,
You jump Jim Crow.

Put yō' han's upon yō' hips,
Bow low to yō' beau;
An' ebry time you tu'n 'round,
You jump Jim Crow.

21 Jaybird

This song is to be distinguished from the more familiar "Jaybird Died with the Whooping Cough" (cf. below, item 50). Similar texts appear in Scarborough (191–92), Browne (447), and White (243), but none is quite like this. The references to "Br'er Rabbit" suggest some literary influence, and remind us that Talley was a fan of Joel Chandler Harris and even emulates him to some extent in *Negro Traditions* (the manuscript). Note the refrain "I loves dem shorten gals!" which Talley did not include in the original printed text. This is one of the few pieces for which Talley provided music in the original edition. Talley explains the superstition (asterisk) in his "Study" (below).

De Jaybird jump from lim' to lim',
An' he tell Br'er Rabbit to do lak him.
Br'er Rabbit say to de cunnin' elf:
"You jes want me to fall an' kill myself."

   Chorus
   I loves dem shorten gals!
   I loves dem shorten gals!
   Oh, have mercy on my soul!

Dat Jaybird a-settin' on a swingin' lim'.
He wink at me an' I wink at him.
He laugh at me w'en my gun "crack."
It kick me down on de flat o' my back.

Nex' day de Jaybird dance dat lim'.
I grabs my gun fer to shoot at him.
W'en I "crack" down, it split my chin.
"Ole Aggie Cunjer" fly lak sin.

Way down yon'er at de risin' sun,
Jaybird a-talkin' wid a forked tongue.
* He's been down dar whar de bad mens dwell.
"Ole Friday Devil," fare — you — well!

22   Off from Richmond

Music is from "Leading Themes" notebook, #85.

I'se off from Richmon' sooner in de mornin'.
I'se off from Richmon' befō' de break o' day.
I slips off from Mosser widout pass an' warnin'
Fer I mus' see my Donie wharever she may stay.

23   He Is My Horse

Scarborough (162–63) prints a variant of this that she found in an 1867 collection of slave songs, under the title "Charleston Gals."

One day as I wus a-ridin' by,
Said dey: "Ole man, yō' hoss will die" —
    "If he dies, he is my loss;
    An' if he lives, he is my hoss."

Nex' day w'en I come a-ridin' by,
Dey said: "Ole man, yō' hoss may die."—
   "If he dies, I'll tan 'is skin;
   An' if he lives, I'll ride 'im ag'in."

Den ag'in w'en I come a-ridin' by,
Said dey: "Ole man, yō' hoss mought die."—
   "If he dies, I'll eat his co'n;
   An' if he lives, I'll ride 'im on."

24   Judge Buzzard

Talley notes that this rhyme is "one of a kind. In the Negro version of the race between the hare and the tortoise ('rabbit and terrapin'), the tortoise wins not through the hare's going to sleep, but through a gross deception of all concerned, including even the buzzard who acted as Judge. The rhyme is a laugh on 'Jedge Buzzard.' It was commonly repeated to Negro children in olden days when they passed erroneous judgments."

Dere sets Jedge Buzzard on de Bench.
Go tu'n him off wid a monkey wrench!
Jedge Buzzard try Br'er Rabbit's case;
An' he say Br'er Tarepin win dat race.
Here sets Jedge Buzzard on de Bench.
Knock him off wid dat monkey wrench!

25   Sheep and Goat

Stanzas similar to this have been published as early as 1843, in Dan Emmett's minstrel song "Old Dan Tucker." The lyric has also survived in the modern repertoires of Appalachian musicians Doc Watson and fiddler Buddy Thomas.

Sheep an' goat gwine to de paster;
Says de goat to de sheep: "Cain't you walk a liddle faster?"

De sheep says: "I cain't, I'se a liddle too full."
Den de goat say: "You can wid my ho'ns in yō' wool."

But de goat fall down an' skin 'is shin
An' de sheep split 'is lip wide a big broad grin.

26 Jackson, Put That Kettle On!

Talley notes that "Sassfac tea" (line 6) is sassafras tea.

Jackson, put dat kittle on!
Fire, steam dat coffee done!
Day done broke, an' I got to run
Fer to meet my gal by de risin' sun.

My ole Mosser say to me,
Dat I mus' drink sassfac tea;
But Jackson stews dat coffee done,
An' he shō' gits his po'tion: Son!

27 Dinah's Dinner Horn

The first two stanzas here appear in collections of primarily white songs; see Randolph (2:365–66) and Brown (3:543). "Shu't" (stanza 1) is "shirt," and "Poke—sallid" (stanza 7) is "poke sallet," a common southern green.

It's a cōl', frosty mornin',
An' de Niggers goes to wo'k;
Wid deir axes on deir shoulders,
An' widout a bit o' shu't.

Dey's got ole husky ashcake,
Widout a bit o' fat;
An' de white folks'll grumble,
If you eats much o' dat.

I runs down to de henhouse,
An' I falls upon my knees;
It's 'nough to make a rabbit laugh
To hear my tucky sneeze.

I grows up on dem meatskins,
I comes down on a bone;
I hits dat co'n bread fifty licks,
I makes dat butter moan.

It's glory in yō' honor!
An' don't you want to go?
I sholy will be ready
Fer dat dinnah ho'n to blow.

Dat ole bell, it goes "Bangity—bang!"
Fer all dem white folks bo'n.
But I'se not ready fer to go
Till Dinah blows her ho'n.

"Poke—sallid!" "Poke-sallid!"
Dat ole ho'n up an' blow.
Jes think about dem good ole greens!
Say? Don't you want to go?

28   My Mule

Las' Saddy mornin' Mosser said:
"Jump up now, Sambo, out'n bed.
Go saddle dat mule, an' go to town;
An' bring home Mistiss' mornin' gown."

I saddled dat mule to go to town.
I mounted up an' he buck'd me down.
Den I jumped up from out'n de dust,
An' I rid him till I thought he'd bust.

29   Bullfrog Put on the Soldier Clothes

Bullfrog put on de soldier clo's.
He went down yonder fer to shoot at de crows;
Wid a knife an' a fo'k between 'is toes,
An' a white hankcher fer to wipe 'is nose.

Bullfrog put on de soldier clo's.
He's a "dead shore shot," gwineter kill dem crows."
He takes "Pot," an' "Skillet" from de Fiddler's Ball.
Dey're to dance a liddle jig while Jim Crow fall.

Bullfrog put on de soldier clo's.
He went down de river fer to shoot at de crows.
De powder flash, an' de crows fly 'way;
An' de Bullfrog shoot at 'em all nex' day.

30   Sail Away, Ladies

For other versions, see Brown (1:153), Brewer (165), and a 1903 collection by William W. Newell, *Games and Songs of American Children* (170). It appears in a modern collection of African-American songs and games, Jones and Hawes's *Step It Down* (174, as "Horse and Buggy"). The song was very popular with white fiddlers and banjo players in Middle Tennessee; Uncle Dave Macon recorded a vocal version that was very popular (Vocalion 5155, 1927), and Bunt Stephens, Henry Ford's champion fiddler from near Tullahoma, in the same region Talley was from, recorded it as a fiddle solo (Columbia 15701, 1926). Talley's text is somewhat different from Macon's.

Sail away, ladies! Sail away!
Sail away, ladies! Sail away!
Nev' min' what dem white folks say,
May de Mighty bless you. Sail away!

Nev' min' what yo daddy say,
Shake yo liddle foot an' fly away.
Nev' min' if yo' mammy say:
"De Devil'll git you." Sail away!

31   The Banjo Picking

Not found in most of the standard folksong collections, this song is possibly of literary or minstrel origin. The "bones" in stanza 1 were a standard rhythm accompaniment for most minstrel shows and have nothing to do with the "graveyard" reference. Talley noted that, of the five banjo songs mentioned here, "Walk Tom Wilson" and "Dinah's Dinner Ho'n" appear in this collection. "We were unable to find the other three," he concluded. These include "Sweep dat Kittle Wid a Bran' New Broom," which might be related to a tune mid-South fiddlers still play called "New Broom," and "You Cain't Dance Lak ole Zipp Coon," which may or may not be related to the "Zip Coon" family of minstrel songs from the 1840s.

Hush boys! Hush boys! Don't make a noise,
While ole Mosser's sleepin'.
We'll run down de Graveyard, an' take out de bones,
An' have a liddle Banjer pickin'.

I takes my Banjer on a Sunday mornin'.
Dem ladies, dey 'vites me to come.
We slips down de hill an' picks de liddle chune:
"Walk, Tom Wilson Here Afternoon."

"Walk Tom Wilson Here Afternoon";
"You Cain't Dance Lak ole Zipp Coon."
Pick "Dinah's Dinner Ho'n" "Dance 'Round de Room."
"Sweep dat Kittle Wid a Bran' New Broom."

32   Old Molly Hare

This is apparently a minstrel song that went into oral tradition among both
blacks and whites. Brown (3:211–13) contains many references to it, most from
black informants. However, Richardson, in her *American Mountain Songs*, collected from white informants in the mid-1920s, prints a good version (98,
118), and Randolph (2:359) offers a number of Ozarks versions from white
sources. There seems to be little localization of the piece, though a version
does appear in Robert Mason's dissertation on songs of Cannon County (Tennessee), near Talley's native county. Parts of the song appeared in nineteenth-
century minstrel songbooks, such as *The Negro Singer's Own Book* (32). A
number of old-time music artists recorded the piece in the 1920s: Riley Puckett and Clayton McMichen, from north Georgia (Columbia 15295, 1927);
Fiddling Powers and his family, from East Tennessee (Okeh 45268, 1928);
and the Crockett Family, from Kentucky (Brunswick 291, 1928). The music
is #42 in the "Leading Themes" notebook.

Ole Molly har'!
What's you doin' thar?
"I'se settin' in de fence corner, smokin' seegyar."

Ole Molly har'!
What's you doin' thar?
"I'se pickin' out a br'or, settin' on a Pricky-p'ar."

Ole Molly har'!
What's you doin' thar?
"I'se gwine cross de Cotton Patch, hard as I can t'ar."

Molly har' to-day,
So dey all say,
Got her pipe o' clay, jes to smoke de time 'way.

"De dogs say 'boo!'
An' dey barks too.
I hain't got no time fer to talk to you."

33   An Opossum Hunt

Written and performed by black minstrel Sam Lucas about 1870, "An Opossum Hunt" does not appear in many collections of black traditional song, though Odum and Johnson cite it in their 1925 book, *The Negro and His Songs* (240–41). Randolph (2:357) reports that it was often printed in the Hamlin's Wizard Oil Songbooks, printed in the 1890s in Chattanooga, Tennessee. The title usually attached to the song is "Carve Dat Possum," and that is the title used in an influential recording of the piece made by Middle Tennessee singer Uncle Dave Macon in 1927 (Vocalion 5151). Talley provided music in the 1922 edition of *Negro Folk Rhymes*.

Possum meat is good an' sweet   Charve him to de heart,
I always finds it good to eat,   Charve him to de heart,

Chorus
Charve dat possum!
Charve dat possum!
Charve dat possum!
Oh charve 'im to de heart!

My dog tree, I went to see,   Charve him to de heart,
A great big possum up dat tree,   Charve him to de heart,
I retch up an' pull him in,   Charve him to de heart,
Dat ol' possum 'gin to grin,   Charve him to de heart,

(*Chorus*)

I tuck him home an' dressed him off,   Charve him to de heart,
Dat night I laid him in de' fros',   Charve him to de heart,
De way I cooked dat possum sound,   Charve him to de heart,
I fust parboiled, den baked him brown,   Charve him to de heart,
I put sweet taters in de pan,   Charve him to de heart,
'Twus de bigges' eatin' in de lan.'   Charve him to de heart,

(*Chorus*)

34   Devilish Pigs

I have been unable to locate any analogues to this piece. The music is from
the "Leading Themes" notebook, #1.

I wish I had a load o' poles,
To fence my new-groun' lot;
To keep dem liddle bitsy debblish pigs
Frum a-rootin' up all I'se got.

Dey roots my cabbage, roots my co'n;
Dey roots up all my beans.
Dey speilt my fine sweet-tater patch,
An' dey ruint my tunnup greens.

I'se rund dem pigs, an' I'se rund dem pigs.
I'se gittin' mighty hot;
An' one dese days w'en nobody look,
Dey'll root 'round in my pot.

35 Promises of Freedom

The first stanza, at least, is very common in black folksong collections. See Scarborough (164–65, 223–25), White (152), and Brown (3:502–503, 535). Version A is that which originally appeared in the first 1922 edition of *Negro Folk Rhymes*; the B version was sent to Talley by Joe H. Bishop of Belfast, Tennessee, one of Talley's former students, in 1920, and was found in manuscript form in the Talley papers.

A

My ole Mistiss promise me,
W'en she died, she'd set me free.
She lived so long dat 'er head got bal',
An' she give out'n de notion a dyin' at all.

My ole Mistiss say to me:
"Sambo, I'se gwine ter set you free."
But w'en dat head git slick an' bal',
De Lawd couldn' a' kiled 'er wid a big green maul.

My ole Mistiss never die,
Wid 'er nose all hooked an' skin all dry.
But my ole Miss, she's somehow gone,
An' she lef' "Uncle Sambo" a-hillin' up co'n.

Ole Mosser lakwise promise me,
W'en he died, he'd set me free.
But Ole Mosser go an' make his Will
Fer to leave me a-plowin' ole Beck still.

Yest, my ole Mosser promise me;
But "his papers" didn' leave me free.
A dose of pizen he'ped 'im along.
May de Devil preach 'is fūner'l song.

B

My old mistress promised me,
When she died she'd set me free,
She lived so long her head got bald,
I thought she wasn't going to die at all.
We had a silver spade to dig her grave,
A golden chain to let her down,
A Conquer shell to blow her to hell,
Oh old Mistress a long farewell.

36   When My Wife Dies

Numerous black versions of stanzas 2 and 4 appear in White's *American Negro Folk-Songs*, collected from Alabama, North Carolina, Tennessee, and Mississippi (cf. 276–77, 368, et al.). White suggests the general form of the stanzas ("When I die . . .") might have originated with spirituals. Stanza 4 has currency in white tradition; see Brown (3:69). It is also common in an old-time country song from the 1920s, "Cotton Mill Girls," which stayed in currency through the 1960s. (See, for instance, the influential version by north Georgia singer Lester Smallwood [Victor 40181, 1928].)

W'en my wife dies, gwineter git me anudder one;
A big fat yaller one, jes lak de yudder one.
I'll hate mighty bad, w'en she's been gone.
Hain't no better 'oman never nowhars been bo'n.

W'en I comes to die, you mus'n' bury me deep,
But put Sogrum molasses close by my feet.

Pu a pone o' co'n bread way down in my han'.
Gwineter sop on de way to de Promus' Lan'.

W'en I goes to die, Nobody mus'n' cry,
Mus'n' dress up in black, fer I mought come back.
But w'en I'se been dead, an' almos' fergotten;
You mought think about me an' keep on a-trottin'.

Railly, w'en I'se been dead, you needn' bury me at tall.
You mought pickle my bones down in alkihall;
Den fold my han's "so," right across my breas';
An' go an' tell de folks I'se done gone to "res'."

37   Baa! Baa! Black Sheep

Distinct from the "Poor Little Lamb Cried 'Mammy'" elsewhere in this collection, this song originally appeared with music intact; the same tune appears in the manuscript notebook (#73).

"Baa! Baa! Black Sheep,
Has you got wool?"
"Yes, good Mosser,
Free bags full.
One fer ole Mistis,
One fer Miss Dame,

An' one fer de good Nigger
Jes across de lane."

Pōōr liddle Black Sheep,
Pōōr liddle lammy;
Pōōr liddle Black Sheep's
Got no mammy.

38   He will Get Mr. Coon

Talley had a fondness for hunting songs—a genre generally neglected by other collectors. This has some of the earmarks of a minstrel piece, many of which dealt with hunting.

Ole Mistah Coon, at de break o' day,
You needn't think youse gwineter git 'way.
Caze ole man Ned, he know how to run,
An' he's shō' gone fer to git 'is gun.

You needn' clam to dat highes' lim',
You cain't git out'n de retch o' him.
You can stay up dar till de sun done set.
I'll bet you a dollar dat he'll git you yet.

Ole Mistah Coon, you'd well's to give up.
You had well's to give up, I say.
Caze ole man Ned is straight atter you,
An' he'll git you shō' this day.

39   Bring on Your Hot Corn

This song is in the repertoires of a number of black and white traditional singers. Leadbelly recorded a version he called "Green Corn, Come Along Charlie," and bluegrass duo Lester Flatt and Earl Scruggs routinely performed it as "Hot Corn, Cold Corn." Talley's seems to have been the first publication of it, though Randolph (2:342–43) has a version called "I'll Meet You in the Evening." For a version popular in the 1960s folk circuits, see *New Lost City Ramblers Songbook* (180–81). An early commercial recording by old-time country artists Asa Martin and Ray Hobbs appeared on Champion 45065 (1928). Talley also used the song in the story "The Parrot Overseer" in his "Negro Traditions" manuscript. Talley explained the term "Jimmy-john" (stanza 1) as "a whiskey jug."

Bring along yō' hot co'n,
Bring along yō' col' con;
But I say bring along,
Bring along yō' Jimmy-john.

Some loves de hot co'n,
Some loves de col' co'n;
But I loves, I loves,
I loves dat Jimmy-john.

40 The Little Rooster

I had a liddle rooster,
He crowed befō' day.
'Long come a big owl,
'An toted him away.

But de rooster fight hard,
An' de owl let him go.
Now all de pretty hens
Wants dat rooster fer deir beau.

41 Sugar in Coffee

There are few printed analogues of this song, though stanza 2 is very close to the lyrics of a commercial record by old-time white fiddler John Carson, "Little More Sugar in My Coffee" (Okeh 45542, 1930). See Gene Wiggins, *Fiddlin' Georgia Crazy* (174–75). Middle Tennessee songster Uncle Dave Macon recorded a song called "She Wouldn't Give Me Sugar in My Coffee" (Vocalion 15440, 1926) which contains lines similar to those in stanza 1. Both white old-time musicians recorded their versions several years after Talley collected his. Also on record is a fiddle tune called "Sugar in My Coffee" by the Kentucky string band The Crockett Family (Crown 3075, ca. 1931).

Sheep's in de meader a-mowin' o' de hay.
De honey's in de bee-gum, so dey all say.
My head's up an' I'se boun' to go.
Who'll take sugar in de coffee-o?

I'se de prettiest liddle gal in de county-o.
My mammy an' daddy, dey bofe say so.
I looks in de glass, it don't say, "No";
So I'll take sugar in de coffee-o.

42   The Turtle's Song

Talley notes, in his "Study" (see below), that this song belongs with Joel
Chandler Harris's, story "Mr. Terrapin Shows His Strength," "though the
Rhyme was not collected by him." Talley was fond of Harris's work and men-
tions it often in his own collection of black dialect stories "Negro Traditions."
The music is #104 in the "Leading Themes" notebook.

Mud turkle setin' on de end of a log,
A-watchin' of a tadpole a-turnin' to a frog.
He sees Br'er B'ar a-pullin' lak a mule.
He sees Br'er Tearpin a-makin' him a fool.

Br'er B'ar pull de rope an' he puff an' he blow;
But he cain't git de Tearpin out'n de water from below.
Dat big clay root is a-holdin' dat rope,
Br'er Tearpin's got 'im fooled, an' dere hain't no hope.

Mud turkle settin' one de end o' dat log;
Sing fer de tadpole a-turnin' to a frog,

Sing to Br'er B'ar a-pullin' lak a mule,
Sing to Br'er Tearpin a-makin' 'im a fool: —

"Oh, Br'er Rabbit! Yō' eyes mighty big!"
"Yes, Br'er Turkle! Dey're made fer to see."
"Oh, Br'er Tearpin! Yō' house mighty cu'ous!"
"Yes, Br'er Turkle, but it jest suits me."

"Oh, Br'er B'ar! You pulls mighty stout."
"Yes, Br'er Turkle? Dat's right smart said!"
"Right, Br'er B'ar! Dat sounds bully good,
But you'd oughter git a liddle mō' pull in de head."

43   Raccoon and Opossum Fight

See White (385–86); Brown (3:548); and, for more modern versions still found
in African-American games, see Jones and Hawes (210).

De raccoon an' de 'possum
Under de hill a-fightin';
Rabbit almos' bust his sides
Laughin' at de bitin'.

De raccoon claw de 'possum
Along de ribs an' head;
'Possum tumble over an' grin,
Playin' lak he been dead.

44   Cotton Eyed Joe

Surviving today primarily as a popular western swing fiddle tune, the song
has deep roots in black traditional lore. This version is apparently the earliest
published, though Scarborough (*On the Trail of Negro Folk-Songs*, 69) prints
a version "from Texas and Louisiana" that she calls "an authentic slavery time
song." Versions of it also appear in White (359–60), collected from black
sources in Alabama in 1915–16. For details of the song's history as a fiddle
tune, see Alan Jabbour, notes to *North American Fiddle Tunes* (30). In his
manuscript of stories, "Negro Traditions," Talley inclues a story entitled "Cot-

ton Eyed Joe, or The Origin of the Weeping Willow"; it includes a short
stanza from the song, but more importantly details a bizarre tale of a well-
known pre–Civil War plantation musician, Cotton Eyed Joe, who plays a
fiddle made from the coffin of his dead son. The music here comes from
the "Leading Themes" notebook, where it is listed as #66.

Hol' my fiddle an' hol' my bow,
Whilst I knocks ole Cotton Eyed Joe.

I'd a been dead some seben years ago,
If I hadn' a danced dat Cotton Eyed Joe.

Oh, it makes dem ladies love me so,
W'en I comes 'roun' pickin' ole Cotton Eyed Joe!

Yes, I'd a been married some forty year ago,
If I hadn' stay'd 'roun' wid Cotton Eyed Joe.

I hain't seed ole Joe, since way las' Fall;
Dey say he's been sol' down to Guinea Gall.

45   Rabbit Soup

The music is from the "Leading Themes" notebook, #36. See Brown (3:213–14)
for another version.

Rabbit Soup! Rabbit sop!
Rabbit e't my tunnup top.

Rabbit hop, rabbit jump,
Rabbit hide behin' dat stump.

Rabbit stop, twelve o'clock,
Killed dat rabbit wid a rock.

Rabbit's mine. Rabbit's skin'.
Dress 'im off an' take 'im in.

Rabbit's on! Dance an' whoop!
Makin' a pot o' rabbit soup!

46 Old Gray Mink

I once did think dat I would sink,
But you know I wus dat ole gray mink.

Dat ole gray mink jes couldn' die,
W'en he thought about good chicken pie.

He swum dat creek above de mill,
An' he's killing an' eatin' chicken still.

47 Run, Nigger, Run

Prior to Talley's printing of this well-documented song are versions in White's
Serenader's Songbook (1851), p. 66; Joel Chandler Harris's *Uncle Remus and His
Friends: Old Plantation Stories, Songs, and Ballads* (200); and E.C. Perrow's "Songs

and Rhymes from the South" (1915), p. 138. Furthermore, two early commercial recordings of the piece were made by well-known Middle Tennessee performers: Dr. Humphrey Bate (Brunswick 275, 1928) and Uncle Dave Macon (Vocalion 15032, 1925). Other references are in Scarborough (23), White (168), Brown (3:531–533), and numerous other collections. In the original edition, Talley noted, in re the first line: "Patrollers, or white guards; on duty at night during the days of slavery; whose duty it was to see that slaves without permission to go, stayed at home." The music is from the "Leading Themes" notebook, #41.

Run, Nigger, run! De Patter-rollers'll ketch you.
Run, Nigger, run! It's almos' day.

Dat Nigger run'd, dat Nigger flew,
Dat Nigger tore his shu't in two.

All over dem woods and frou de paster,
Dem Patter-rollers shot; but de Nigger git faster,

Oh, dat Nigger whirl'd, dat Nigger wheel'd,
Dat Nigger tore up de whole co'n field.

48   Shake the Persimmons Down

For representative variants, see Brown (3:206–207); White (237); Botkin (295–96); and, to show the piece is still found in modern tradition, Jones and Hawes (127, as "Possum-ha").

A

This is the version found in Talley's original edition.

De raccoon up in de 'simmon tree.
Dat 'possum on de groun'.
De 'possum say to de raccon: "Suh!"
Please shake dem 'simmons down."

De raccoon say to de 'possum: "Suh!"
(As he grin from down below),
If you wants dese good 'simmons, man,
Jes clam up whar dey grow."

B

This alternate version was sent to Talley by Joe Bishop of Belfast, Tennessee, in 1920 and was found in Talley's manuscripts.

Opossum in persimmon tree,
One eye looking down on me,
I up with a rock sorta sly,
I hit that opposum above the eye.

Laid him that night in the frost,
Then took him down and dressed him off,
Asked Mariah to make fire,
And cook a good old possum pie.

49 The Cow Needs a Tail in Fly-Time

Dat ole black sow, she can root in de mud,
She can tumble an' roll in de slime;
But dat big red cow, she git all mired up,
So dat cow need a tail in fly-time.

Dat ole gray hoss, wid 'is ole bob tail,
You mought buy all 'is ribs fer a dime;
But dat ole gray hoss can git a kiver on,
Whilst de cow need a tail in fly-time.

Dat Nigger Overseer, dat's a-ridin' on a mule,
Cain't make hisse'f white lak de lime;
Mosser mought take 'im down fer a notch or two,
Den de cow'd need a tail in fly-time.

50   Jaybird Died with the Whooping Cough

The first two stanzas of this piece have been widely collected from both white
and black sources, and print versions are found as far back as 1846; see White
(243), Brown (3:201), Browne (447), among others. An early Tennessee variant
is found in the *Tennessee Folklore Society Bulletin* 2, p. 30. The last two stanzas
are relatively rare. Music from "Leading Themes" notebook, #48.

De Jaybird died wid de Whoopin' Cough,
De Sparrer died wid de colic;
'Long come de Red-bird, skippin' 'round,
Sayin': "Boys, git ready fer de Frolic!"

De Jaybird died wid de Whoopin' Cough,
De Bluebird died wid de Measles;
'Long come a Nigger wid a fiddle on his back,
'Vitin' Crows fer to dance wid de Weasels.

Dat Mockin'-bird, he romp an' sing;
Dat ole Gray Goose come prancin'.

Dat Thrasher stuff his mouf wid plums,
Den he caper on down to de dancin'.

Dey hopped it low, an' dey hopped it high;
Dey hopped it to, an' dey hopped it by;
Dey hopped it fer, an' dey hopped it nigh;
Dat fiddle an' bow jes make 'em fly.

51   Wanted! Cornbread and Coon

I'se gwine now a-huntin' to ketch a big fat coon.
Gwineter bring him home, an' bake him, an' eat him wid a spoon.
Gwineter baste him up wid gravy, an' add some onions too.
I'se gwineter shet de Niggers out, an' stuff myse'f clean through.

I wants a piece o' hoecake; I wants a piece o' bread,
An' I wants a piece o' Johnnycake as big as my ole head.
I wants a piece o' ash cake: I wants dat big fat coon!
An' I shō' won't git hongry 'fore de middle o' nex' June.

52   Little Red Hen

See Brown (3:206). The phrase "Anudder liddle drink wouldn' do us no harm"
appears in a number of old-time country songs.

My liddle red hen, wid a liddle white foot,
Done built her nes' in a huckleberry root.
She lay mō' aigs dan a flock on a fahm.
Anudder liddle drink wouldn' do us no harm.

My liddle red hen hatch fifty red chicks
In dat little ole nes' of huckleberry sticks.
Wid one mō' drink, ev'y chick'll make two!
Come, bring it on, Honey, an' let's git through.

53   Ration Day

Dat ration day come once a week,
Ole Mosser's rich as Gundy;
But he gives us 'lasses all de week,
An' buttermilk fer Sund'y.

Ole Mosser give me a pound o' meat.
I e't it all on Mond'y;
Den I e't 'is 'lasses all de week.
An' buttermilk fer Sund'y.

Ole Mosser give me a peck o' meal,
I fed and cotch my tucky;
But I e't dem 'lasses all de week,
An' buttermilk fer Sund'y.

Oh laugh an' sing an' don't git tired.
We's all gwine home, some Mond'y,
To de honey ponds an' fritter trees;
An' ev'ry day'll be Sund'y.

54   My Fiddle

If my old fiddle wus jes in chune,
She'd bring me a dollar ev'y Friday night in June.
W'en my old fiddle is fixed up right,
She bring me a dollar in nearly ev'y night.
W'en my old fiddle begin to sing,
She make de whole plantation ring.
She bring me in a dollar an' sometime mō'.
Hurrah fer my old fiddle an' bow!

55   Die in the Pig-Pen Fighting

Dat ole sow said to de barrer:
"I'll tell you w'at let's do:

Let's go an' git dat broad-axe
And die in de pig-pen too."

"Die in de pig-pen fightin'!
Yes, die, die in de wah!
Die in de pig-pen fightin',
Yes, die wid a bitin' jaw!"

56   Master Is Six Feet One Way

Mosser is six foot one way, an' free foot tudder;
An' he weigh five hundred pound.
Britches cut so big dat dey don't suit de tailor,
An' dey don't meet half way 'round.

Mosser's coat come back to a claw-hammer p'int.
(Speak sof' or his Bloodhound'll bite us.)
His long white stockin's mighty clean an' nice,
But a liddle mō' holier dan righteous.

57   Fox and Geese

Brown (3:178) lists numerous citations for this well-known song, a few of them
from black sources; Scarborough (70) offers a related version supposedly sung
by slaves in Virginia. "Ole mammy Sopentater" (stanza 2) is apparently a
nonsense name; in other versions it appears as "old mother Wibble-Wabble"
(Randolph, 1:387), "old mother Lollypopper" (Randolph, 1:389), and "old
mother Whittle" (Brown, 3:179). For variants and comments on stanza 2, see
White (177).

Br'er Fox wa'k out one moonshiny night,
He say to hisse'f w'at he's a gwineter do.
He say, "I'se gwineter have a good piece o' meat,
Befō' I leaves dis townyoo!
Dis townyoo, dis townyoo!
Yes, befō' I leaves dis townyoo!"

Ole mammy Sopentater jum up out'n bed,
An' she poke her head outside o' de dō'.

She say: "Ole man, my gander's gone.
I heared 'im w'en he holler 'quinny-quanio,'
'Quinny-quanio, quinny-quanio!'
Yes, I heard 'im w'en he holler 'quinny-quanio.'

58   Gooseberry Wine

The second stanza here appears to derive from a pre–Civil War minstrel song (see *The Popular National Songster* [Philadelphia, 1848, pp. 157–158]) and has been chronicled both in Brown (3:557) and White (381). "Dr. Ginger Blue" was probably a stock character from minstrel shows. The song was well known to white old-time country musicians; north Georgia singer Arthur Tanner made a popular recording in 1929 (Columbia 15479) and Kentuckian Asa Martin included a version in an album recorded in the 1970s (Rounder LP).

Now 'umble Uncle Steben,
I wonders whar youse gwine?
Don't never tu'n yō' back, Suh,
On dat good ole gooseberry wine!

Oh walk chalk, Ginger Blue!
Git over double trouble.
You needn' min' de wedder
So's de win' don't blow you double.

Now!
Uncle Mack! Uncle Mack!
Did you ever see de lak?
Dat good ole sweet gooseberry wine
Call Uncle Steben back.

59   I Would Rather Be a Negro
Than a Poor White Man

A version in White was supposedly "sung by Negro at Reconstruction political meeting" (170); also see versions in Odum and Johnson's *The Negro and His Songs* (217–18). Some of the couplets became popular with white fiddlers; see the 1927 commercial recording by Fiddlin' John Carson "Hell Bound for

Alabama" (Okeh 45159) and its transcription in Gene Wiggins's *Fiddlin' Georgia Crazy* (209–11). The music here comes from the "Leading Themes" notebook (#13); see also Talley's comments on this song in his "Study," below.

My name's Ran, I wuks in de san';
But I'd druther be a Nigger dan a pō' white man.

Gwineter hitch my oxes side by side,
An' take my gal fer a big fine ride.

Gwineter take my gal to de country stō';
Gwineter dress her up in red calico.

You take Kate, an' I'll take Joe.
Den off we'll go to de pahty-o.

Gwineter take my gal to de Hulla-baloo,
Whar dere hain't no Crackers in a mile or two.

Interlocution

(Fiddler) "Oh, Sal! Whar's de milk strainer cloth?"

(Banjo Picker) "Bill's got it wropped 'round his ole sore leg."
(Fiddler) "Well, take it down to de gum spring an' give it a cold water rench; I 'spizes nastness anyway. I'se got to have a clean cloth fer de milk."

He don't lak whisky but he jest drinks a can.
Honey! I'd druther be a Nigger dan a pō' white man.

I'd druther be a Nigger, an' plow ole Beck
Dan a white Hill Billy wid his long red neck.

60   The Hunting Camp

Sam got up one mornin'
A mighty big fros'.
Saw "A louse, in de huntin' camp
As big as any hoss!"

Sam run 'way down de mountain;
But w'en Mosser got dar,
He swore it twusn't nothin'
But a big black b'ar.

61   The Ark

This appears to be a folk version of a popular poem from the 1870s by the Mississippi dialect writer Irwin Russell (1853–79). Russell, from a well-to-do white family, trained for the law, yet had a fondness and fascination for folk music; he once described himself as "something of a banjoist." In his brief career, he published his poems in local newspapers as well as national magazines like *Puck*. According to Joel Chandler Harris, he was "among the first — if not the very first — of Southern writers to appreciate the literary possibilities of the negro character"; his book of collected poems, published in 1888, was *Christmas Night in the Quarters*. The title piece, called a "negro operetta" by Harris, is a series of shorter poems, one of which seems to be the source for "The Ark." Russell's text is twice as long as Talley's, and there are enough major differences to suggest that Talley took his from a source honed and simplified from several decades of oral transmission. Like the work of many dialect writers, Russell's poems were popular as oral recitations, and this might help explain how "The Ark" became a "Negro folk rhyme." The overall influence of such recitations on black tradition, however, has not been determined, nor has the extent to which such pieces have been put to music — as here. The music here is found in the "Leading Themes" notebook, labeled #75.

Ole Nora had a lots o' hands
A clearin' new ground patches.
He said he's gwineter build a Ark,
An' put tar on de hatches.

He had a sassy Mo'gan hoss
An' gobs of big fat cattle;
An' he driv' em all aboard de Ark,
W'en he hear de thunder rattle.

An' den de river riz so fas'
Dat it bust de levee railin's.
De lion got his dander up,
An' he lak to a broke de palin's.

An' on dat Ark was daddy Ham;
No udder Nigger on dat packet.
He soon got tired o' de Barber Shop,
Caze he couln' stan' de racket.

An' den jes to amuse hisse'f,
He steamed a board an' bent it, Son.
Dat way he got a banjer up,
Fer ole Ham's de fust to make one.

Dey danced dat Ark from ēen to ēen,
Ole Nora called de Figgers.
Ole Ham, he sot an' knocked de chunes,
De happiest of de Niggers.

62   Gray and Black Horses

Possibly originating as a minstrel piece, the song has remained in black tradition up through the 1950s and is sometimes associated with the play-party song "Mary Mack." For the version closest to Talley's, see Harold Courlander's *Negro Folk Music U.S.A.* (158); for earlier variants, see White (195, 229) and Scarborough (185); none of these is clearly identified as Tennessee texts. Preceeding Talley's version in print was one published by E.C. Perrow (1913), p. 124.

> I went down to de woods an' I couldn' go 'cross,
> So I paid five dollars fer an ole gray hoss.
> De hoss wouldn' pull, so I sōl' 'im fer a bull.
> De bull wouldn' holler, so I sōl' 'im fer a dollar.
> De dollar wouldn't pass, so I throwed it in de grass.
> Den de grass wouldn' grow. Heigho! Heigho!
>
> Through dat huckleberry woods I couldn't git far,
> So I paid a good dollar fer an ole black mar'.
> W'en I got down dar, de trees wouldn' bar;
> So I had to gallop back on dat ole black mar'.
> "Bookitie-bar!" Dat ole black mar';
> "Bookitie-bar!" Dat ole black mar'.
> Yes she trabble so hard dat she jolt off my ha'r.

63   Rattler

An early version of a hunting song that has become a standard in bluegrass and country music, largely on the strength of a hit recording by Kentucky singer Marshall "Grandpa" Jones ("Old Rattler," King 668, 1947). A version earlier than Talley's was printed by Natalie Curtis Burlin in *Hampton Series Negro Folk Songs*, volume 4 (p. 38), in 1919, under the title "Hyar, Rattler." See also White (232) and an early commercial recording by blind singer George Reneau, from East Tennessee, "Here, Rattler, Here" (Vocalion 14814, 1924).

> Go call ole Rattle from de bo'n.
> Here Rattler! Here!

He'll drive de cows out'n de co'n,
Here Rattler! Here!

Rattler is my huntin' dog.
Here Rattler! Here!
He's good fer rabbit, good fer hog,
Here Rattler! Here!

He's good fer 'possum in de dew.
Here Rattler! Here!
Sometimes he gits a chicken, too.
Here Rattler! Here!

64   Brother Ben and Sister Sal

Ole Br'er Ben's a mighty good ole man,
He don't steal chickens lak he useter.
He went down de chicken roos' las' Friday night,
An' tuck off a dominicker rooster.

Dere's ole Sis Sal, she climbs right well,
But she cain't 'gin to climb lak she useter.
So younder she sets a shellin' out co'n
To Mammy's ole bob-tailed rooster.

Yes, old Sis Sal's a mighty fine ole gal,
She's shō' extra good an' clever.
She's done tuck a notion all her own,
Dat she hain't gwineter marry never.

Ole Sis Sal's got a foot so big,
Dat she cain't wear no shoes an' gaiters.
So all she want is some red calico,
An' dem big yaller yam sweet taters.

Now looky, looky here! Now looky, looky there!
Jes looky! — Looky 'way over yonder! —
Don't you see dat ole gray goose
A-smilin' at de gander?

65   Simon Slick's Mule

Browne, in his *The Alabama Folk Lyric* (442–44), cites a number of printed minstrel songster appearances for this piece between 1879 and 1883; Brown offers a similarly long list of other references (3:567). See also White (157). The song seems especially well known in Middle Tennessee and northern Alabama, primarily among whites; it was featured for years on the Grand Ole Opry by Sam and Kirk McGee, from Williamson County in Middle Tennessee, who also recorded it numerous times (cf. "Kickin' Mule," by Kirk McGee with Blythe Poteet, Conqueror 7257, 1928).

> Dere wus a liddle kickin' man,
> His name wus Simon Slick.
> He had a mule wid cherry eyes.
> Oh, how dat mule could kick!
>
> An', Suh, w'en you go up to him,
> He shet one eye an' smile;
> Den 'e telegram 'is foot to you,
> An' sen' you half a mile!

66   Nobody Looking

> Well: I look dis a way, an' I look dat a way,
>   An' I heared a mighty rumblin'.
>   W'en I come to find out, 'twus dad's black sow,
>   A-rootin' an' a-grumblin'.
>
> Den: I slipped away down to de big White House.
>   Miss Sallie, she done gone 'way.
>   I popped myse'f in de rockin' chear,
>   An' I rocked myse'f all day.
>
> Now: I looked dis a way, an' I looked dat a way,
>   An' I didn' see nobody in here.
>   I jest run'd my head in de coffee pot,
>   An' I drink'd up all o' de beer.

67   Hoecake

This song is commonly known as "Snake Baked a Hoecake," but less commonly reported with as many stanzas as here. Evidence in White (158, 246–47) suggests the song was known as early as 1810–12 and was mentioned in a notebook of Washington Irving. See also Brown (3: 223–24).

If you wants to bake a hoecake,
To bake it good an' done;
Jes' slap it on a Nigger's heel,
An' hol' it to de sun.

Dat snake, he bake a hoecake,
An' sot de toad to mind it;
Dat toad he up an' go to sleep,
An' a lizard slip an' find it!

My mammy baked a hoecake,
As big as Alabamer.
She threwed it 'g'inst a Nigger's head
An' it ring jes' lak a hammer.

De way you bakes a hoecake,
In de ole Virginy 'tire;
You wrops it 'round a Nigger's heel,
An' hōl's it to de fire.

68   I Went Down the Road

I went down de road,
I went in a whoop;
An' I met Aunt Dinah
Wid a chicken pot o' soup.
Sing: "I went away from dar; hook-a-doo-dle, hook-a-doo-dle."
        "I went away from dar; hook-a-doo-dle-doo!"
        I drunk up dat soup,
        An' I let her go by;
        An' I tōl' her nex' time
        To bring Missus' pot pie.
Sing: "Oh far'-you-well; hook-a-doo-dle, hook-a-doo-dle;
        Oh far'-you-well, an' a hook-a-doo-dle-doo!"

69   The Old Hen Cackled

Though conspicuously absent from most standard collections of black folk songs, this piece became a favorite with mid-South string bands, both black and white. North Georgia native Fiddlin' John Carson used a version of it on one of the first country music recordings made, "The Old Hen Cackled and the Rooster's Going to Crow" (Okeh 4890, 1923), issued just a year after Talley's first edition came out. On this record, Carson sings three stanzas similar to those found here. Closer to Talley's base, two well-known black string bands knew and recorded the piece. From south-central Tennessee, the team of Joe Evans and Arthur McClain recorded a vocal and string band version of it for the American Recording Company in 1931, a record that was issued on four Depression-era labels (cf. Oriole 8095, Perfect 12751). The Knoxville string band headed by fiddler Howard Armstrong also knew the piece, though they did not record it until 1985 (Arhoolie LP 1095). The music here is from the "Leading Themes" notebook, #2.

De ole hen she cackled,
An' stayed down in de bo'n.
She git fat an' sassy,
A-eatin' up de co'n.

De ole hen she cackled,
Git great long yaller laigs.
She swaller down de oats,
But I don't git no aigs.

De ole hen she cackled,
She cackled in de lot,
De nex' time she cackled,
She cackled in de pot.

70   I Love Somebody

Better known among white repertoires than black, one of the earliest prints
of this song is in Perrow, "Songs and Rhymes from the South," (1915), p. 125.
There are also fragments in Brown (3:140–41). Very popular as a fiddle tune
in Middle Tennessee, it was often heard on the Grand Ole Opry in the 1920s
and 1930s. Two popular commercial recordings — both instrumentals — are
those by Uncle Dave Macon with Sid Harkreader (Vocalion 14857, 1924) and
the Crook Brothers Barn Dance Orchestra (Victor 40099, 1928). Music here
is taken from "Leading Themes" notebook, #20.

I loves somebody, yes, I do;
An' I wants somebody to love me too.
Wid my chyart an' oxes stan'in' 'roun',
Her pretty liddle foot needn' tetch de groun'.

I loves somebody, yes, I do,
Dat randsome, handsome, Stickamastew.
Wid her reddingoat an' waterfall,
She's de pretty liddle gal dat beats 'em all.

71   We Are "All the Go"

Yes! We's "All-de-go," boys; we's "All-de-go."
    Me an' my Lulu gals "All-de-go."
        I jes' loves my sweet pretty liddle Lulu Ann,

But de way she gits my money I cain't hardly understan'.
W'en she up an' call me "Honey!" I fergits my name is Sam,
An' I hain't got one nickel lef' to git a me a dram.

Still: We's "All-de-go," boys; we's "All-de-go."
    Me an' my Lulu gal's "All-de-go."
        She's always gwine a-fishin', w'en she'd oughter not to go;
        An' now she's all a troubled wid de frostes an' de snow.
        I tells you jes one thing dat I'se done gone an' foun':
        De Nigs cain't git no livin' 'round de Cō't
            House steps an' town.

72   Aunt Dinah Drunk

Probably an amalgam of diverse minstrel stanzas, this particular version does not appear in standard black collections. The third part, with the refrain, "Way down on de old plank road," appears in the recorded repertoire of Uncle Dave Macon (Vocalion 15321, 1926). Talley's papers contain two versions; the A version below is the one printed in the original edition.

A

Ole Aunt Dinah, she got drunk.
She fell in de fire, an' she kicked up a chunk.
Dem embers got in Aunt Dinah's shoe,
An' dat black Nigger shō' got up an' flew.

I likes Aunt Dinah mighty, mighty well,
But dere's jes' one thing I hates an' 'spize:
She drinks mō' whisky dan de bigges' fool,
Den she up an' tell ten thousand lies.

Yes, I won't git drunk an' kick up a chunk.
    I won't git drunk an' kick up a chunk.
    I won't git drunk an' kick up a chunk,
    'Way down on de ole Plank Road.
    Oh shoo my Love! My turkle dove.
    Oh shoo my Love! My turkle dove.
    Oh shoo my Love! My turkle dove.
    'Way down on de ole Plank Road.

B

This variant was sent to Talley by his friend Joe H. Bishop from Belfast, Tennessee, in 1920, and found with the Talley manuscripts.

> Old aunt Dinah she got drunk,
> She fell in the fire and kicked up a chunk,
> A red hot coal got in her shoe,
> Lord have mercy, how the ashes flew.
>
> Old Dinah sick in bed,
> Out the window she poked her head,
> Snowball hit her in the eyeball brim!
> Look here, Mr. Negro, don't do that again.

73 The Old Woman in the Hills

> Once: Dere was an ole 'oman
>   Dat lived in de hills;
>   Put rocks in 'er stockin's,
>   An' sent 'em to mill.
>
>   Den: De ole miller swore,
>   By de pint o' his knife;
>   Dat he never had ground up
>   No rocks in his life.
>
>   So: De ole 'oman said
>   To dat miller nex' day:
>   "You railly must 'scuse me,
>   It's de onliest way."
>
>   "I heared you made meal,
>   A-grindin' on stones.
>   I mus' 'ave heared wrong,
>   It mus' 'ave been bones."

74   A Sick Wife

Music from "Leading Themes" notebook, #58.

Las' Sadday night my wife tuck sick,
An' what d'you reckon ail her?
She e't a tucky gobbler's head
An' her stomack, it jes' fail her.

She squall out: "Sam, bring me some mint!
Make catnip up an' sage tea!"
I goes an' gits her all dem things,
But she throw 'em back right to me.

Says I: "Dear Honey! Mind nex' time!"
    "Don't eat from 'A to Izzard'"
    "I thinks you won' git sick at all,
    If you saves pō' me de gizzard."

75   My Wonderful Travel

I come down from ole Virginny,
'Twas on a Summer day;
De wedder was all frez up,
'An' I skeeted all de way!

Interlocution:
Hand my banjer down to play,
Wanter pick fer dese ladies right away;

"W'en dey went to bed,
Dey couldn' shet deir eyes,"
An' "Dey was stan'in' on deir heads,
A-pickin' up de pies."

76   I Would Not Marry a Black Girl

The "I wouldn't marry" family of songs can be traced as far back as minstrel songsters of the 1850s; see White (324–25) and Brown (3:30–36). Talley discusses the racial implications of the song in his "Study" (below). Music from the "Leading Themes" notebook, #76.

I wouldn' marry a black gal,
I'll tell you de reason why:
When she goes to comb dat head
De naps'll 'gin to fly.

I wouldn' marry a black gal,
I'll tell you why I won't:
When she'd oughter wash her face —
Well, I'll jes say she don't.

I woudn' marry a black gal,
An' dis is why I say:
When you has her face around,
It never gits good day.

77   Harvest Song

Individual stanzas of this song have been reported from various sources. Stanza 4 appears in White (329), and is well known as an Anglo-American square dance call. Stanza 3 is found in the popular bluegrass song "Roll in My Sweet Baby's Arms," which seems to have first been recorded in 1931 by Buster Carter and Preston Young (Columbia 15690).

> Las' year wus a good crap year,
> An' we raised beans an' 'maters.
> We didn' make much cotton an' co'n;
> But, Goodness Life, de taters!
>
> You can plow dat ole gray hoss,
> I'se gwineter plow dat mulie;
> An' w'en we's geddered in de craps,
> I'se gwine down to see Julie.
>
> I hain't gwineter wo'k on de railroad.
> I hates to wo'k on de fahm.
> I jes wants to set in de cool shade,
> Wid my head on my Julie's ahm.
>
> You swing Lou, an' I'll swing Sue.
> Dere hain't no diffunce 'tween dese two.
> You swing Lou, I'll swing my beau;
> I'se gwineter buy my gal red calico.

78   Year of Jubilee

An oral variation of Henry Clay Work's 1861 song "Kingdom Coming," this was widely published in songsters in the early 1860s; Scarborough (125) and White (170–72) offer other early folk versions, the latter collected in 1916 and called "Savannah River." Talley's version shows more departure from the printed text than most others. The song is generally found in white rather than black repertoires. White country singers Sam and Kirk McGee, who grew up a county away from Talley's home county in Middle Tennessee and who learned the song from their father circa 1910, recorded a version of the song in 1927 (Vocalion 5167), with text quite different from Talley's. It is possible that the uniqueness of Talley's text can be ascribed to the fact that it came from a black informant.

> Niggers, has you seed ole Mosser;
> (Red mustache on his face.)
> A-gwine 'roun' sometime dis mawnin',
> 'Spectin' to leave de place?
>
> Nigger Hands all runnin' 'way,
> Looks lak we mought git free!
> It mus' be now de Kingdom Come
> In de Year o' Jubilee.
>
> Oh, yon'er comes ole Mosser
> Wid his red mustache all white!
> It mus' be now de Kingdom Come
> Sometime to-morrer night.
>
> Yanks locked him in de smokehouse cellar,
> De key's throwed in de well:
> It shō' mus' be de Kingdom Come.
> Go ring dat Nigger field-bell!

79   Sheep Shell Corn

The second stanza is in Brown (3:239); also see Brown (3:233). Music is from the "Leading Themes" notebook, #28.

Oh: De Ram blow de ho'n an' de sheep shell co'n;
  An' he sen' it to de mill by de buck-eyed Whippoorwill.
  Ole Joe's dead an' gone but his Hant blows de ho'n;
  An' his hound howls still from de top o' dat hill.

Yes: De Fish-hawk said unto Mistah Crane;
  I wishes to de Lawd dat you'd sen' a liddle rain;
  Fer de water's all muddy, an de creek's gone dry;
  If it 'twasn't fer de tadpoles we'd all die."

Oh: When de sheep shell co'n wid de rattle of his ho'n
  I wishes to de Lawd I'd never been bo'n;
  Caze when he Hant blows de ho'n, de sperits all dance,
  An' de hosses an' de cattle, dey whirls 'round an' prance.

Oh: Yonder comes Skillet an' dere goes Pot;
  An' here comes Jawbone 'cross de lot.
  Walk Jawbone! Beat de Skillet an' de Pan!
  You cut dat Pigeon's Wing, Black Man!

Now: Take keer, gemmuns, an' let me through;
  Caze I'se gwineter dance wid liddle Mollie Lou.
  But I'se never seed de lak since I'se been bo'n,
  When de sheep shell co'n wid de rattle of his ho'n!

80 Plaster

Music from "Leading Themes" notebook, #77.

Chilluns: Mammy an' daddy had a hoss,
  Dey want a liddle bigger.

        Dey sticked a plaster on his back
        An' drawed a liddle Nigger.

Den: Mammy an' daddy had a dog,
        His tail wus short an' chunky.
        Dey slapped a plaster 'round dat tail,
        An' drawed it lak de monkey.

Well: Mammy an' daddy's dead an' gone.
        Did you ever hear deir story?
        Dey sticked some plasters on deir heels,
        An' drawed 'em up to Glory!

81   Uncle Ned

This Stephen Foster song was copyrighted in 1848 and widely reprinted in songsters of the period. See Brown(3:305–306); White (164-66) offers four oral variants collected around 1915-16 from black sources in Alabama. The song was quite popular with early country music singers; Uncle Dave Macon recorded a version of it in 1926 (Vocalion 15450), as did Georgia pioneer Fiddlin' John Carson (Okeh 40263, 1924), WLS radio singer Chubby Parker (Gennett 6287, 1928), and others.

        Jes lay down de shovel an' de hoe.
        Jes hang up de fiddle an' de bow.
        No more hard work fer ole man Ned,
        Fer he's gone whar de good Niggers go.

        He didn' have no years fer to hear,
        Didn' have no eyes fer to see,
        Didn' have no teeth fer to eat corn cake,
        An' he had to let de beefsteak be.

        Dey called 'im "Ole Uncle Ned,"
        A long, long time ago.
        Dere wusn't no wool on de top o' his head
        In de place whar de wool oughter grow.

        When ole man Ned wus dead,
        Mosser's tears run down lak rain;

But ole Miss, she wus a liddle sorter glad,
Dat she wouldn' see de ole Nigger 'gain.

82   The Master's "Stolen" Coat

Talley explains the quotation marks in his title by noting that "stole, here, means taken temporarily with intention to return."

Ole Mosser bought a brand new coat,
He hung it on de wall.
Dat Nigger stole dat coat away,
An' wore it to de Ball.

His head look lak a Coffee pot,
His nose look lak de spout,
His mouf look lak de fier place,
Wid de ashes all tuck out.

His face look lak a skillet lid,
His years lak two big kites.
His eyes look lak two big biled aigs,
Wid de yallers in de whites.

His body 'us lak a stuffed toad frog,
His foot look lak a board.
Oh-oh! He thinks he is so fine,
But he's greener dan a gourd.

83   I Wouldn't Marry a Yellow or a White Negro Girl

See song number 76 in this collection, and references there; see also Talley's comments in his "Study" (below). Talley further notes, regarding the quotation marks around "Black" in line 1: "'Black' here is not the real name. The name is applied because of the complexion of the girls to whom it was sung."

I sho' loves dat gal dat dey calls Sally "Black,"
An' I sorter loves some of de res';

I first loves de gals fer lovin' me,
Den I loves myse'f de bes'.

I wouldn' marry dat yaller Nigger gal,
An' I'll tell you de reason why:
Her neck's drawed out so stringy an' long,
I'se afeared she 'ould never die.

I wouldn' marry dat White Nigger gal,
(Fer gracious sakes!) dis is why:
Her nose look lak a kittle spout;
An' her skin, it hain't never dry.

84   Don't Ask Me Questions

Don't ax me no questions,
An' I won't tell you no lies;
But bring me dem apples,
An' I'll make you some pies.

An' if you ax questions,
'Bout my havin' de flour;
I fergits to use 'lasses
An' de pie'll be all sour.

Dem apples jes wa'k here;
An' dem 'lasses, dey run.
Hain't no place lak my house
Found un'er de sun.

85   The Old Section Boss

Widely known under titles such as "Bill Stafford," "State of Arkansas," "Misery in Arkansas," and "Arkansas Traveler" (different from the comic dialogue), this piece has been studied extensively and its provenance traced to an eighteenth-century Scots love song called "Caledonia." A good summary of its history is presented by Cohen in his edition of *Ozark Folksongs* (228). Talley's is one of the very few black versions collected. He also used it in his story "Why the Irishman is a Railroad Section Boss" in the "Negro Traditions" manuscript. The "Iron Mountain" reference in stanza 4 is likewise rare, and probably refers to the Iron Mountain Railway, a midwestern line of the 1870s which Jesse James reportedly robbed. An entry appears in the "Leading Themes" notebook, item #106(a), but the score was obviously incomplete and unedited by Talley; we have chosen not to include it here.

I once knowed an ole Sexion Boss but he done been laid low.
I once knowed an ole Sexion Boss but he done been laid low.
He "Caame frum gude ole Ireland some fawhrty year ago."

W'en I ax 'im fer a job, he say: "Nayger, w'at can yer do?"
W'en I ax 'im fer a job, he say: "Nayger, w'at can yer do?"
"I can line de track; tote de jack, de pick an' shovel too."

Says he: "Nayger, de railroad's done, an' de chyars is on de track,"
Says he: "Nayger, de railroad's done, an' de chyars is on de track,"
"Transportation brung yer here, but yō' money'll take yer back."

I went down to de Deepo, an' my ticket I shō' did draw.
I went down to de Deepo, an' my ticket I shō' did draw.
To take me over dat ole Iron Mountain to de State o' Arkansaw.

As I went sailin' down de road, I met my mudder-in-law.
I wus so tired an' hongry, man, dat I couldn' wuk my jaw.
Fer I hadn't had no decent grub since I lef' ole Arkansaw.

Her bread wus hard corndodgers; dat meat, I couldn' chaw.
Her bread wus hard corndodgers; dat meat, I couldn' chaw.
You see; dat's de way de Hoosiers feeds way out in Arkansaw.

86   The Negro and the Policeman

White's *American Negro Folk-Songs* (361) offers some fragments similar to stanza 1; the overall song may either be a precursor to or derivative from a 1906 "coon" song, "Mister Johnson, Turn Me Loose," written by a songwriter named Ben Harney. See also Paul Oliver *Songsters and Saints* (50). Uncle Dave Macon recorded a Tennessee variant as "Mister Johnson" in 1929 (Vocalion 5341).

Oh Mistah Policeman, tu'n me loose;
Hain't got no money but a good excuse."
Oh hello, Sarah Jane!

Dat ole Policeman treat me mean,
He make me wa'k to Bowlin' Green.
Oh hello, Sarah Jane!

De way he treat me wus a shame.
He make me wear dat Ball an' Chain.
Oh hello, Sarah Jane!

I runs to de river, I can't git 'cross;
Dat Police grab me an' swim lak a hoss.
Oh hello, Sarah Jane!

I goes up town to git me a gun,
Dat ole Police shō' make me run.
Oh hello, Sarah Jane!

I goes crosstown sorter walkin' wid a hump
An' dat ole Police shō' make me jump.
Oh hello, Sarah Jane!

Sarah Jane, is dat yō' name?
Us boys, we calls you Sarah Jane.
Well, hello, Sarah Jane!

87 Ham Beats All Meat

Middle Tennessee musician and Grand Ole Opry pioneer Dr. Humphrey
Bate performed a version of the song almost identical to Talley's; he recorded
it on Vocalion 5238 (1928). Another Opry pioneer, Uncle Dave Macon, knew
the song and adapted it for his use, recording it as "Country Ham and Red
Gravy" (Bluebird 7951, 1938). Music from "Leading Themes" notebook (#23),
with a melody very similar to that of Dr. Bate's.

Dem white folks set up in a Dinin' Room
An' dey charve dat mutton an' lam'.
De Nigger, he set 'hind de kitchen door,
An' he eat up de good sweet ham.

Dem white folks, dey set up an' look so fine,
An' dey eats dat ole cow meat;
But de Nigger grin an' he don't say much,
Still he know how to git what's sweet.

Deir ginger cakes taste right good sometimes,
An' deir Cobblers an' deir jam.
But fer every day an' Sunday too,
Jest gimme de good sweet ham.

Ham beats all meat,
Always good an' sweet.
Ham beats all meat,
I'se always ready to eat.
You can bake it, bile it, fry it, stew it,
An' still it's de good sweet ham.

88   Suze Ann

This song is probably of minstrel origin, especially considering the reference to "Jubal Jew" (stanza 3), a dance step. The first stanza appears in an Uncle Dave Macon song, "Give Me the Girl with the Red Dress On," which he copyrighted in 1937 (CE unpub 330696) but did not publish or record.

Yes: I loves dat gal wid a blue dress on,
        Dat de white folks calls Suze Ann.
        She's jes' dat gal what stole my heart,
        'Way down in Alabam'.

But: She loves a Nigger about nineteen,
        Wid his lips all painted red;
        Wid a liddle fuz around his mouf;
        An' no brains in his head.

Now: Looky, looky Eas'! Oh, looky, looky Wes'!
        I'se been down to ole Lou'zan';
        Still dat ar gal I loves de bes'
        Is de gal what's named Suze Ann.
        Oh, head 'er! Head 'er! Ketch 'er!
        Jump up an' "Jubal Jew."
        Fer de Banger Picker's sayin':
        He hain't got nothin' to do.

89   Walk Tom Wilson

Another minstrel piece that became well known as a banjo and fiddle tune in southern Tennessee and northern Alabama. Uncle Dave Macon recorded a version in 1927 (Vocalion 5154), using only the last two lines of the text here as a refrain for a newly composed song about his trip to New York. The song does not appear in any of the standard black folk song collections, but it is in Byron Arnold's *Folksongs of Alabama* (30–31), collected from a white woman who called it "a banjo song."

Ole Tom Wilson, he had 'im a hoss;
His legs so long he couldn' git 'em 'cross.
He laid up dar lak a bag o' meal,
An' he spur him in de flank wid his toenail heel.

Ole Tom Wilson, he come an' he go,
Frum cabin to cabin in de county-o.
W'en he go to bed, his legs hang do'n,
An' his foots makes poles fer de chickens t' roost on.

Tom went down to de river, an' he couldn' go 'cross.
Tom tromp on a 'gater an' 'e think 'e wus a hoss.
Wid a mouf wide open, 'gater jump from de san',
An' dat Nigger look clean down to de Promus' Lan'.

Wa'k Tom Wilson, git out'n de way!
Wa'k Tom Wilson, don't wait all de day!
Wa'k Tom Wilson, here afternoon;
Sweep dat kitchen wid a bran' new broom.

90   Chicken Pie

"Bake Dat Chicken Pie" was a commercial "coon song" published by M. Witmark and Sons in 1906, with composer credits to Frank Dumont; it was recorded several times in the late teens by white vaudeville performers, and in 1927 by Tennessee singer Uncle Dave Macon (Vocalion 5148). Assuming that Talley was collecting around 1920, it is remarkable that such a currently popular vaudeville song would have already gone into oral tradition.

If you wants to make an ole Nigger feel good,
Let me tell you w'at to do:
Jes take off a chicken from dat chicken roost,
An' take 'im along wid you.
Take a liddle dough to roll 'im up in,
An' it'll make you wink yō' eye;
W'en dat good smell gits up yō' nose,
Frum dat home-made chicken pie.

Jes go round w'en de night's sorter dark,
An' dem chickens, dey can't see.
Be shore dat de bad dog's all tied up,
Den slip right close to de tree.
Now retch out yo' han' an' pull 'im in,
Den run lak a William goat;

An' if he holler, squeeze 'is neck,
An' shove 'im un'er yō' coat.

Bake dat Chicken pie!
It's mighty hard to wait
When you see dat Chicken pie,
Hot, smokin' on de plate.
Bake dat Chicken pie!
Yes, put in lots o' spice.
Oh, how I hopes to Goodness
Dat I gits de bigges' slice.

91   I Am Not Going to Hobo Any More

The opening formula is found in Brown (3:370).

My mammy done tol' me a long time ago
To always try fer to be a good boy;
To lay on my pallet an' to waller on de flō';
An' to never leave my daddy's house.
I hain't never gwineter hobo no mō'. By George!
I hain't never gwineter hobo no mō'.

Yes, befō' I'd live dat ar hobo life,
I'll tell you what I'd jes go an' do:
I'd court dat pretty gal an' take 'er fer my wife,
Den jes lay 'side dat ar hobo life.
I hain't never gwineter hobo no mō'. By George!
I hain't never gwineter hobo no mō'.

92   Forty-Four

This particular song does not appear in any of the standard collections of
black folksongs; it may, however, be related to the complex of blues songs
Paul Oliver calls "The Forty-Fours" and discusses in his *Screening the Blues:
Aspects of the Blues Tradition* (90–128).

If de people'll jes gimme
Des a liddle bit o' peace,

I'll tell 'em what happen
To de Chief o' Perlice.
He met a robber
Right at de dō'!
An' de robber, he shot 'im
Wid a forty-fō'!
He shot dat Perliceman.
He shot 'im shō'!
What did he soot 'im wid?
A forty-fō'.

Dey sent fer de Doctah
An' de Doctah he come.
He come in a hurry,
He come in a run.
He come wid his instriments
Right in his han',
To progue an' find
Dat forty-fō', Man!
De Doctah he progued;
He progued 'im shō'!
But he jes couldn' find
Dat forty-fō'.

Dey sent fer de Preachah,
An' de preachah he come.
He come in a walk,
An' he come in to talk.
He come wid 'is Bible,
Right in 'is han',
An' he read from dat chapter,
Forty-fō', Man!
Dat Preachah, he read.
He read, I know.
What Chapter did he read frum?
'Twus Forty-fō'!

Play Rhyme Section

93 Blindfold Play Chant

Oh blin' man! Oh blin' man!
You cain't never see.
Just tu'n 'round three times
You cain't ketch me.

Oh tu'n Eas'! Oh tu'n Wes'!
Ketch us if you can.
Did you thought dat you'd cotch us,
Mistah blin' man?

94 Fox and Geese Play

"For explanation of 'call,' and 'sponse,' see Study in Negro Folk Rhymes"
(Talley).

(Fox *Call*)   "Fox in de mawnin'!"
(Goose *Sponse*) "Goose in de evenin'!"
(Fox *Call*)   "How many geese you got?"
(Goose *Sponse*) "More 'an you're able to ketch!"

95 Hawk and Chickens Play

William Newell, in his *Games and Songs of American Children*, offers several
different descriptions of this "Hawk and Chickens" game (155–57); Scarborough

(138) also offers a version, as well as a description of the game as played by black children in rural Texas. The "witch" sits alone in the center while other children (the hen and her chicks) circle around and chant the rhyme. When the witch answers "Twelve o'clock," she can leap forward and catch one of the chicks. See also Randolph (3:382–83).

(Chicken's *Call*)	"Chickamee, chickamee, cranie-crow."
	I went to de well to wash my toe.
	W'en I come back, my chicken wus gone.
	W'at time, ole Witch?

(Hawk *Sponse*)	"One"
(Hawk *Call*)	"I wants a chick."
(Chicken's *Sponse*)	"Well, you cain't git mine."
(Hawk *Call*)	"I shall have a chick!"
(Chicken's *Sponse*)	"You shan't have a chick!"

96   Caught by the Witch Play

(Human *Call*)	"Molly, Molly, Molly-bright!"
(Witch *Sponse*)	"Three scō' an' ten!"
(Human *Call*)	"Can we git dar 'fore candle-light?"
(Witch *Sponse*)	"Yes, if yō' legs is long an' light."
(Conscience's Warning *Call*)	"You'd better watch out, Or de witches'll git yer!"

97   Goosie-Gander Play Rhyme

Talley discusses this rhyme in his "Study," below.

"Goosie, goosie, goosie-gander!
Waht d'you say?"—Say: 'Goose!'—
Ve'y well, go right along, Honey!
I tu'ns yō' years a-loose."

"Goosie, goosie, goosie-gander!
What d'you say?"—Say: 'Gander'
Ve'y well. Come in de ring, Honey!
I'll pull yō' years way yander!"

98   Hawk and Buzzard

Talley also used this song in his story "Why the Buzzard Is Black" in the "Negro Traditions" manuscript.

Once: De Hawk an' de buzzard went to roost,
   An' de hawk got up wid a broke off tooth.

Den: De hawk an' de buzzard went to law,
   An' de hawk come back wid a broke up jaw.

But lastly: Dat buzzard tried to plead his case,
   Den he went home wid a smashed in face.

99   Likes and Dislikes

I sho' loves Miss Donie! Oh, yes, I do!
   She's neat in de waist,
   Lak a needle in de case;
   An' she suits my taste.

I'se gwineter run wid Mollie Roalin'! Oh, yes, I will!
   She's pretty an' nice
   Lak a bottle full o' spice,
   But she's done drap me twice.

I don't lak Miss Jane! Oh no, I don't.
   She's fat an' stout,
   Got her mouf sticked out,
   An' she laks to pout.

100   Susie Girl

Brown (3:140) suggests a minstrel origin for this piece that has been collected as a dance tune in North Carolina. Music from "Leading Themes" notebook, where two different melodies are suggested (#5 and #6).

MELODY #5

MELODY #6

Ring 'round, Miss Susie gal,
Ring 'round, "My Dovie."
Ring 'round, Miss Susie gal.
Bless you! "My Lovie."

Back 'way, Miss Susie gal.
Back 'way, "My Money."
Now come back, Miss Susie gal.
Dat's right! "My Honey."

Swing me, Miss Susie gal.
Swing me, "My Starlin'."
Jes swing me, my Susie gal.
Yes "Love!" "My Darlin'."

101 Susan Jane

Variations of stanza 3 appear in White (243).

> I know somebody's got my Lover;
> Susan Jane! Susan Jane!
> Oh, cain't you tell me; help me find 'er?
> Susan Jane! Susan Jane!

> If I lives to see nex' Fall;
> Susan Jane! Susan Jane!
> I hain't gwineter sow no wheat at all.
> Susan Jane! Susan Jane!

> 'Way down yon'er in de middle o' de branch;
> Susan Jane! Susan Jane!
> De ole cow pat an' de buzzards dance.
> Susan Jane! Susan Jane!

102 Peep Squirrel

Other references to this common game song include: Botkin (159–60); Scarborough (134–35); Seeger, *American Folk Songs for Children* (18–19); Courlander's *Negro Folk Music U.S.A.* (160); and, more recently, Jones and Hawes (214).

> Peep squir'l, ying-ding-did-lum;
> Peep squir'l, it's almos' day,
> Look squir'l, ying-ding-did-lum,
> Look squir'l, an' run away.

> Walk squir'l, ying-ding-did-lum;
> Walk squir'l, fer dat's de way.
> Skip squir'l, ying-ding-did-lum;
> Skip squir'l, all dress in gray.

> Run squir'l! Ying-ding-did-lum!
> Run squir'l! Oh, run away!
> I cotch you squir'l! Ying-ding-did-lum!
> I cotch you squir'l! Now stay, I say.

103   Did You Feed My Cow?

A similar early text from black sources is found in Scarborough (141–42).
Music from "Leading Themes" notebook, #70.

"Did yer feed my cow?" "Yes, Mam!"
"Will yer tell me how?" "Yes Mam!"
"Oh, w'at did yer give 'er?" "Cawn an' hay."
"Oh, w'at did yer give 'er?" "Cawn 'an hay."

"Did yer milk 'er good?" "Yes, Mam!"
"Did yer do lak yer should?" "Yes, Mam!"
"Oh, how did yer milk 'er?" "Swish! Swish! Swish!"
"Oh, how did yer milk 'er?" "Swish! Swish! Swish!"

"Did dat cow git sick?" "Yes, Mam!"
"Wus she kivered wid tick?" "Yes, Mam!"
"Oh, how wus she sick?" "All bloated up."

"Oh, how wus she sick?" "All bloated up."
"Did dat cow die?" "Yes, Mam!"
"Wid a pain in 'er eye?" "Yes, Mam!"
"Oh, how did she die?" "Uh-! Uh-! Uh-!"
"Oh, how did she die?" "Uh-! Uh-! Uh-!"

"Did de Buzzards come?" "Yes, Mam!"
"Fer to pick 'er bone?" "Yes, Mam!"
"Oh, how did they come?" "Flop! Flop! Flop!"
"Oh, how did they come?" "Flop! Flop! Flop!"

104 A Budget

If I lives to see nex' Spring
I'se gwineter buy my wife a big gold ring.

If I lives to see nex' Fall,
I'se gwineter buy my wife a waterfall.

"When Christmas comes?" You cunnin' elf!
I'se gwineter spen' my money on myself.

105 The Old Black Gnats

Another rare song not found in standard collections. Talley suggests in his "Study" that the refrain "I can't git out'n here" in fact acts as a "response" to the "call" of line 1. Music from the "Leading Themes" notebook, #17.

Dem ole black gnats, dey is so bad
I cain't git out'n here.
Dey stings, an' bites, an' runs me mad;
I cain't git out'n here.

Dem ole black gnats dey sings de song,
"You cain't git out'n here.
Ole Satan'll git you befo' long;
You cain't git out'n here."

Dey burns my years, gits in my eye;
An' I cain't git out'n here.
Dey makes me dance, dey makes me cry;
An' I cain't git out'n here.

I fans an' knocks but dey won't go 'way!
I cain't git out'n here.
Dey makes me wish 'twus Jedgment Day;
Fer I cain't git out'n here.

106   Sugar Loaf Tea

According to Talley, the terms "Sugar-lo-tea" and "Candy" are "nicknames applied in imagination to the women engaged in playing in the Play Song."

Bring through yō' Sugar-lō'-tea, bring through yō' Candy,
All I want is to wheel, an' tu'n, an' bow to my Love so handy.

You tu'n here on Sugar-lō'-tea, I'll tu'n there on Candy.
All I want is to wheel, an' tu'n, an' bow to my Love so handy.

Some gits drunk on Sugar-lō'-tea, some gits drunk on Candy,
But all I wants is to wheel, an' tu'n, an' bow to my Love so handy.

107   Green Oak Tree! Rocky'o

For other variants, see Courlander (280), Newell (56), and, for a more recent collection, Jones and Hawes (74, as "Oh Green Fields, Roxie").

Green oak tree! Rocky'o! Green oak tree! Rocky'o!
Call dat one you loves, who it may be,
To come an' set by de side o' me.
"Will you hug 'im once an' kiss 'im twice?"
"W'y! I wouldn' kiss 'im once fer to save 'is life!"
Green oak tree! Rocky'o! Green oak tree! Rocky'o!

108   Kissing Song

A sleish o' bread an' butter fried,
Is good enough fer yō' sweet Bride.
Now choose yō' Lover, w'ile we sing,
An' call 'er nex' onto de ring.

"Oh my Love, how I loves you!
Nothin' 's in dis worl' above you.
Dis right han', fersake it never.
Dis heart, you mus' keep forever.
One sweet kiss, I now takes from you;
Caze I'se gwine away to leave you."

109　Kneel on this Carpet

Jes choose yō' Eas'; jes choose yō' Wes'.
Now choose de one you loves de bes'.
If she hain't here to take 'er part
Choose some one else wid all yō' heart.

Down on dis chyarpet you mus' kneel,
Shore as de grass grows in de fiel'.
Salute yō' Bride, an' kiss her sweet,
An' den rise up upon yō' feet.

110　Salt Rising Bread

Talley was apparently the first to present a black-derived version of this piece, more commonly known as "Shortenin' Bread." Only Perrow (1915) printed an earlier version, one collected from East Tennessee white singers. Other 1920s publications included those in Scarborough (149–153), White (193), and Richardson (81); versions, with annotations, are also found in Brown (3:535) and Randolph (2:328–29). Talley's version seems unique in its use of "saltin'" bread rather than "shorten'" bread; the former seems to refer to bread made from water-ground corn meal; the latter, according to Scarborough (149), to bread mixed with bacon bits or bacon gravy. She also notes that such bread is also called "cracklin'"—such as mentioned in the third stanza here.

I loves saltin', saltin' bread.
I loves saltin', saltin' bread.
Put on dat skillet, nev' mind de lead;
Caze I'se gwineter cook dat saltin' bread;
Yes, ever since my mammy's been dead,
I'se been makin' an' cookin' dat saltin' bread.

I loves saltin', saltin' bread.
I loves saltin', saltin' bread.
You loves biscuit, butter, an' fat?
I can dance Shiloh better 'an dat.
Does you turn 'round an' shake yō' head?—
Well; I loves saltin', saltin' bread.

I loves saltin', saltin' bread.
I loves saltin', saltin' bread.
W'en you ax yō' mammy fer butter an' bread,
She don't give nothin' but a stick across yō' head.
On cracklin's, you say, you wants to git fed?
Well, I loves saltin', saltin' bread.

III   Precious Things

Talley notes that "Gooshen Ben'" in line 2 means "Grecian Bend"; that, in turn, refers to an angle at which women walked in the era when bustles and wasp waists were in fashion.

Hol' my rooster, hōl' my hen,
Pray don't tetch my Gooshen Ben'.

Hol' my bonnet, hōl' my shawl,
Pray don't tetch my waterfall.

Hōl' my han's by de finger tips,
But pray don't tetch my sweet liddle lips.

112   He Loves Sugar and Tea

Mistah Buster, he loves sugar an' tea.
Mistah Buster, he loves candy.
Mistah Buster, he's a Jim-dandy!
He can swing dem gals so handy.

Charlies' up an' Charlie's down.
Charlie's fine an' dandy.

Ev'ry time he goes to town,
He gits dem gals stick candy.

Dat Niggah, he love sugar an' tea.
Dat Niggah love dat candy.
Fine Niggah! He can wheel 'em 'round,
An' swing dem ladies handy.

Mistah Sambo, he love sugar an' tea.
Mistah Sambo love his candy.
Mistah Sambo; he's dat han'some man
What goes wid sister Mandy.

113   Here Comes a Young Man Courting

See Botkin (328–30); Brown (1:89–93); Newell (47–50), for representative annotations; a more recent collection is in Jones and Hawes (71, as "Johnny Cuckoo"). Music from Talley's "Leading Themes" notebook, #21.

Here comes a young man a courtin'! Courtin'! Courtin'!
Here comes a young man a-courtin'! It's Tidlum Tidelum Day.
"Say! Won't you have one o' us? Us, Sir? Us, Sir?
Say! Won't you have one o' us, Sir?" dem brown skin ladies say.

"You is too black an' rusty! Rusty! Rusty!
You is too black an' rusty!" said Tidlum Tidelum Day.
We hain't no blacker 'an you, Sir! You, Sir! You, Sir!
We hain't no blacker 'an you, Sir!" dem brown skin ladies say.

"Pray! Won't you have one o' us, Sir? Us, Sir? Us, Sir?
Pray! Won't you have one o' us, Sir?" say yaller gals all gay.
"You is too ragged an' dirty! Dirty! Dirty!
You is too ragged an' dirty!" said Tidlum Tidelum Day.

"You shore is got de bighead! Bighead! Bighead!
You shore is got de bighead! You needn' come dis way.
We's good enough fer you, Sir! You, Sir! You, Sir!
We's good enough fer you, Sir!" dem yaller gals all say.

"De fairest one dat I can see, dat I can see, dat I can see,
De fairest one dat I can see," said Tidlum Tidelum Day.
"My Lulu, come an' wa'k wid me, wa'k wid me, wa'k wid me.
My Lulu, come an' wa'k wid me. 'Miss Tidlum Tidelum Day.'"

114   Anchor Line

The Anchor Line, formerly known as the St. Louis and New Orleans, was
one of the best-known nineteenth-century steamship lines of the West. Among
its other accomplishments, it was the first line to put regular uniforms on
its crew. The music here is from the "Leading Themes" notebook, #38.
(Note: measure 6 contains an apparent missing eighth note count; no attempt has been made to "correct" it.)

I'se gwine out on de Anchor Line, Dinah!
I won't git back 'fore de summer time, Dinah!
W'en I come back be "dead in line,"
I'se gwineter bring you a dollar an' a dime,
Shore as I gits in from de Anchor Line, Dinah!

If you loves me lak I loves you, Dinah!
No Coon can cut our love in two, Dinah!
If you'll jes come an' go wid me,

Come go wid me to Tennessee,
Come go wid me; I'll set you free,—Dinah!

115 Sallie

Music is from the "Leading Themes" notebook (#69); not found in most of the standard black folksong collections.

Sallie! Sallie! don't you want to marry?
Sallie! Sallie! do come an' tarry!
Sallie! Sallie! Mammy says to tell her when.
Sallie! Sallie! She's gwineter kill dat turkey hen!

Sallie! Sallie! When you goes to marry,
(Sallie! Sallie!) Marry a fahmin man(!)
(Sallie! Sallie!) Ev'ry day'll be Mond'y,
(Sallie! Sallie!) Wid a hoe-handle in yō' han'!

116 Song to the Runaway Slave

Talley notes: "The story went among Negroes that a runaway slave husband returned every night, and knocked on the window of his wife's cabin to get food. Other slaves having betrayed the secret that he was still in the vicinity, he was sold in the woods to a slave trader at reduced price. This trader was to come next day with bloodhounds to hunt him down. On the night after the sale, when the runaway slave husband knocked, the slave wife pinched their baby to make it cry. Then she sang the [below] song (as if singing to the baby), so that he might, if possible, effect his escape."

Though the song is not readily found in many standard collections, in the late 1920s it was popularized over NBC radio and WSM's Grand Ole Opry by a singing group called The Pickard Family, from a county just north of Nashville. In 1928, they recorded the song (as "Get Away from that Window) for the Plaza Company in New York, and this recording remained popular throughout the 1930s, appearing on no fewer than twelve different record labels, including these sold by Sears-Roebuck. In the early 1960s, the song gained renewed popularity during the folk revival, when it was performed and recorded under the title "Razors in the Air" by the Kingston Trio. White (325) offers a stanza collected in Alabama and cites an earlier appearance in William Cameron's *Volk's Theatre Songster* (11).

Go 'way from dat window, "My Honey, My Love!"
Go 'way from dat window! I say.
De baby's in de bed, an' his mammy's lyin' by,
But you cain't git yō' lodgin' here.

Go 'way from dat window, "My Honey, My Love!"
Go 'way from dat window! I say;
Fer ole Mosser's got 'is gun, an' to Miss'ip' youse been sōl';
So you cain't git yō' lodgin' here.

Go 'way from dat window, "My Honey, My Love!"
Go 'way from dat window! I say.
De baby keeps a-cryin'; but you'd better un'erstan'
Dat you cain't git yō' lodgin' here.

Go 'way from dat window, "My Honey, My Love!"
Go 'way from dat window! I say;
Fer de Devil's in dat man, an' you'd better un'erstan'
Dat you cain't git yō' lodgin' here.

117   Down in the Lonesome Garden

Hain't no use to weep, hain't no use to moan;
Down in a lonesome gyardin.
You cain't git no meat widout pickin' up a bone,
Down in a lonesome gyardin.

Look at dat gal! How she puts on airs,
Down in de lonesome gyardin!
But what did she git dem closes she w'ars,
Down in de lonesome gyardin?

It hain't gwineter rain, an' it hain't gwineter snow;
Down in my lonesome gyardin.
You hain't gwinter eat in my kitchen doo',
Nor down in my lonesome gyardin.

118   Little Sister, Won't You Marry Me?

Liddle sistah in de barn, jine de weddin'.
Youse de sweetest liddle couple dat I ever did see.
Oh Love! Love! Ahms all 'round me!
Say, liddle sistah, won't you marry me?

Oh step back, gal, an' don't you come a nigh me,
Wid all dem sassy words dat you say to me.
Oh Love! Love! Ahms all 'roun' me!
Oh liddle sistah, won't you marry me?

119   Raise a "Rucus" To-night

In *Folk Song U.S.A.* (1947), John A. and Alan Lomax note that this is "an ante-bellum Negro hoedown or jig tune with an overlay of minstrel-show influence" (111). Again, Talley was one of the first to publish a text, though most early printed versions come from black sources. See Odum and Johnson, *Negro Workaday Songs* (173–174), which contains versions from Georgia, Tennessee, and North Carolina; and Brown (3:558–59). The stanza 1 seen here is similar to a stanza in White (194), while stanza 2 appears in the same source (385). There were at least two commercial recordings from the 1920s by black singers: one by the Norfolk Jazz Quartet (a singing group) on Paramount 12032 (1923), and one by the Southern Negro Quartet on Columbia 14048 (1924). However, as is often the case with Talley's songs, "Raise a Rucus" was also popular with early white country recording groups. Two Tennessee artists were among these: East Tennessee fiddler/singer Charlie Bowman (Columbia 15455, 1929). North Georgia singer Bill Chitwood also recorded a version as "Raise Rough House Tonight" for Okeh in 1928 (Okeh 45236). The song enjoyed renewed popularity in the 1960s during the folk revival.

> Two liddle Niggers all dressed in white,
>   (Raise a rucus to-night.)
> Want to go to Heaben on de tail of a kite.
>   (Raise a rucus to-night.)
> De kite string broke; dem Niggers fell;
>   (Raise a rucus to-night.)
> Whar dem Niggers go, I hain't gwineter tell.
>   (Raise a rucus to-night.)
>
> A Nigger an' a w'ite man a playin' seben up;
>   (Raise a rucus to-night.)
> De Nigger beat de w'ite man, but 'ē's skeered to pick it up.
>   (Raise a rucus to-night.)
> Dat Nigger grabbed de money, an' de w'ite man fell.
>   (Raise a rucus to-night.)
> How de Nigger run, I'se not gwineter tell.
>   (Raise a rucus to-night.)
>
> Look here, Nigger! Let me tell you a naked fac':
>   (Raise a rucus to-night.)
> You mought a been cullud widout bein' dat black;
>   (Raise a rucus to-night.)
> Dem 'ar feet look lak youse shō' walkin' back;
>   (Raise a rucus to-night.)
> An' yō' ha'r, it look lak a chyarpet tack.
>   (Raise a rucus to-night.)
>
> Oh come 'long, chilluns, come 'long,
> W'ile dat moon are shinin' bright.
> Let's git on board, an' float down de river,
> An' raise dat rucus to-night.

120   Sweet Pinks and Roses

Music from "Leading Themes" notebook, #50.

Sweet pinks an' roses, strawbeers on de vines,
Call in de one you loves, an' kiss 'er if you minds.
Here sets a pretty gal,
Here sets a pretty boy;
Cheeks painted rosy, an' deir eyes battin' black.
You kiss dat pretty gal, an' I'll stan' back.

Pastime Rhyme Section

121 Satan

De Lawd made man, an' de man made money.
De Lawd made de bees, an 'de bees made honey.
De Lawd made ole Satan, an' ole Satan he make sin.
Den de Lawd, He make a liddle hole to put ole Satan in.

Did you ever see de Devil, wid his iron handled shovel,
A scrapin' up de san' in his ole tin pan?
He cuts up mighty funny, he steals all yō' money,
He blinds you wid his san'. He's tryin' to git you, man!

122 Johnny Bigfoot

Johnny, Johnny Bigfoot!
Want a pair o' shoes?
Go kick two cows out'n deir skins.
Run Brudder, tell de news!

123 The Thrifty Slave

Apparently a version of "Root Hog or Die," a song that has obscure origins
in the pre–Civil War minstrel stage. Further annotations are found in Randolph (3:162) and Brown (3:441–42), though neither offers a text exactly like
this one.

Jes wuk all day,
Den go huntin' in de wood.

Ef you cain't ketch nothin',
Den you hain't no good.
Don't look at Mosser's chickens,
Caze dey're roostin' high.
Big pig, liddle pig, root hog or die!

124   Wild Negro Bill

I'se wild Nigger Bill
Frum Redpepper Hill.
I never did wo'k, an' I never will.

I'se done killed de Boss.
I'se knocked down de hoss.
I eats up raw goose widout apple sauce!

I'se Run-a-way Bill,
I knows dey mought kill;
But ole Mosser hain't cotch me, an' he never will!

125   You Love Your Girl

You loves yō' gal?
Well, I loves mine.
Yō' gal hain't common?
Well, my gal's fine.

I loves my gal,
She hain't no goose —
Blacker 'an blackberries,
Sweeter 'an juice.

126   Frightened Away from a Chicken-Roost

A familiar stanza found in most early black folksong collections. See White (372) and Scarborough (194); even earlier variants appear in pre–Civil War minstrel songsters, such as *The Negro Singer's Own Book* (1846), p. 312. Evidence of its popularity in white tradition comes from its inclusion in Richardson's *American Mountain Songs* (1927), p. 103, as part of the longer piece called "Jest Talking." In 1926 a white South Carolina singer named Chris Bouchillon made a very popular commercial phonograph record, "Talking Blues," Columbia 15120, which utilized this stanza. His rendition of "Talking Blues" became a country music favorite in the 1930s, when it was adapted and performed almost weekly by Robert Lunn on the Grand Ole Opry from Nashville.

> I went down to de hen house on my knees,
> An' I thought I heared dat chicken sneeze.
> You'd oughter seed dis Nigger a'gittin' 'way frum dere,
> But 'twusn't nothin' but a rooster sayin' his prayer.
> How I wish dat rooster's prayer would en',
> Den perhaps I mought eat dat ole gray hen.

127   Bedbug

Part of a large family of songs involving three-way comparisons; some deal with women, some with animals, some with insects. The basic form of the song may date as far back as the 1840s. A good annotation is found in White (316–21).

> De June-bug's got de golden wing,
> De Lightning-bug de flame;
> De Bedbug's got no wing at all,
> But he gits dar jes de same.
>
> De Punkin-bug's got a punkin smell,
> De Squash-bug smells de wust;
> But de puffume of dat ole Bedbug,
> It's enough to make you bust.
>
> W'en dat Bedbug come down to my house,
> I wants my walkin' cane.
> Go git a pot an' scald 'im hot!
> Good-by, Miss Lize Jane!

128   How to Get to Glory Land

Another floating verse that has been incorporated into the country music "Talking Blues" (cf. item 126, above), this verse was also included in the Bouchillon text cited above. This particular stanza by itself appears twice in White (135, 144), in Scarborough (225), and Perrow (1913), p. 158.

> If you wants to git to Glory Land,
> I'll tell you what to do:
> Jes grease yō' heels wid mutton sue,
> W'en de Devil's atter you.
> Jes grease yō' heel an' grease yō' han',
> An' slip 'way—over into Glory Lan'.

129   Destitute Former Slave Owners

> Missus an' Mosser a-walkin' de street,
> Deir han's in deir pockets an' nothin' to eat.
> She'd better be home a-washin' up de dishes,
> An' a-cleanin' up de ole man's raggitty britches.
> He'd better run 'long an' git out de hoes
> An' clear out his own crooked weedy corn rows;
> De Kingdom is come, de Niggers is free.
> Hain't no Nigger slaves in de Year Jubilee.

130   Fattening Frogs for Snakes

A song by this name was recorded in the 1940s by a black string band called The Mobile Strugglers (cf. Paul Oliver, *The Meaning of the Blues* (73–74), but except for the final line, that one seems to have little in common with this version. "Fattenin' frogs fer snakes" is a proverbial expression of futility.

> You needn' sen' my gal hoss apples
> You needn' sen' her 'lasses candy;
> She would keer fer de lak o' you,
> Ef you'd sen' her apple brandy.

W'y don't you git some common sense?
Jes git a liddle! Oh fer land sakes!
Quit yō' foolin', she hain't studyin' you!
Youse jes fattenin' frogs fer snakes!

131   The Mule's Kick

Is dis me, or not me,
Or is de Devil got me?
Wus dat a muskit shot me?
Is I laid here more'n a week?—
Dat ole mule do kick amazin',
An' I 'spec's he's now a-grazin'
On de t'other side de creek.

132   Christmas Turkey

I prayed to de Lawd fer tucky-o.
Dat tucky wouldn' come.
I prayed, an' I prayed 'til I'se almos' daid.
No tucky at my home.

Chrismus Day, she almos' here;
My wife, she mighty mad.
She want dat tucky mo' an' mo'.
An' she want 'im mighty bad.

I prayed 'til de scales come on my knees,
An' still no tucky come.
I tuck myse'f to my tucky roos',
An' I brung my tucky home.

133   A Full Pocketbook

De goose at de barn, he feel mighty funny,
Caze de duck find a pocketbook chug full o' money.
De goose say: "Whar is you gwine, my Sonny?"
An' de duck, he say: "Now good-by, Honey."

De duck chaw terbacker an' de goose drink wine,
Wid a stuffed pocketbook dey shō had a good time;
De grasshopper played de fiddle on a punkin vine
'Till dey all fall over on a sorter dead line.

134   No Room to Poke Fun

Nev' mîn' if my nose are flat,
An' my face are black an' sooty;
De Jaybird hain't so big in song,
An' de Bullfrog hain't no beauty.

135   Crooked Nose Jane

I courted a gal down de lane.
Her name, it wus Crooked Nose Jane.
Her face wus white speckled, her lips wus all red,
An' she look jes as lean as a weasel half-fed.

136   Bad Features

Blue gums an' black eyes;
Run 'round an' tell lies.
Liddle head, liddle wit;
Big long head, not a bit.

Wid his long crooked toes,
An' his heel right roun';
Dat flat-footed Nigger
Make a hole in de groun'.

137   Miss Slippy Sloppy

Ole Miss Slippy Sloppy jump up out'n bed,
Den out'n de winder she poke 'er nappy head,
"Jack! O Jack! De gray goose's dead.
Dat fox done gone an' bit off 'er head!"

Jack run up de hill an' he call Mosser's hounds;
An' w'en dat fox hear dem turble sounds,
He sw'ar by his head an' his hide all 'round,
Dat he don't want no dinner, but a hole in de ground.

138   How to Make It Rain

Go kill dat snake an' hang him high,
Den tu'n his belly to de sky.
De storm an' rain'll come bye an' bye.

139   A Wind-Bag

A Nigger come a-struttin' up to me las' night;
In his han' wus a walkin' cane,
He tipped his hat an' give a low bow;
"Howdy-doo! Miss Lize Jane!"

But I didn' ax him how he done,
Which make a hint good pinned,
Dat I'd druther have a paper bag,
When it's sumpin' to be filled up wid wind.

140   Going to Be Good Slaves

Ole Mosser an' Missus has gone down to town,
Dey said dey'd git us somethin' an' dat hain't no jokes.
I'se gwineter be good all de whilst dey're all 'way,
An' I'se gwineter wear stockin's jes lak de white folks.

141 Page's Geese

Apparently this was a local song. Talley explains in his original note: "The Northern soldiers during the Civil War took all of a southern planter's geese except one lone gander. They put one penny, for each goose taken, into a small bag and tied the bag around the gander's neck. They then sent him home to his owner with the pay of one penny for each goose taken. The Negroes of the community at once made up this little song."

> Ole man Page'll be in a turble rage,
> W'en he find out, it'll raise his dander.
> Yankee soldiers bought his geese, fer one cent a-piece,
> An' sent de pay home by de gander.

142 To Win a Yellow Girl

> If you wants to win a yaller gal,
> I tell you what you do;
> You "borrow" Mosser's Beaver hat,
> An' slip on his Long-tailed Blue.

143 Sex Laugh

> "You'se heared a many a gal laugh,
> An' say: "He! He-he! He-he-he!"
> But you hain't heared no boy laugh,
> An' say: "She! She-she! She-she-she!"

144 Outrunning the Devil

Brown (3:221) has a stanza similar to the second one here.

> I went upon de mountain,
> An' I seed de Devil comin'.
> I retched an' got my hat an' coat,
> An' I beat de Devil runnin'.

As I run'd down across de fiel',
A rattlesnake bit me on de heel.
I rears an' pitches an' does my bes',
An' I falls right back in a hornet's nes'.

For w'en I wus a sinnah man,
I rund by leaps an' boun's.
I wus afeard de Devil 'ould ketch me
Wid his ole three legged houn's.

But now I'se come a Christun,
I kneels right down an' prays,
An' den de Devil runs from me —
I'se tried dem other ways.

145 How to Keep or Kill the Devil

If you wants to see de Devil smile,
Simpully do lak his own chile.

If you wants to see de Devil git spunk,
Swallow whisky, an' git drunk.

If you wants to see de Devil live,
Cuss an' swar an' never give.

If you wants to see de Devil run,
Jes tu'n a loose de Gospel gun.

If you wants to see de Devil fall,
Hit him wid de Gospel ball.

If you wants to see de Devil beg,
Nail him wid a Gospel peg.

If you wants to see de Devil sick,
Beat him wid a Gospel stick.

If you wants to see de Devil die,
Feed him up on Gospel pie.

But de Devil w'ars dat iron shoe,
An' if you don't watch, he'll slip it on you.

146 John Henry

For a good summary of the complex history of this famous ballad, see Norm
Cohen, *Long Steel Rail: The Railroad in American Folksong*. Parts of the ballad
have appeared in print since about 1900, though, as Cohen notes, "the earliest
collected versions, the earliest printed version, and the earliest recorded versions . . . were all by whites" (70). Talley's text might well be one of the first
black-derived versions to reach print, though he was followed in 1926 by both
Odum and Johnson *The Negro and His Songs* (222) and Scarborough (218).
The first commercial recording of the song was by the white entertainer
Fiddlin' John Carson (Okeh 7004, 1924); the first recording by a black singer
was that by Texas songster Henry Thomas (Vocalion 1094, 1927), who used
a guitar and the reed-pipes (cf. Talley's "Study," below) as accompaniment.
Three artists from Talley's collecting area also made recordings shortly after
Talley's book came out; they were Grand Ole Opry stars DeFord Bailey (a
black harmonica player), on Victor 23336 (1928); and Harkreader and Moore,
Paramount 3023 (1928). A black string band headed by Evans and McClain,
"The Two Poor Boys," recorded a version in 1930 for the American Record
Company that was issued on numerous labels.

John Henry, he wus a steel-drivin' man.
He died wid his hammer in his han'.
O come long boys, an' line up de track,
For John Henry, he hain't never comin' back.

John Henry said to his Cappun: "Boss,
A man hain't nothin' but a man,
An' 'fore I'll be beat in dis sexion gang,
I'll die wid a hammer in my han'."

John Henry, he had a liddle boy,
He helt 'im in de pam of his han';
An' de las' word he say to dat chile wus:
"I wants you to be my steel-drivin' man."

John Henry, he had a pretty liddle wife,
An' her name, it wus Polly Ann.

She walk down de track, widout lookin' back,
For to see her big fine steel-drivin' man.

John Henry had dat pretty liddle wife,
An' she went all dress up in red.
She walk ev'y day down de railroad track
To de place whar her steel-drivin' man fell dead.

147   The Nashville Ladies

Talley notes: "The name of the place was used where the rhyme was repeated."

Dem Nashville ladies dress up fine.
Got longpail hoopskirts down behīn'!
Got deir bonnets to deir shoulders an' deir noses in de sky!
Big pig! Liddle pig! Root hog, or die!

148   The Rascal

I'se de bigges' rascal fer my age.
I now speaks from dis public stage.
I'se stole a cow; I'se stole a calf,
An' dat hain't more 'an jes 'bout half.

Yes, Mosser! — Lover of my soul! —
"How many chickens has I stole?"
Well; three las' night, an' two night befo';
An' I'se gwine 'fore long to git four mō'.

But you see dat hones' Billy Ben,
He done e't more dan erry three men.
He e't a ham, en e't a side;
He would a e't mō', but you know he died.

149   Coffee Grows on White Folks' Trees

The annals of traditional white folk music are filled with versions of a play-party song called "Coffee Grows on White Oak Trees." Versions of this appear as early as 1914 (Perrow, 187); see also Randolph (3:309–311) and Brown (3:110). Edwin C. Kirkland's "Check List of The Titles of Tennessee Folksongs" (423–76) lists two versions of the song, both from Middle Tennessee. John and Alan Lomax print a version in *Folk Song U.S.A.* (140–41). Textual similarities show clearly that these songs are the same as Talley's, except for the significant change in tone brought about by switching the phonetically similar "white oak" to "white folks." This change, and the attendant references to "de Nigger can git dat w'en he please," make the Talley text quite unusual. As to which version came first, the only clue is that coffee traditionally does not grow on white oak trees in a literal sense, but does grow on "white folks trees" in the surrealistic landscape where rivers run with milk and brandy, as they do in the Talley version.

Talley offered two tunes for this song in the "Leading Themes" notebook, #67 and #102.

MELODY #67

MELODY #102

Note: the key signature of A major (three sharps) was scratched out on the original score.

Coffee grows on w'ite folks' trees,
But de Nigger can git dat w'en he please.
De w'ite folks loves deir milk an' brandy,
But dat black gal's sweeter dan 'lasses candy.

Coffee grows on w'ite folks trees,
An' dere's a river dat runs wid milk an' brandy.
De rocks is broke an' filled wid gold,
So dat yaller gal loves dat high-hat dandy.

150   Aunt Jemima

"Leading Themes" notebook, #10.

Ole Aunt Jemima grow so tall,
Dat she couldn' see de groun'.
She stumped her toe, an' down she fell
From de Blackwoods clean to town.

W'en Aunt Jemima git in town,
An' see dem "tony" ways,
She natchully faint an' back she fell
To de Backwoods whar she stays.

151   The Mule's Nature

If you sees a mule tied up to a tree,
You mought pull his tail an' think about me.
For if a Nigger don't know de natcher of a mule,
It makes no diffunce what 'comes of a fool.

152   I'm a "Round-Town" Gentleman

I hain't no wagon, hain't no dray,
Jes come to town wid a load o' hay.
I hain't no cornfield to go to bed
Wid a lot o' hay-seeds in my head.
I'se a "round-town" Gent an' I don't choose
To wuk in de mud, an' do widout shoes.

153   This Sun Is Hot

Dis sun are hot,
Dis hoe are heavy,
Dis grass grow furder dan I can reach;
An' as I looks
At dis Cotton fiel',
I thinks I mus' 'a' been called to preach.

154   Uncle Jerry Fants

Has you heared 'bout Uncle Jerry Fants?
He's got on some cu'ious shapes.
He'd de one what w'ars em white duck pants,
An' he sot down on a bunch o' grapes.

155   Kept Busy

Jes as soon as de sun go down,
My True-love's on my min'.
An' jes as soon as de daylight breaks
De white folks is got me a gwine.

She's de sweetes' thing in town;
An' when I sees dat Nig,
She make my heart go "pitty-pat,"
An' my head go "whirly-gig."

156   Crossing a Foot-Log

A verse from the popular white folk song "Little Brown Jug." White (213)
prints a similar version from a black source. For other references, see Randolph (3:141–42).

Me an' my wife an' my bobtail dog
Start 'cross de creek on a hick'ry log.
We all fall in an' git good wet,
But I helt to my liddle brown jug, you bet!

157   Watermelon Preferred

This appears to be the refrain for the well-known minstrel song "Watermelon
on the Vine"; for comments and references, see Brown (3:529, 540). The song
was another popular with early country music players; Uncle Dave Macon
recorded a version in 1925 (Vocaliion 5063), and the Georgia string band The
Skillet Lickers recorded a version in 1926 (Columbia 15091) which was a
best-seller.

Dat hambone an' chicken are sweet.
Dat 'possum meat are sholy fine.
But give me, — now don't you cheat! —
(Oh, I jes wish you would give me!)
Dat watermillion, smilin' on de vine.

158   "They Steal" Gossip

Brown (3:508–509) offers several texts of this song, notes that the piece seems as common with blacks as with whites, and suggests a source as far back as an 1845 songster. See also White (370–72).

> *You know:*
>   Some folks say dat a Nigger won't steal,
>   But Mosser cotch six in a watermillion fiel';
>   A-cuttin', an' a-pluggin' an' a-tearin' up de vines,
>   A-eatin' all de watermillions, an' a-stackin' up de rinds.
>
> *Uh-huh! Yes, I heared dat:*
>   Ole Mosser stole a middlin' o' meat,
>   Ole Missus stole a ham;
>   Dey sent 'em bofe to de Wuk-house,
>   An' dey had to leave de land.

159   Fox and Rabbit Drinking Proposition

> Fox on de low ground,
> Rabbit on de hill.
> Says he: "I'll take a drink,
> An' leave you a gill."
>
> De fox say: "Honey,
> (You sweet liddle elf!)
> Jes hand me down de whole cup;
> I wants it fer myself."

160   A Turkey Funeral

> Dis tucky once on earth did dwell;
> An' "Gobble! Gobble! Gobble!"
> But now he gives me bigges' joy,
> An' rests from all his trouble.
>
> Yes, now he's happy, so am I;
> No hankerin' fer a feas':

Because I'se stuffed wid tucky meat,
An' he struts in tucky peace.

161   Our Old Mule

We had an ole mule an' he wouldn' go "gee";
So I knocked 'im down wid a single-tree.
To daddy dis wus some mighty bad news,
So he made me jump up an' outrun de Jews.

162   The College Ox

Ole Ox! Ole Ox! How'd you come up here?
You'se shō' plowed de cotton fields for many a, many a year.
You'se been kicked an' cuffed about wid heaps an' heaps abuse.
Now! Now, you comes up here fer some sort o' College use.

163   Care in Bread-Making

W'en you sees dat gal o' mine,
Jes tell 'er fer me, if you please,
Nex' time she goes to make up bread
To roll up 'er dirty sleeves.

164   Why Look at Me?

What's you lookin' at me fer?
I didn' come here to stay.
I wants dis bug put in yō' years,
An' den I'se gwine away.

I'se got milk up in my bucket,
I'se got butter up in my bowl;
But I hain't got no Sweetheart
Fer to sae my soul.

165　A Short Letter

She writ me a letter
As long as my eye.
An' she say in dat' letter:
"My Honey!—Good-by!"

166　Does Money Talk?

Dem whitefolks say dat money talk.
If it talk lak dey tell,
Den ev'ry time it come to Sam,
It up an' say: "Farewell!"

167　I'll Eat When I'm Hungry

A version of the "Rye Whiskey"/"Jack of Diamonds" tune complex, this song
is widely collected from white folk sources but seldom found in black collections; in fact, Talley's might be one of the first such printings of it. Cohen's
edition of Randolph's *Ozark Folk Songs* (344–45) offers a good set of citations
and notes that this, too, was another of Talley's songs that was taken up by
early country music singers in the 1920s and 1930s, with at least four recordings for commercial companies.

The tune here is from the "Leading Themes" notebook (identified as #40),
and is the familiar tune associated with other versions of the song. Talley's
original notation here contained several fermatas, or holds, which are also
reproduced here.

I'll eat when I'se hongry,
An' I'll drink when I'se dry;
An' if de whitefolks don't kill me,
I'll live till I die.

In my liddle log cabin,
Ever since I'se been born;
Dere hain't been no nothin'
'Cept dat hard salt parch corn.

But I knows whar's a henhouse,
An' de tucky he charve;
An' if ole Mosser don't kill me,
I cain't never starve.

168   Hear-Say

Hello! Br'er Jack. How do you do?
I'se been a-hearin' a heaps o' things 'bout you.
I'll jes declar! It beats de Dickuns!
Dey's been tryin' to say you's been a-stealin' chickens!

169   Negro Soldier's Civil War Chant (Old Abe)

Tune from "Leading Themes" notebook, #33.

Ole Abe (God bless 'is ole soul!)
Got a plenty good victuals, an' a plenty good clo'es.
Got powder an' shot, an' lead,
To bust in Adam's liddle Confed'
In dese hard times.

Oh, once dere wus union, an' den dere wus peace;
De slave, in de cornfield, bare up to his knees.
But de Rebel's in gray, an' Sesesh's in de way,
An' de slave'll be free
In dese hard times.

170 Parody on "Now I Lay Me Down to Sleep"

Parody was by no means uncommon in black traditional music; see White's entire chapter on it in *American Negro Folk-Songs* (130–47).

Uh-huh: "Now I lays me down to sleep!"—
While deadl oudles o' bedbugs 'round me creep,—
Well: If dey bites me befo' "I" wake,
I hopes "deir" ole jawbones'll break.

171 I'll Get You, Rabbit!

For a similar song collected from Mississippi, see Seeger, *American Folk Songs for Children* (98).

Rabbit! Rabbit! You'se got a mighty habit,
A-runnin' through de grass,
Eatin' up my cabbages;
But I'll git you shore at las'.

Rabbit! Rabbit! Ole rabbit in de bottoms,
A-playin' in de san',
By to-morrow mornin',
You'll be in my fryin' pan.

172   The Elephant

African-American jump-rope rhyme, versions of which appear in Abrahams, *Jump-Rope Rhymes: A Dictionary* (72); Brown (1:172); and, more recently, Jones and Hawes (25–26).

> My mammy gimme fifteen cents
> Fer to see dat elephan' jump de fence.
> He jump so high, I didn' see why,
> If she gimme a dollar he mought not cry.
>
> So I axed my mammy to gimme a dollar,
> Fer to go an' hear de elephan' holler.
> He holler so loud, he skeered de crowd.
>
> Nex' he jump so high, he tetch de sky;
> An' he won't git back 'fore de fo'th o' July.

173   A Few Negroes by State

> Alabammer Nigger say he love mush.
> Tennessee Nigger say: "Good Lawd, hush!"
>
> Fifteen cents in de panel of de fence,
> South Ca'lina Nigger hain't got no sense.
>
> Dat Kentucky Nigger jes think he's fine,
> 'Cause he drink dat Gooseberry wine.
>
> I'se done heared some twenty year ago
> Dat de Missippi Nigger hafter sleep on de flō'.
>
> Lousanner Nigger fall out'n de bed,
> An' break his head on a pone o' co'n bread.

174   How to Please a Preacher

Often called "Preacher Blues," this is seldom found in printed collections, but has appeared on numerous commercial recordings, such as ones by Hi Henry Brown (Vocalion 1728, 1932), and by Memphis singer Frank Stokes. In 1937, University of Tennessee professor Edwin Kirkland recorded a version of the song from two North Carolina blues singers (cf. Tennessee Folklore Society LP TFS 106). There were also recordings by early country singers, such as that by Bill Chitwood, a Georgia singer, in 1927 (Okeh 45131).

> If you wants to see dat Preachah laugh,
> Jes change up a dollar, an' give 'im a half.
> If you wants to make dat Preachah sing,
> Kill dat tucky an' give him a wing.
> If you wants to see dat Preachah cry,
> Kill dat chicken an' give him a thigh.

175   Looking for a Fight

> I went down town de yudder night,
> A-raisin' san' an a-wantin' a fight.
> Had a forty dollar razzer, an' a gatlin' gun,
> Fer to shoot dem Niggers down one by one.

176   I'll Wear Me a Cotton Dress
(Milly Biggers)

An unusual black version of the familiar song "Jenny Jenkins," which has been collected from Vermont to Missouri; see Brown (3:102–103) for basic references. Kirkland, in his 1946 list of "Tennessee Folksongs," cites two versions collected in the 1930s in East Tennessee. None of these versions appear, however, to have come from black sources. The references in this text to "cooperse" (copperas, or sulphate of iron, as Talley notes) as a dye marks this version as very early and authentic.

Music from "Leading Themes" notebook, #27.

Oh, will you wear red? Oh, will you wear red?
Oh, will you wear red, Milly Biggers?
"I won't wear red,
It's too much lak Missus' head.
I'll wear me a cotton dress,
Dyed wid copperse an' oak-bark."

Oh, will you wear blue? Oh, will you wear blue?
Oh, will you wear blue, Milly Biggers?
"I won't wear blue,
It's too much lak Missus' shoe.
I'll wear me a cotton dress,
Dyed wid copperse an' oak-bark."

You sholy would wear gray? You sholy would wear gray?
You sholy would wear gray, Milly Biggers?
"I won't wear gray,
It's too much lak Missus' way.
I'll wear me a cotton dress,
Dyed wid copperse an' oak-bark."

Well, will you wear white? Well, will you wear white?
Well, will you wear white, Milly Biggers?
"I won't wear white,
I'd get dirty long 'fore night.
I'll wear me a cotton dress,
Dyed wid copperse an' oak-bark."

Now, will you wear black? Now, will you wear black?
Now, will you wear black, Milly Biggers?
"I mought wear black,
Case it's de color o' my back;
An' it looks lak my cotton dress,
Dyed wid copperse an' oak-bark."

177 Half Way Doings

Another traditional variant of a printed poem by the white Mississippi poet Irwin Russell, dating from the 1870s and printed in the posthumous collection *Christmas Night in the Quarters.* (An earlier Russell redaction, with information about his career, is found in the headnotes to item 61, "The Ark," above.) Talley does not mention Russell in any of his notes or letters, though he must have been aware of his work, since Talley's role model, Joel Chandler Harris, wrote the introduction to Russell's book. As with "The Ark," it is quite possible that "Half Way Doings" got into black oral tradition as a recitation, since the differences in the original text and the one presented here are significant but consist in many cases of merging or dislocation of couplets. For example, in Russell's orginal (longer than Talley's), the third stanza begins with a series of references to Biblical stories absent in Talley. Russell's stanza 7 then becomes Talley's stanza 3.

To illustrate the nature of the textual differences between Russell and Talley, here are the two opening stanzas of Russell's original:

> Belubbed fellah-trabelers: — In holdin' forth to-day,
> I doesn't quote no special verse fur what I has to say:
> De sermon will be berry short, an' dis here am de tex':
> Dat half-way doins' ain't no 'count fur dis worl' or de nex.'
>
> Dis worl' dat we's a-libbin' in is like a cotton-row,
> Whar ebery cullud gentleman has got his line to hoe;
> An' ebery time a lazy nigger stops to take a nap,
> De grass keeps on a-growin' fur to smudder up his crap.

Only one line of Talley's ("An' w'en de cotton's all laid by," stanza 6) does not have a corresponding reference to Russell's original.

> My dear Brudders an' Sisters,
> As I comes here to-day,
> I hain't gwineter take no scripture verse
> Fer what I'se gwineter say.
>
> My words I'se gwineter cut off short
> An' I 'spects to use dis tex':
> "Dis half way doin's hain't no 'count
> Fer dis worl' nor de nex.'"

Dis half way doin's, Brudderin,
Won't never do, I say.
Go to yō' wuk, an' git it done,
An' den's de time to play.

Fer w'en a Nigger gits lazy,
An' stops to take short naps,
De weeds an' grass is shore to grow
An' smudder out his craps.

Dis worl' dat we's a livin' in
Is sumpen lak a cotton row:
Whar each an' ev'ry one o' us
Is got his row to hoe.

An' w'en de cotton's all laid by,
De rain, it spile de bowls,
If you don't keep busy pickin'
In de cotton fiel' of yō' souls.

Keep on a-plowin', an' a-hoein';
Keep on scrapin' off de rows;
An' w'en de year is over
You can pay off all you owes.

But w'en you sees a lazy Nigger
Stop workin', shore's you're born,
You'se gwineter see him comin' out
At de liddle end of de horn.

178 Two Times One

Two times one is two.
Won't you jes keep still till I gits through?
Three times three is nine.
You 'tend to yō' business, an' I'll tend to mine.

179   He Paid Me Seven (Parody)

"Our Fadder, Which are in Heaben!"—
White man owe me leben and pay me seben.
"D'y Kingdom come! D'y Will be done!"—
An' if I hadn't tuck dat, I wouldn' git none.

180   Parody on "Reign, Master Jesus, Reign!"

Oh, rain! Oh rain! Oh rain, "good" Mosser!
Rain, Mosser, rain! Rain hard!
Rain flour an' lard an' a big hog head
Down in my back yard.

An' w'en you comes down to my cabin,
Come down by de corn fiel'.
If you cain't bring me a piece o' meat,
Den bring me a peck o' meal.

Oh rain! Oh rain! Oh rain, "good" Mosser!
Dat good rain gives mō' rest.
"What d'you say? You Nigger, dar!"—
"Wet ground grows grass best."

181   A Request to Sell

Gwineter ax my daddy to sell ole Rose,
So's I can git me some new clō's.
Gwineter ax my daddy to sell ole Nat,
So's I can git a bran' new hat.
Gwineter ax my daddy to sell ole Bruise,
Den I can git some Brogan shoes.
Now, I'se gwineter fix myse'f "jes so,"
An' take myse'f down to Big Shiloh.
I'se gwine right down to Big Shiloh
To take dat t'other Nigger's beau.

182   We'll Stick to the Hoe

Both the melody and words suggest this song is related to one called "Rise When the Rooster Crows," which was very popular among early country entertainers in the Nashville area. It possibly originated with a piece called "Dem Golden Shoes," written in 1881 by Harry Jackson. Its popularity was reflected more in commercial recordings than printed sources or folksong collections; Uncle Dave Macon recorded it in 1925 (Vocalion 15321) and singer Jack Jackson, accompanied by the Nashville-based Binkley Brothers band, did it in 1928, on a record for Victor (V-40048). The tune is #26 in the "Leading Themes" notebook.

We'll stick to de hoe, till de sun go down.
We'll rise w'en de rooster crow,
An' go to de fiel' whar de sun shine hot,
To de fiel' whar de sugar cane grow.
Yes, Chilluns, we'll all go!
We'll go to de fiel' whar de sun shine hot.
To de fiel' whar de sugar cane grow.

Oh, sing 'long boys, fer de wuk hain't hard!
Oh scrape an' clean up de row.
Fer de grass musn' grow, while de sun shine hot,
In de fiel' whar de sugar cane grow.
No, Chilluns. No, No!

Dat grass musn' grow, while de sun shine hot,
In de fiel' whar de sugar cane grow.

Don't think 'bout de time, fer de time hain't long.
Yō' life soon come an' go;
Den good-bye fiel' whar de sun shine hot,
To de fiel' whar de sugar cane grow.
Yes, Chillins. We'll all go!
Good-by to de fiel' whar de sun shine hot,
To de fiel' whar de sugar cane grow.

183   A Fine Plaster

W'en it's sheep skin an' beeswax,
It shō's a mighty fine plaster:
De mō' you tries to pull it off,
De mō' it sticks de faster.

184   A Day's Happiness

This is an unusual version of "Turkey in the Straw," itself derived from an 1834 blackface minstrel song called "Old Zip Coon." Extensive annotation references for it are found in Cohen's edition of *Ozark Folk Songs* (234–37), and in the brochure notes to the historical LP album *Minstrels and Tunesmiths: The Commercial Roots of Early Country Music* (JEMF 109). There are dozens of recordings of the piece by early country artists, though very few by blacks.

Fust: I went out to milk an' I didn' know how,
I milked dat goat instid o' dat cow;
While a Nigger a-settin' wid a gapin' jaw,
Kept winkin' his eye at a tucky in de straw.

Den: I went out de gate an' I went down de road,
An' I met Miss 'Possum an' I met Mistah Toad;
An' ev'y time Miss 'Possum 'ould sing,
Mistah Toad 'ould cut dat Pigeon's Wing.

But: I went in a whoop, as I went down de road;
    I had a bawky team an' a heavy load.
    I cracked my whip, an' ole Beck sprung,
    An' she busted out my wagin tongue.

Well: Dat night dere 'us a-gittin' up, shores you're born.
    De louse go to supper, an' de flea blow de horn.
    Dat raccoon paced, an' dat 'possum trot;
    Dat ole goose laid, an' de gander sot.

185   Master Killed a Big Bull

Mosser killed a big bull,
Missus cooked a dish full,
Didn't give poor Nigger a mouf full.
    Humph! Humph!

Mosser killed a fat lam'.
Missus brung a basket,
An' give poor Nigger de haslet.
    Eh-eh! Eh-eh!

Mosser killed a fat hog
Missus biled de middlin's,
An' give poor Nigger de chitlin's.
    Shō! Shō!

186   You Had Better Mind Master

'Way down yon'er in 'Possum Trot,
(In ole Miss'sip' whar de sun shines hot)
Dere hain't no chickens an' de Niggers eats c'on;
You hain't never see'd de lak since youse been bo'n,
You'd better mīn' Mosser an' keep a stiff lip,
So's you won't git sōl' down to ole Miss'sip'.

Love Rhyme Section

187 Pretty Little Pink

Found in Brown (3:111), this song was also a staple in the repertoires of 1930s country radio singers Bradley Kincaid, Skyland Scotty, and Grandpa Jones. See Loyal Jones, *Radio's Kentucky Mountain Boy, Bradley Kincaid* (120–21).

> My pretty liddle Pink,
> I once did think,
> Dat we-uns shō' would marry;
> But I'se done give up,
> Hain't got no hope,
> I hain't got no time to tarry.
> I'll drink coffee dat flows,
> From oaks dat grows,
> 'Long de river dat flows wid brandy.

188 A Bitter Lovers' Quarrel—One Side

> You nasty dog! You dirty hog!
> You thinks somebody loves you.
> I tells you dis to let you know
> I thinks myse'f above you.

189   Roses Red

Rose's red, vi'lets blue.
Sugar is sweet but not lak you.
De vi'lets fade, de roses fall;
But you gits sweeter, all in all.

As shore as de grass grows 'round de stump,
You is my darlin' Sugar Lump.
W'en de sun don't shine de day is cold,
But my love fer you do not git old.

De ocean's deep, de sky is blue;
Sugar is sweet, an' so is you;
De ocean waves an' de sky gits pale,
But my love are true, an' it never fail.

190   You Have Made Me Weep

You'se made me weep, you'se made me mourn,
You'se made me tears an' sorrow.
So far' you well, my pretty liddle gal,
I'se gwine away to-morrow.

191   Mourning Slave Fiancees

A combination of two familiar, widely known, and much-traveled lyric quatrains. The first stanza is very common both in black and white collections and recordings; see White (300–301), Odum (*Negro Workaday Songs*, 46), and Brown (3:347) for representative citations. The second stanza is often associated with the Anglo-American lyric complex called "In the Pines"; see Brown (3:332–34). Talley's melody (identified in the "Leading Themes" notebook as #25) more resembles the one generally associated with the "In the Pines" complex, or with one often called "Sweet Wine" by Appalachian singers.

Look down dat lonesome road! Look down!
De way are dark an' cōl'.
Dey makes me weep, dey makes me mourn;
All 'cause my love are sōl'.

O don't you see dat turkle dove,
What mourns from vine to vine?
She mourns lak I moans fer my love,
Lef' many a mile behin'.

192 Do I Love You?

Does I love you wid all my heart?—
I loves you wid my liver;
An' if I had you in my mouf,
I'd spit you in de river.

193 Lovers' Goodnight

Cotton fields white in de bright moonlight,
Now kiss yō' gal' an' say "Good-night."
If she don't kiss you, jes go on 'way;
Hain't no need a-stayin' ontel nex' day.

194 Vinie

Though the opening couplet is very familiar as a play-party and jump-rope
rhyme (see Brown [3:128–29] for references and citations), Talley's text is
much better integrated than many random collections of floating couplets.
Such extended lyrics are rare in traditional music, and nothing quite like
Talley's appears in standard collections.

I loves coffee, an' I loves tea.
I axes you, Vinie, does you love me?

My day's study's Vinie, an' my midnight dreams,
My apples, my peaches, my tunnups, an' greens.

Oh, I wants dat good 'possum, an' I wants to be free;
But I don't need no sugar, if Vinie love me.

De river is wide, an' I cain't well step it.
I loves you, dear Vinie; an' you know I cain't he'p it.

Dat sugar is sweet, an' dat butter is greasy;
But I loves you, sweet Vinie; don't be oneasy.

Some loves ten, an' some loves twenty,
But I loves you, Vinie, an' dat is a plenty.

Oh silver, it shine, an' lakwise do tin.
De way I loves Vinie, it mus' be a sin.

Well, de cedar is green, an' so is de pine.
God bless you, Vinie! I wish you 'us mine.

Love Song Rhyme Section

195　She Hugged Me and Kissed Me

The first two stanzas are similar to verses of "Cindy"; see White (333 and 616) for another black Tennessee version; also see Brown (3: 482–84), Scarborough (67), and Randolph (3:376–77). The final stanza is unusual, with its reference to "bed-cord" strong — referring to the eighteenth-century practice of using ropes strung across bed frames in lieu of a regular mattress. Music is #9 in "Leading Themes" notebook.

I see'd her in de Springtime,
I see'd her in de Fall,
I see'd her in de Cotton patch,
A cameing from de Ball.

She hug me, an' she kiss me,
She wrung my han' an' cried.
She said I wus de sweetes' thing
Dat ever lived or died.

She hug me an' she kiss me.
Oh Heaben! De touch o' her hand'!
She said I wus de puttiest thing
In de shape o' mortal man.

I told her dat I love her,
Dat my love wus bed-cord strong;
Den I axed her w'en she'd have me,
An' she jes say "Go long!"

196   It Is Hard to Love

Featured in the 1940s on the Grand Ole Opry by Beecher Kirby (Oswald), with Roy Acuff's band.

It's hard to love, yes, indeed 'tis.
It's hard to be broke up in min'.
You'se all lugged up in some gal's heart,
But you hain't gwineter lug up in mine.

197   Me and My Lover

See White (137) and Brown (3:129) for sample comparisons.

Me an' my Lover, we fall out.
How d'you reckon de fuss begun?
She laked licker, an' I laked fun,
An' dat wus de way de fuss begun.

Me an' my Lover, we fall out.
W'at d'you reckon de fuss wus 'bout?
She loved bitters, an' I loved kraut,
An' dat wus w'at de fuss wus 'bout.

Me an' my Lover git clean 'part.
How d'you reckon dat big fuss start?
She's got a gizzard, an' I'se got a heart,
An' dat's de way dat big fuss start.

198 I Wish I Was an Apple

Oh: I wish I wus an apple,
      An' my Sallie wus anudder.
      What a pretty match we'd be,
      Hangin' on a tree togedder!

But: If I wus an apple,
      An' my Sallie was anudder;
      We'd grow up high, close to de sky,
      Whar de Niggers couldn' git 'er.

      We'd grow up close to de sun
      An' smile up dar above;
      Den we'd fall down 'way in de groun'
      To sleep an' dream 'bout love.

And: W'en we git through a dreamin',
      We'd bofe in Heaben wake.
      No Nigger shouldn' git my gal
      W'en 'is time come to bake.

199 Rejected by Eliza Jane

See White (172–74) with annotations; see also Brown (3:532) and especially Scarborough (7–8). Two popular commercial recordings from the 1920s helped spread the song in white country music; these are "Mountaineer's Love Song" by the East Tennessee string band The Hill Billies (Vocalion 5115, ca. 1926) and "Miss Liza, Poor Gal" by another band from the same area, The Tenneva Ramblers, on Victor 21141 (1927). Music is #65 from the "Leading Themes" notebook.

W'en I went 'cross de cotton patch
I give my ho'n a blow.
I thought I heared pretty Lizie say:
"Oh, yon'er come my beau!"

So: I axed pretty Lizie to marry me,
An' what d'you reckon she said?
She said she wouldn' marry me,
If ev'ybody else wus dead.

An': As I went up de new cut road,
An' she go down de lane;
Den I though I heared somebody say:
"Good-bye, ole Lize Jane!"

Well: Jes git 'long, Lizie, my true love.
Git 'long, Miss Lizie Jane.
Perhaps you'll sack "Ole Sour Bill"
An' git choked on "Sugar Cain."

Courtship Rhyme Section

200 Antebellum Courtship Inquiry

(He) Is you a flyin' lark or a settin' dove?
(She) I'se a flyin' lark, my honey Love.
(He) Is you a bird o' one fedder, or a bird o' two?
(She) I'se a bird o' one fedder, w'en it comes to you.
(He) Den, Mam:
       I has desire, an' quick temptation,
       To jine my fence to yō' plantation.

201 Invited to Take the Escort's Arm

Miss, does you lak strawberries?
. . . .
Den hang on de vine.
. . . .
Miss, does you lak chicken?
. . . .
Den have a wing dis time.

135

202 Sparking or Courting

I'se heaps older dan three.
I'se heaps thicker dan barks;
An' de older I gits,
De mō' harder I sparks.

I sparks fast an' hard,
For I'se feared I mought fail.
Dough I'se gittin' ole,
I don't co't lak no snail.

203   A Clandestine Letter

Kind Miss: If I sent you a letter,
       By de crickets,
       Through de thickets,
       How'd you answer better?

Kind Suh: I'd sen' you a letter,
       By de mole,
       Not to be tōl';
       Fer dat's mō' secretter.

204   Antebellum Marriage Proposal

"(A proposal of marriage with the answer deferred)" (Talley).

(He) De ocean, it's wide; de sea, it's deep.
       Yes, in yō' arms I begs to sleep,
       Not for one time, not fer three;
       But long as we-uns can agree.
(She) Please gimme time, Suh, to "reponder;"
       Please gimme time to "gargalize;"
       Den 'haps I'll tu'n to "cattlegog,"
       An' answer up 'greeable fer a s'prise.

205   If You Frown

If you frowns, an' I frowns,
W'en we goes out togedder;
Den all de t'other folks aroun'
Will say: "De rain is fallin' down
Right in de sunshine wedder!"

206 "Let's Marry" Courtship

"(A *proposal* of *marriage, with a provisional acceptance*)" (Talley).

> (He) Oh Miss Lizie, how I loves you!
>   My life's jes los' if you hain't true.
>   If you loves me lak I loves you,
>   No knife cain't cut our love in two.
>
> (She) Grapevine warp, an' cornstalk fillin';
>   I'll marry you if mammy an' daddy's willin'.
> (He) Rabbit hop an' long dog trot!
>   Let's git married if dey say "not."

207 Courtship

"(*A proposal of marriage with its acceptance*)" (Talley). In a footnote, Talley notes that "cravenate" in line 4 means "to consider."

> Kind Miss: I'se on de stage o' action,
>   Pleadin' hard fer satisfaction,
>   Pleadin' 'fore de time-thief late;
>   Darfore, Ma'm, now, "cravenate."
>
>   If I brung to you a gyarment;
>   To be cut widout scissors,
>   An' to be sewed widout thread;
>   How (I ax you) would you make it,
>   Widout de needle sewin'
>   An' widout de cloth spread?
>
> Kind Suh: I'd make dat gyarment
>   Wid love from my heart,
>   Wid tears on yō' head;
>   We never would part.

208   I Walked the Roads

Well: I walked de roads, till de roads git muddy.
     I talked to dat pretty gal, till I couldn' stan' study.

Den: I say: "Love me liddle," I say; "Love me long."
     I say: "Let dat liddle be 'doggone' strong!
     For, shore as dat rat runs 'cross de rafter,
     So shore you'se de gal, you'se de gal I'se after."

209   Presenting a Hat to Phoebe

Sister Phoebe: Happy wus we,
W'en we sot under dat Juniper tree.
Take dis hat, it'll keep yō' head warm.
Take dis kiss, it'll do you no harm.

Sister Phoebe: De hours, dey're few;
But dis hat'll say I'se thinkin' 'bout you.
Sugar, it's sugar; an' salt, it's salt;
If you don't love me, it's shō' yō' own fault.

210   Wooing

W'at is dat a wukin
At yō' han' bill on de wall,
So's yō' sperit, it cain't res',
An' a gemmun's heat, it call?

Is you lookin' fer sweeter berries
Growin' on a higher bush?
An' does my combersation suit?
If not, w'at does you wush?

Courtship Song Rhyme Section

211 The Courting Boy

This may be related to the group of songs presented by Randolph (3:48–50).

W'en I wus a liddle boy,
Jes fifteen inches high;
De way I court de pretty gals,
It make de ole folks cry.

De geese swim in de middle pon'.
De ducks fly 'cross de clover.
Run an' tell dem pretty gals,
Dat I'se a-comin' over.

Ho! Marindie! Ho!
Ho! Missindie! Ho!
Ho! Malindie! Ho! my gal!
I'se gwine now to see ole Sal.

212 Pretty Polly Ann

I'se gwineter marry, if I can.
I'se gwineter marry pretty Polly Ann.

I axed Polly Ann, fer to marry me.
She say she's a-lookin' fer a Nigger dat's free.

Pretty Polly Ann's jes dressed so fine!
I'll bet five dollars she hain't got a dime.

Pretty Polly Ann's jes a-puttin' on airs,
She won't notice me, but nobody cares.

I'll drop Polly Ann, a-lookin' lak a crane;
I 'spec's I'll marry Miss Lize Jane.

Marriage Rhyme Section

213   Slave Marriage Ceremony Supplement

Dark an' stormy may come de wedder;
I jines dis he-male an' dis she-male to-gedder.
Let none, but Him dat makes de thunder,
Put dis he-male an' dis she-male asunder.
I darfore 'nounce you bofe de same.
Be good, go 'long, an' keep up yō' name.
De broomstick's jumped, de worl's not wide.
She's now yō' own. Salute yō' bride!

Married Life Rhyme Section

214 The Newly Weds

First Mont': "Set down in my cabin, Honey!"
Nex' Mont': "Stan' up, my Pie."
Third Mont': "You go to wuk, you Wench!
You well to wuk as I!"

215 When I Go to Marry

W'en I goes to marry,
I wants a gal wid money.
I wants a pretty black-eyed gal
To kiss an' call me "Honey."

Well, w'en I goes to marry,
I don't wanter git no riches.
I wants a man 'bout four foot high,
So's I can w'ar de britches.

216 Bought Me a Wife

Often considered a play-party song; versions are in Newell *Games and Songs of American Children* (115), Parsons *Folk-Lore of the Sea Islands, South Carolina* (184), Brown (3:172–74), and, more recently, Jones and Hawes (192), as "I Had an Old Rooster." Music is #61 in "Leading Themes" notebook.

Bought me a wife an' de wife please me,
I feeds my wife un'er yon'er tree.
My wife go: "Row-row!"
My guinea go: "Potrack! Potrack!
My chicken go: "Gymsack! Gymsack!"
My duck go: "Quack-quack! Quack-quack!"
My dog go: "Bow-bow!"
My hoss go: "Whee-whee! Whee-whee!"
My cat go: "Fiddle-toe! Fiddle-toe!"

217 When I Was a "Roustabout"

Black banjo players in Virginia and North Carolina play a tune called
"Roustabout," but it is usually sung with a set of commonplace lyrics that
are quite different from the sustained narrative of this piece. Though similar
in theme to the familiar traditional jest called "The Taming of the Shrew"
or "That's Once," this song appears in none of the major black folksong collections. Music is #78 in "Leading Themes" notebook.

W'en I wus a "Roustabout," wild an' young,
I co'ted my gal wid a mighty slick tongue.
I tōl' her some oncommon lies dere an' den.
I tōl' her dat we'd marry, but I didn' say w'en.

So on a Mond'y mornin' I tuck her fer my wife.
Of co'se I wus 'spectin' an agreeable life.
But on a Chuesd'y mornin' she chuned up her pipe,
An' she 'bused me more 'an I'd been 'bused all my life.

On a Wednesd'y evenin', as I come 'long home,
I says to myse'f dat she wus all my own;
An' on a Thursd'y night I went out to de woods,
An' I cut me two fig fine tough leatherwoods.

So on a Frid'y mornin' w'en she roll me 'er eyes,
I retched fer my leatherwoods to give 'er a s'prise,
Dem long keen leatherwoods wuked mighty well,
An' 'er tongue, it jes rattle lak a clapper in a bell.

On a Sadd'y mornin' she sleep sorter late;
An' de las' time I see'd her, she 'us gwine out de gate.
I wus feedin' at de stable, lookin' out through a crack,
An' she lef' my log cabin 'fore I could git back.

On a Sund'y mornin', as I laid on my bed,
I didn' have no Nigger wife to bother my head.
Now whisky an' brandy jug's my biges' bes' friend,
An' my long week's wuk is about at its end.

218　My First and My Second Wife

My fust liddle wife wus short an' fat.
Her face wus as black as my ole hat,
Her nose all flat, an' her eyes sunk in,
An' dat lip hang down below her chin.
　　　　Now wusn't I sorrowful in mind?

W'en I went down to dat wife's brother;
He said: "She 'us tired. Gwineter marry 'nother."
If I ever ketches dat city Coon,
He railly mought see my razzer soon.
　　　　Den I 'spec's he'd be troubled in mind!

My nex' wife hug an' kiss me,
She call me "Sugar Plum!"
She throw her arms 'round me,
Lak a grapevine 'round de gum!
　　　　Wusn't dat glory to my soul!

Her cheeks, dey're lak de cherry;
Dat Cherry, it's lak de rose.
Wid a liddle dimple in her chin,
An' a liddle tu'ned up nose!
　　　　Oh, hain't I happy in mind!

I'se got you, Lou, now fer my wife.
Keep new Coons 'way, "My Pie!"
Caze, if you don't, I tells you now,
Dat we all three mought die.
　　　　Den we'd be troubled in min'!

219 Good-By, Wife!

Music is #64 in "Leading Themes" notebook. (Note: there is an apparent missing eighth note count in the second complete measure.)

I had a liddle wife,
An' I didn' want to kill 'er;
So I tuck 'er by de heels,
An' I throwed 'er in de river.
"Good-by, Wife! Good-by, Honey!
Hadn' been fer you,
I'd a had a liddle money."

My liddle fussy wife
Up an' say she mus' have scissors;
An' druther dan to fight,
I'd a throwed 'er in three rivers.
But she crossed dem fingers, w'en she go down,
An' a liddle bit later
She walk out on de groun'.

Nursery Rhyme Section

220 Awful Harbingers

In the original edition, Talley appended the following note: "This little rhyme is based upon a superstition once current among Negroes, to the effect that bad luck would come when a screech owl called near your home at night unless, upon hearing him, you would stick the handle of a shovel into the fire about which you were sitting, or would throw salt into it. The word 'hant' means ghost or spirit."

> W'en de big owl whoops,
> An' de screech owl screeks,
> An' de win' makes a howlin' sound;
> You liddle wooly heads
> Had better kiver up,
> Caze de "hants" is comin' 'round.

221 The Last of Jack

Though this text and the following two may be related, Brown (3:217) gives a text close to this one, noting that the more common form offers a horse or mule instead of a dog as the subject. See also White (232). Music is #34 in "Leading Themes" notebook, where it is titled "I Had a Little Dog and His Name Was Jack."

I had a liddle dog, his name wus Jack;
He run forty mile 'fore he look back.
W'en he look back, he fall in a crack;
W'en he fall in a crack, he break 'is back;
An' dat wus de las' o' poor liddle Jack.

222   Little Dogs

Items 222, 223, and 259 below all seem to be part of the same basic formula, which has been traced by White (207–208) as far back as 1850-era songsters. The most common couplet is stanza 3 here, usually associated with the well-known "Old Blue." For other variants and references, see: Randolph (3:385); Perrow 1913 (pp. 127–32); and Scarborough (171).

I had a liddle dog; his name wus Ball'
W'en I give him a liddle, he want it all.

I had a liddle dog, his name wus Trot:
He helt up his tail, all tied in a knot.

I had a liddle dog, his name wus Blue;
I put him on de road, an' he almos' flew.

I had a liddle dog, his name wus Mack;
I rid his tail fer to save his back.

I had a liddle dog, his name wus Rover;
W'en he died, he died all over.

I had a liddle dog, his name wus Dan;
An' w'en he died, I buried 'im in de san'.

223   My Dog, Cuff

I had a liddle dog, his name wus Cuff;
I sent 'im to town to buy some snuff.
He drapped de bale, an' he spilt de snuff,
An' I guess dat speech is long enough.

224   Sam Is a Clever Fellow

Music from "Leading Themes" notebook, #63.

Sam Is a Clever Fellow

Say! Is yō' peaches ripe, my boy,
An' is yō' apples meller?
Go an' tell Miss Katie Jones
Dat Sam's a clever feller.

Say! Is yō' cherries red, my boy,
An' is yō' plums all yeller?
Oh please run tell Miss Katie Jones
Dat Sam's a clever feller.

225   The Great Owl's Song

Ah-hoo-hoo? Ah-hoo-hoo? Ah-hoo-hoo —?
An' who'll cook fer Kelline, an' who'll cook fer you —?
   I will cook fer myse'f, I won't cook fer you.
   Ah-hoo-hoo! Ah-hoo-hoo! Ah-hoo —!

Ah-hoo-hoo! Ah-hoo-hoo! Ah-hoo-hoo! Ah-hoo —!
I wonder if Kelline would not cook fer Hue —?

Fer dis is Big Sandy! It's Big Sandy Hue—!
Ah-hoo-hoo! Ah-hoo-hoo! Ah-hoo-hoo! Ah-hoo—

Ah-ha-hah! Ah-ha-hah! Ah-ha-hah! Ah-hah—!
I thought you 'us ole Bill Jack as black as de tah.
You really must 'scuse me, my "Honey Lump Pa."
Ah-ha-hah! Ah-ha-hah! Ah-ha-hah! Ah-hah—!

An' since I'se been Kelline, an' you'se Big Sandy Hue;
I will cook fer myse'f, an' I will cook fer you.
I'll love you forever, an' sing in de dew:
"Ah-hoo-hoo! Ah-hoo-hoo! Ah-hoo-hoo! Ah-hoo—"

Yes!—Ah-hoo-hoo! Ah-hoo-hoo! Ah-hoo-hoo! Ah-hoo-all!
Now, we'll cook fer ourse'fs, but who'll cook fer you all?
Fer Tom Dick an' his wife, fer Pete Snap an' Shoe-Awl,
Rough Shot De Shoe-boot, an' de Lawd He knows who all?

226   Here I Stand

Scarborough (137) reports the first stanza as a playground chant from Texas;
White (179) reports another variant and notes that the couplet goes back in
print as far as *The Negro Singer's Own Book* (1846), p. 227.

Here I stan', raggity an' dirty;
If you don't come kiss me, I'll run lak a tucky.

Here I stan' on two liddle chips,
Pray, come kiss my sweet liddle lips.

Here I stan' crooked lak a horn;
I hain't had no kiss since I'se been born.

227   Pig Tail

Run boys, run!
De pig tail's done.
If you don't come quick,
You won't git none.

Pig ham's dere,
Lakwise middlin's square;
But dese great big parts
Hain't no Nigger's bes' fare.

228   A, B, C

For a sample of similar alphabet rhymes, see Randolph (4:399–405).

A, B, C,
Doubled down D;
I'se so lazy you cain't see me.

A, B, C,
Doubled down D
Lazy Chilluns gits hick'ry tea.

A, B, C,
Doubled down D,
Dat "cat's" in de cupboard an' hid. You see?

A, B, C,
Doubled down D,
You'd better come out an' wuk lak me.

229   Negro Baker Man

Patty cake! Patty cake! Nigger Baker man.
Missus an' Mosser gwineter ketch 'im if dey can.
Put de liddle Nigger in Mosser's dish pan,
An' scrub 'im off good fer de ole San' Man.

230   Stick-a ma-stew

Stick-a-ma-stew, he went to town.
Stick-a-ma-stew, he tore 'is gown.
All dem folks what live in town
Cain't mend dat randsome, handsome gown.

231   Bob-White's Song

Bob-white! Bob-white!
Is yō' peas all ripe?
No—! not—! quite!

Bob-white! Bob-white!
W'en will dey be ripe?
To-mor—! row—! might!

Bob-white! Bob-white!
Does you sing at night?
No—! not—! quite!

Bob-white! Bob-white!
W-en is de time right?
At can—! dle—! light!

232   Cooking Dinner

"A Negro reel tune which has become universally popular among white square dance musicians," writes Allan Lomax in his *Folk Songs of North America* (506). Similar texts are reported in White (303–304), Scarborough (124, 168), and Brown (3:319)—all from black informants. Talley, however, seems to have been first to publish this now-famous text; his fellow Middle Tennessean Uncle Dave Macon, the white banjoist, recorded one of the first versions of the song in 1924 (Vocalion 14849).

Go: Bile dem cabbage down.
   Turn dat hoecake 'round,
   Cook it done an' brown.

Yes: Gwineter have sweet taters too.
    Hain't had none since las' Fall,
    Gwineter eat 'em skins an' all.

233 Chuck Will's Widow Song

The chuck-will's-widow is a bird of the goatsucker family, so named because of the sound of its call.

Oh nimber, nimber Will-o!
My crooked, crooked bill-o!
I'se settin' down right now, on de sweet pertater hill-o.

Oh nimber, nimber Will-o!
My crooked, crooked bill-o!
Two liddle naked babies, my two brown aigs now fill-o.

Oh nimber, nimber Will-o!
My crooked, crooked bill-o!
Don't hurt de liddle babies; dey is too sweet to kill-o.

234 Bridle up a Rat

Bridle up er rat,
Saddle up er cat,
An' han' me down my big straw hat.

In come de cat,
Out go de rat,
Down go de baby wid 'is big straw hat.

235 My Little Pig

You see: I had a liddle pig,
           I fed 'im on slop;
           He got so fat
           Dat he almos' pop.

An' den: I tuck de liddle pig,
            An' I rid 'im to school;
            He e't ginger cake,
            An' it tu'n 'im a fool.

            But he grunt de lessons,
            An' keep all de rule,
            An' he make 'em all think
            Dat he learn in de cool.

236 In a Mulberry Tree

Jes looky, looky yonder; w'at I see!
Two liddle Niggers in a Mulberry tree.
One cain't read, an' de t'other cain't write.
But dey bofe can smoke deir daddy's pipe.

"One ma two! One ma two!"
Dat Mulberry Witch, he titterer too.
"Big bait o'Mulberries make 'em bofe sick.
Dem liddle Niggers gwineter roll an' kick!"

237 Animal Attire

Dat Coon, he w'ar a undershirt;
Dat 'Possum w'ar a gown.
Br'er Rabbit, he w'ar a overcoat
Wid buttons up an' down.

Mistah Gobbler's got beads 'roun' 'is nec'.
Mistah Pattridge's got a collar, Hun!
Mistah Peacock, a fedder on his head!
But dese don't stop no gun.

238 Aspiration

If I wus de President
Of dese United States,
I'd eat good 'lasses candy,
An' swing on all de gates.

239 Animal Fair

See Brown (3:219), Randolph (3:207), and Jones and Hawes (61) for representative variants and annotations.

Has you ever hearn tell 'bout de Animal Fair?
Dem birds an' beasts wus all down dere.
Dat jaybird a-settin' down on 'is wing!
Has you ever hearn tell about sitch a thing
As whut 'us at dat Animal Fair?

Well, dem animals had a Fair.
Dem birds an' beasts wus dere.
De big Baboon,
By de light o' de moon,
Jes comb up his sandy hair.

De monkey, he git drunk,
He kick up a red hot chunk.
Dem coals, dey 'rose;
An' bu'nt 'is toes!
He clumb de Elephan's trunk.

I went down to de Fair.
Dem varmints all wus dere.
Dat young Baboon
Wunk at Miss Coon;
Dat curled de Elephan's hair.

De Camel den walk 'bout,
An' tromped on de Elephan's snout.
De Elephan' sneeze,
An' fall on his knees;
Dat pleased all dem monkēys.

240 Little Boy Who Couldn't Count Seven

Once der wus a liddle boy dat couldn' count one.
Dey pitched him in a fedder bed; 'e thought it great big fun.

Once der wus a liddle boy dat couldn' count two.
Dey pitched him in a fedder bed; 'e thought 'e 'us gwoine through.

Once der wus a liddle boy dat couldn' count three.
Dey pitched him in a fedder bed; 'e thought de Niggers 'us free.

Once der wus a liddle boy dat couldn' count fō'.
Dey pitched him in a fedder bed; 'e jumped out on de flō'.

Once der wus a liddle boy dat couldn' count five.
Dey pitched him in a fedder bed; 'e thought de dead alive.

Once der wus a liddle boy dat couldn' count six.
Dey pitched him in a fedder bed; 'e never did git fix!

Once der wus a liddle boy dat couldn' count seben.
Dey pitched him in a fedder bed; 'e thought he's gwine to Heaben!

241 Miss Terrapin and Miss Toad

Annotations and variants appear in White (247–48) and Scarborough (106, 162, 164); versions of stanza 1 date from pre-Civil War minstrel songsters such as *The Negro Singer's Own Book* (407) and *Christy's Nigga Songster* (250).

As I went marchin' down de road,
I met Miss Tearpin an' I met Miss Toad.
An' ev'ry time Miss Toad would jump,
Miss Tearpin would peep from 'hind de stump.

I axed dem ladies fer to marry me,
An' bofe find fault wid de t'other, you see.
"If you marries Miss Toad," Miss Tearpin said,
"You'll have to hop 'round lak you'se been half dead!"

"If you combs yō' head wid a Tearpin comb,
You'll have to creep 'round all tied up at home."
I run'd away frum dar, my foot got bruise,
For I didn't know zackly which to choose.

242 From Slavery

Chile: I come from out'n slavery,
Whar de Bull-whup bust de hide;
Back dar, whar dis gineration
Natchully widdered up an' died!

243 The End of Ten Little Negroes

Ten liddle Niggers, a-eatin', fat an' fine;
One choke hisse'f to death, an' dat lef' nine.
Nine liddle Niggers, dey sot up too late;
One sleep hisse'f to death, an' dat lef' eight.
Eight liddle Niggers want to go to Heaben;
One sing hisse'f to death, an' dat lef' seben.
Seben liddle Niggers, a-pickin' up sticks;
One wuk himme'f to death, an' dat lef' six.
Six liddle Niggers went out fer to drive;
Mule run away wid one, an' dat lef' five.
Five liddle Niggers in a cold rain pour;
One coughed hisse'f to death, an' dat lef' four.
Four liddle Niggers, climb a' apple tree'
One fall down an' out, an' dat lef' three.
Three liddle Niggers a-wantin' sumpin new;
One, he quit de udders, an' dat lef' two.
Two liddle Niggers went out fer to run;
One fell down de bluff, an' dat lef' one.
One liddle Nigger, a-foolin' wid a gun;
Gun go off "bang!" an' dat lef' none.

244   The Alabama Way

For other traditional variants, see White (138–39) and Perrow 1915 (135). A minstrel version is in *Christy's Nigga Songster* (69,239).

> 'Way down yon'er "in de Alerbamer way,"
> De Niggers goes to wo'k at de peep o' de day.
> De bed's too short, an' de high posts rear;
> De Niggers needs a ladder fer to climb up dere.
> De cord's wore out, an' de bed-tick's gone.
> Niggers' legs hang down fer de chickens t' roost on.

245   Mother Says I Am Six Years Old

> My mammy says dat I'se too young
> To go to Church an' pray;
> But she don't know how bad I is
> W'en she's been gone away.
>
> My mammy says I'se six years old,
> My daddy says I'se seben.
> Dat's all right how old I is,
> Jes since I'se a gwine to Heaben.

246   The Origin of the Snake

See Brown (3:137) for a slightly different variant from about the same time.

> Up de hill an' down de level!
> Up de hill an' down de level!
> Granny's puppy treed de Devil.
>
> Puppy howl, an' Devil shake!
> Puppy howl, an' Devil shake!
> Devil leave, an' dere's yō' snake.
>
> Mash his head; de sun shine bright!
> Mash his head; de sun shine bright;
> Tail don't die ontel it's night.

Night come on, an' sperits groan!
Night come on, an' sperits groan!
Devil come an' gits his own.

247 Wild Hog Hunt

Often associated with the song "Oh Monah," a complex piece that became
very popular in country music in the 1930s. For comments and variants, see
White (139–40).

> Nigger in de woods, a-settin' on a log;
> Wid his finger on de trigger, an' his eyes upon de hog.
> De gun say "bam!" an' de hog say "bip!"
> An' de Nigger grab dat wild hog wid all his grip.

248 A Strange Brood

> De ole hen sot on tucky aigs,
> An' she hatch out goslin's three.
> Two wus tuckies wid slender legs,
> An' one wus a bumblebee.
> All dem hens say to one nudder:
> "Mighty queer chickens! See?"

249 The Town and the Country Bird

Stanza 3 is almost identical to one in Brown (3:203); see also Brown (3:127
and 130) for annotations. Music from "Leading Themes" notebook, #94.

Jaybird a-swingin' a two hoss plow;
"Sparrer, why not you?"
"W'y—! My legs so liddle an' slender, man,
I'se fear'd dey'd break in two."

Jaybird answer: "What'd you say?— —
I sometimes worms terbaccy;
But I'd druther plow sweet taters too,
Dan to be a ole Town Tacky!"

Jaybird up in de Sugar tree,
De sparrer on de groun';
De jaybird shake de sugar down,
An' de sparrer say pass it 'roun'.

De jaybird say: "Save some fer me;
I needs it w'en I bakes."
De sparrer say: "Use 'lasses, Suh!
Dat suits fer Country-Jakes!"

250   Frog in a Mill (Guinea or Ebo Rhyme)

Talley discusses the origin of this rhyme in his "Study," below. Music is #72 in "Leading Themes" notebook.

Once dere wus er frog dat lived in er mill.
He had er raker don la bottom o' la kimebo
Kimebo, nayro, dilldo, kiro
Stimstam, formididdle, all-a-board la rake;
Wid er raker don la bottom o' la kimebo.

251 Strong Hands

Possibly part of a longer toast.

Here's yō' bread, an' here's yō' butter;
An' here's de hands fer to make you sputter.

Tetch dese hands, w'en you wants to tetch a beaver.
If dese hands tetch you, you'll shō' ketch de fever.

Dese hands Samson, good fer a row,
W'en dey hits you, it's "good-by cow!"

252 Tree Frogs (Guinea or Ebo Rhyme)

See Talley's discussion of Ebo rhymes in his "Study," below. Also resembles
well-known Gaelic lullaby "Schule Aroon."

Shool! Shool! Shool! I rule!
Shool! Shool! Shool! I rule!
Shool! Shacker-rack!
I shool bubba cool.

Seller! Beller eel!
Fust to ma tree'l
Just came er bubba.
Buska! Buska-reel!

253   When I Was a Little Boy

W'en I wus a liddle boy
I cleaned up mammy's dishes;
Now I is a great big boy,
I wears my daddy's britches.
I can knock dat Mobile Buck
An' smoke dat corncob pipe.
I can kiss dem pretty gals,
An' set up ev'ry night.

254   Grasshopper Sense

Dere wus a liddle grasshopper
Dat wus always on de jump;
An' caze he never look ahead,
He wus always gittin' a bump.

Huddlety, dumpty, dumpty, dump!
Mind out, or you will git a bump;
Shore as de grass grows 'round de stump
Be keerful, my sweet Sugar Lump.

255   Young Master and Old Master

Hick'ry leaves an' calico sleeves!
I tells you young Mosser's hard to please.
Young Mosser fool you, de way he grin.
De way he whup you is a sin.

De monkey's a-settin' on de end of a rail,
Pickin' his tooth wid de end of his tail.
Mulberry leaves an' homespun sleeves!
Better know dat ole Mosser's not easy to please.

256 My Speckled Hen

Somebody stole my speckled hen.
Dey lef' me mighty pōo'.
Ev'ry day she layed three aigs,
An' Sunday she lay fō'.

Somebody stole my speckled hen.
She crowed at my back dō'.
Fedders, dey shine jes lak de sun;
De Niggers grudged her mō'.

De whis'lin' gal, an' de crowin' hen,
Never comes to no good en'.
Stop dat whis'lin'; go on an' sing!
'Member dat hen wid 'er shinin' wing.

257 The Snail's Reply

Snail! Snail! Come out'n o' yō' shell,
Or I'll beat on yō' back till you rings lak a bell.

"I do ve'y well," sayed de snail in de shell,
"I'll jes take my chances in here whar I dwell."

258 A Strange Family

Once dere's an ole 'oman dat lived in de Wes'.
She had two gals of de very bes'.
One wus older dan de t'other,
T'other's older dan her mother,
An' dey're all deir own gran'mother.
Can you guess?

259   Good-by, Ring

For similar formulas, see items 222 and 223, above.

> I had a liddle dog, his name wus Ring,
> I tied him up to his nose wid a string.
> I pulled dat string, an' his eyes tu'n blue.
> "Good-by, Ring! I'se done wid you."

260   Deedle, Dumpling

> Deedle, deedle, dumplin'! My boy, Pete!
> He went to bed wid his dirty feet.
> Mammy laid a switch down on dat sheet!
> Deedle, deedle, dumplin'! My boy, Pete!

261   Buck and Berry

> Buck an' Berry run a race,
> Buck fall down an' skin his face.
>
> Buck an' Berry in a stall'
> Buck, he try to eat it all.
>
> Buck, he e't too much, you see.
> So he died wid choleree.

262   Pretty Little Girl

About the only print variant seems to be White (68), though the annotations suggest a number of Anglo-American sources as well, occasionally associated with a song called "Frog in the Well." The song was in the repertoire of Grand Ole Opry star Uncle Dave Macon, though he never formally recorded it. Noted fiddler Doc Roberts, accompanied by Asa Martin, recorded an instrumental version of a tune by this title in 1929 (Gennett 6826).

Who's been here since I'se been gone?
  A pretty liddle gal wid a blue dress on.

Who'll stay here when I goes 'way?
  A pretty liddle gal, all dressed in gray.

Who'll wait on Mistress day an' night?
  A pretty liddle gal, all dressed in white.

Who'll be here when I'se been dead?
  A pretty liddle gal, all dressed in red.

263   Two Sick Negro Boys

Two liddle Niggers sick in bed,
One jumped up an' bumped his head.
W'en de Doctah come he simpully said:
"Jes feed dat boy on shorten' bread."

T'other liddle Nigger sick in bed,
W'en he hear tell o' shorten' bread,
Popped up all well. He dance an' sing!
He almos' cut dat Pigeon's Wing!

264   Grasshopper Sitting on a Sweet Potato Vine

Grasshopper a settin' on a sweet tater vine,
 'Long come a Blackbird an' nab him up behind.

Blackbird a-settin' in a sour apple tree;
Hawk grab him up behind; he "Chee! Chee! Chee!"

Big hawk a-settin' in de top of dat oak,
Start to eat dat Blackbird an' he git choke.

265   Doodle-Bug

Doodle-bug! Doodle-bug! Come git sweet milk.
Doodle-bug! Doodle-bug! Come git butter.
Doodle-bug! Doodle-bug! Come git co'n bread.
Doodle-bug! Doodle-bug! Come on to Supper.

266   Raw Head and Bloody Bones

"Repeated to restless children at night to make them lie still and go to sleep" (Talley). The tale of Bloody Bones is familiar even today in the Appalachians.

Don't talk! Go to sleep!
Eyes shet an' don't you peep!
Keep still, or he jes moans:
"Raw Head an' Bloody Bones!"

267   Mysterious Face Washing

I wash my face in de watah
Dat's neider rain nor run.
I wipes my face on de towel
Dat's neider wove nor spun.— —
I wash my face in de dew,
An' I dries it in de sun.

268   Go to Bed

De wood's in de kitchen.
De hoss's in de shed.
You liddle Niggers
Had better go to bed.

269 Buck-Eyed Rabbit! Whoopee!

The first two stanzas are quite similar to a pair in "Do Come Along, Ole Sandy Boy" in *The Negro Singer's Own Book* (ca. 1846), 309. For traditional variants and analogues, see White (235–38) and Scarborough (165–69). The well-known early country string band The Hill Billies, whose members came from Virginia and East Tennessee, had two hit records by the name "Buck-Eyed Rabbits" in the 1926–27 era (Vocalion 5023, Brunswick 104). Talley also discusses this rhyme in his "Study in Negro Folk Rhymes," below.

> Dat Squir'l, he's a cunnin' thing;
> He tote a bushy tail.
> He jes lug off Uncle Sambo's co'n,
> An' heart it on a rail.

> Dat Squir'l, he's a cunnin' thing;
> An' so is ole Jedge B'ar.
> Br'er Rabbit's gone an' los' his tail
> 'Cep' a liddle bunch of ha'r.

> Buckeyed Rabbit! Whoopee!
> Buckeyed Rabbit! Ho!
> Buckeyed Rabbit! Whoopee!
> Squir'l's got a long way to go.

270 Captain Coon

A

This is the original text Talley used in his 1922 edition. For variants and references, see White (317) and Brown (3:208).

> Captain Coon's a mighty man,
> He trabble atter dark;
> Wid nothin' 'tall to 'sturb his mind,
> But to hear my ole dog bark.

> Dat 'Possum, he's a mighty man,
> He trabble late at night.
> He never think to climb a tree,
> 'Till he's feared ole Rober'll bite.

B

This is an unpublished variant found in manuscript in the Talley papers; it was sent to him in 1920 by Joe Bishop, a schoolteacher from Belfast, Tennessee.

> Raccoon is a mighty man,
> He travels after dark,
> He's never known to take a tree,
> Untill he hears old Beaver bark.

271   Guinea Gall

The "Guinea Gall" reference is unclear; it could refer either to the west African countries of that name, or be a metathetic confusion with "Senegal," the former Portugese colony in West Africa.

> Way down yon'er in Guinea Gall,
> De Niggers eats de fat an' all.
> 'Way down yon'er in de cotton fiel',
> Ev'ry week one peck o' meal.
> 'Way down yon'er ole Mosser swar';
> Holler at you, an' pitch, an' r'ar;
>   Wid cat o' nine tails,
>   Wid pen o' nine nails,
>   Tee whing, tee bing,
>   An' ev'ry thing!

272   Fishing Simon

> Simon tuck his hook an' pole,
> An' fished on Sunday we's been told.
> Fish dem water death bells ring,
> Talk from out'n de water, sing— —
> "Bait yō' hook, Simon!
> Drap yō' line, Simon!
> Now ketch me, Simon!
> Pull me out, Simon!
> Take me home, Simon!

Now clean me, Simon!
Cut me up now, Simon!
Now salt me, Simon!
Now fry me, Simon!
Dish me up now, Simon!
Eat me all, Simon!"
Simon e't till he wus full.
Still dat fish keep his plate fall.
Simon want no mō' at all,
Fish say dat he mus' eat all.
Simon's sick, so he throw up!
He give Sunday fishin' up.

273   A Strange Old Woman

Dere wus an ole 'oman, her name wus Nan.
She lived an 'oman, an' died a man.
De ole 'oman lived to be dried up an' cunnin';
One leg stood still, while de tother kep' runnin'

274   In '76

Way down yonder in sebenty-six,
Whar I git my jawbone fix;
All dem coon-loons eatin' wid a spoon!
I'll be ready fer dat Great Day soon.

275   Redhead Woodpecker

Redhead woodpecker: "Chip! Chip! Chee!"
Promise dat he'll marry me.
Whar shall de weddin' supper be?
Down in de lot, in a rotten holler tree.
What will de weddin' supper be?
A liddle green worm an' a bumblebee,
'Way down yonder on de holler tree.
De Redhead woodpecker, "Chip! Chip! Chee!"

276   Old Aunt Kate

Possibly related to "Old Aunt Katy" in Brown (3:374–75).

> Jes look at Ole Aunt Kate at de gyardin gate!
>   She's a good ole 'oman.
>   W'en she sift 'er meal, she give me de husk;
>   W'en she cook 'er bread, she give me de crust.
>   She put de hosses in de stable;
>   But one jump out, an' skin his nable.
> Jes look at Ole Aunt Kate at de gyardin gate!
>   Still she's always late.
>
> Hurrah fer Ole Aunt Kate by de gyardin gate!
>   She's a fine ole 'oman.
>   Git down dat sifter, take down dat tray!
>   Go 'long, Honey, dere hain't no udder way!
>   She put on dat hoe cake, she went 'round de house.
>   She cook dat 'Possum, an' she call 'im a mouse!
> Hurrah fer Ole Aunt Kate by de gyardin gate!
>   She's a fine playmate.

277   Children's Seating Rhyme

> You set outside, an' ketch de cow-hide.
> I'll set in de middle, an' play de gol' fiddle.
> You set 'round about, an' git scrouged out.

278   My Baby

> I'se de daddy of dis liddle black baby.
> He's his mammy's onliest sweetest liddle Coon.
> Got de look on de forehead lak his daddy,
> Pretty eyes jes as big as de moon.
>
> I'se de daddy of dis liddle black baby.
> Yes, his mammy deep de "Sugar" rollin' over.
> She feed him wid a tin cup an' a spoon;
> An' he kick lak a pony eatin' clover.

279   A Race-Starters Rhyme

This familiar quatrain is chronicled in Roger Abrahams, *Jump-rope Rhymes:
A Dictionary* (147).

> One fer de money!
> Two fer de show!
> Three to git ready,
> An' four fer to go!

280   Nesting

> De jaybird build on a swingin' lim',
> De sparrow in de gyardin;
> Dat ole gray goose in de panel o' de fence,
> An' de gander on de t'other side o' Jordan.

281   Baby Wants Cherries

> De cherries, dey're red; de cherries, dey're ripe;
> An' de baby it want one.
> De cherries, dey're hard; de cherries, dey're sour;
> An' de baby cain't git none.
>
> Jew look at dat bird in de cherry tree!
> He's pickin' 'em one by one!
> He's shakin' his bill, he's gittin' it fill',
> An' down dat th'oat dey run!
>
> Nev' mind! Bye an' bye dat bird's gwineter fly,
> An' mammy's gwineter make dat pie.
> She'll give you a few, fer de baby cain't chew,
> An' de Pickaninny sholy won't cry.

282   A Pretty Pair of Chickens

Dat box-legged rooster, an' dat bow-legged hen
Make a mighty pretty couple, not to be no kin.
Dey's jes lak some Niggers wearin' white folks ole britches,
Dey thinks dey's lookin' fine, w'en dey needs lots of stitches.

283   Too Much Watermelon

Compare to a similar text in Brown (3:539), which White suspected was of
"modern vaudeville" origin.

Dere wus a great big watermillion growin' on de vine.
Dere wus a liddle ugly Nigger watchin' all de time.
An' w'en dat great big watermillion lay ripenin' in de sun,
An' de stripes along its purty skin wus comin' one by one,
Dat ugly Nigger pulled it off an' toted it away,
An' he e't dat great big watermillion all in one single day.
He e't de rinds, an' red meat too, he finish it all trim;
An' den, — — dat great big watermillion up an' finish him.

284   Butterfly

Pretty liddle butterfly, yaller as de gold,
My sweet liddle butterfly, you shō' is mighty bold.
You can dance out in de sun, you can fly up high,
But you know I'se bound to git you, yet, my liddle butterfly.

285   The Hated Blackbird and Crow

Dat Blackbird say unto de Crow:
"Dat's why de white folks hates us so;
For ever since ole Adam wus born,
It's been our rule to gedder green corn."

Dat Blackbird say unto de Crow:
"If you's not black, den I don't know.

White folks calls you black, but I say not;
Caze de kittle mustn' talk about de pot."

286   In a Rush

Here I comes jes a-rearin' an' a-pitchin',
I hain't had no kiss since I lef' de ole kitchin.
Candy, dat's sweet; dat's very, very clear;
But a kiss from yō' lips would be sweeter, my dear.

287   Taking A Walk

We's a-walkin' in de green grass dust, dust, dust.
We's a-walkin' in de green grass dust.
If you's jes as sweet as I thinks you to be,
I'll take you by yō' liddle hand to walk wid me.

288   Paying Debts with Kicks

Possibly part of a longer toast or version of the "Dozens."

I owes yō' daddy a peck o' peas.
I'se gwineter pay it wid my knees.
I owes yō' mammy a pound o' meat;
An' I'se gwineter pay dat wid my feet.
Now, if I owes 'em somethin' mō';
You come right back an' let me know.
Please say to dem ('fore I fergets)
I never fails to pay my debts.

289   Getting Ten Negro Boys Together

One liddle Nigger boy whistle an' stew,
He whistle up anudder Nigger an' dat make two.
Two liddle Nigger boys shuck de apple tree,

Down fall anudder Nigger, an' dat make three.
Three liddle Nigger boys, a-wantin' one more,
Never has no trouble a-gittin' up four.
Four liddle Nigger boys, dey cain't drive.
Dey hire a Nigger hack boy, an' dat make five.
Five liddle Niggers, bein' calcullated men,
Call anudder Nigger 'piece an' dat make ten.

290   Hawk and Chicken

Hen an' chickens in a fodder stack,
Mighty busy scratchin'.
Hawk settin' off on a swingin' lim',
Ready fer de catchin'.

Hawk come a-whizzin' wid his bitin' mouf,
Couldn' hold hisself in.
Hen, flyin' up, knock his eye clean out;
An' de Jaybird died a-laughin'.

291   Mud-Log Pond

Another well-traveled stanza that is probably minstrel in origin; in 1929, north Georgia singer-fiddler Clayton McMichen (recording with The Skillet Lickers, a popular string band) used a stanza similar to this as part of his version of "Never Seen the Like Since Gettin' Upstairs" (Columbia 15472). His version went:

I went right down to the muddy, muddy pond,
I met Joe Gump with his new boots on,
His heels were copper and his toes were brass,
The fire kept a-runnin' out of Joe Gump's boots!

Talley's text:

As I stepped down by de Mud-log pon',
I seed dat bullfrog wid his shoe-boots on.
His eyes wus glass, an' his heels wus brass;
An' I give him a dollar fer to let me pass.

292   What Will We Do for Bacon?

What will we do fer bacon now?
I'se shot, I'se shot de ole sandy sow!
She jumped de fence an' broke de rail;
An'—"Bam!"—I shot her on de tail.

293   A Little Pickaninny

In a footnote to the original edition, Talley noted: "Pickaninny appears to
have been an African word used by the early American slaves for the word
baby." Later scholars have suggested its origins in the Spanish word *pequeno,*
meaning "little." Music from "Leading Themes" notebook, #74.

Me an' its mammy is both gwine to town,
To git dis Pickaninny a liddle hat an' gown.
Don't you never let him waller on de flō'!
He's a liddle Pickaninny,
Born in ole Virginy.
Mammy! Don't de baby grow?

Setch a eatin' o' de honey an' a drinkin' o' de wine!
We's gwine down togedder fer to have a good time;
An' we's gwineter eat, an' drink mō' an' mō'.
Oh, sweet liddle Pickaninny,

Born in ole Virginy.
Mammy! How de baby grow!

294   Don't Sing before Breakfast

A well-recorded superstition; see J. Mason Brewer, *American Negro Folklore* (296).

Don't sing out 'fore Breakfast,
Don't sing 'fore you eat,
Or you'll cry out 'fore midnight,
You'll cry 'fore you sleep.

295   My Folks and Your Folks

If you an' yō' folks
Likes me an' my folks,
Lak me an' my folks,
Likes you an' yō' folks;
You's never seed folks,
Since folks 'as been folks,
Like you an' yō' folks,
Lak me an' my folks.

296   Little Sleeping Negroes

One liddle Nigger a-lyin' in de bed;
His eyes shet an' still, lak he been dead.

Two liddle Niggers a-lyin' in de bed;
A-snorin' an' a-dreamin' of a table spread.

Three liddle Niggers a-lyin' in de bed;
Deir heels cracked open lak shorten' bread.

Four liddle Niggers a-lyin' in de bed;
Dey'd better hop out, if dey wants to git fed!

297 Mamma's Darling

Wid flowers on my shoulders,
An' wid slippers on my feet;
I'se my mammy's darlin'.
Don't you think I'se sweet?

I wish I had a fourpence,
Den I mought use a dime.
I wish I had a Sweetheart,
To kiss me all de time.

I has apples on de table,
An' I has peaches on de shelf;
But I wish I had a husband—
I'se so tired stayin' to myself.

298 Stealing a Ride

White (194) has a version collected from black sources in 1919; Perrow (1915,
p. 142) reports a version collected from mountain whites in 1912. Brown (3:540)
also has two versions.

Two liddle Nigger boys as black as tar,
Tryin' to go to Heaben on a railroad chyar.
Off fall Nigger boys on a cross-tie!
Dey's gwineter git to Heaben shore bye-an'-bye.

299 Washing Mamma's Dishes

When I wus a liddle boy
A-washin' my mammy's dishes,
I rund my finger down my th'oat
An' pulled out two big fishes!

When I wus a liddle boy
A-wipin' my mammy's dishes,

I sticked my finger in my eye
An' I shō' seed liddle fishes.

De big fish swallowed dem all up!
It put me jes a-thinkin'.
All dem things looks awful cu'ous!
I wonder wus I drinkin'?

300   Willie Wee

Willie, Willie, Willie Wee!
One, two, three.
If you wanna kiss a pretty gal,
Come kiss me.

301   Frog Went a-Courting

Perhaps the best-known item in the Talley collection, this song has been traced by some scholars as far back as 1580, and some argue it has been in continuous circulation for over four hundred years. Detailed references to its history are found in Randolph (1:402–10), Brown (3:154–66), Scarborough (46–50), White (218) and others. While Sharp (1921) printed what was apparently the first American version taken from oral tradition, Talley's was apparently the first text taken from black oral tradition to reach print. The song has seemed equally popular among whites and blacks, and Jones and Hawes (34) offer a modern version (as part of a clapping game called "Hambone"), showing that the four-hundred-year tradition is still intact with modern children. The music here appears in the "Leading Themes" notebook (#43), but this was also one of the rare songs to which music was provided in the original 1922 edition. (The notebook music and printed music are virtually identical except that Talley had initially transcribed the piece in 2/4 time before changing it to 4/4.) The original notation also explained that this was "one Negro theme" sung to the song.

De frog went a-co'tin', he did ride.   Uh-huh! Uh-huh!
De frog went a-co'tin', he did ride
Wid a sword an' a pistol by 'is side.   Uh-huh! Uh-huh!

He rid up to Miss Mousie's dō'   Uh-hun! Uh-huh!
He rid up to Miss Mousie's dō',
Whar he'd of'en been befō.   Uh-huh! Uh-huh!

Says he: "Miss Mousie, is you in?"   Uh-huh! Uh-huh!
Says he: "Miss Mousie, is you in?"
"Oh yes, Sugar Lump! I kyard an' spin."   Uh-huh! Uh-huh!

He tuck dat Mousie on his knee.   Uh-huh! Uh-huh!
He tuck dat Mousie on his knee,
An' he say: "Dear Honey, marry me!"   Uh-huh! Uh-huh!

"Oh, Suh!" she say, "I cain't do dat."   Uh-huh! Uh-huh!
"Oh Suh!" she say, "I cain't do dat,
Widout de sayso o' uncle Rat."   Uh-huh! Uh-huh!

Dat ole gray Rat, he soon come home.   Uh-huh! Uh-huh!
Dat ole gray Rat, he soon come home,
Sayin': "Whose been here since
    I'se been gone?"   Uh-huh! Uh-huh!

"A fine young gemmun fer to see."   Uh-huh! Uh-huh!
A fine young gemmun fer to see,
An' one dat axed fer to marry me."   Uh-huh! Uh-huh!

Dat Rat jes laugh to split his side.   Uh-huh! Uh-huh!
Dat Rat jes laugh to split his side.
"Jes think o' Mousie's bein' a bride!"   Un-huh! Uh-huh!

Nex' day, dat rat went down to town.   Uh-huh! Uh-huh!
Nex' day dat rat went down to town,
To git up de Mousie's Weddin' gown.   Uh-huh! Uh-huh!

"What's de bes' thing fer de Weddin' gown?"   Uh-huh! Uh-huh!
"What's de bes' thing fer de Weddin' gown?"
"Dat acorn hull, all gray an' brown!"   Uh-huh! Uh-huh!

"Whar shall de Weddin' Infar' be?"   Uh-huh! Uh-huh!
"Whar shall de Weddin' Infar' be?"
"Down in de swamp in a holler tree."   Uh-huh! Uh-huh!

"What shall de Weddin' Infar' be?"   Uh-huh! Uh-huh!
"What shall de Weddin' Infar' be?"—
"Two brown beans an' a blackeyed pea."   Uh-huh! Uh-huh!

Fust to come in wus de Bumblebee.   Uh-huh! Uh-huh!
Fust to come in wus de Bumblebee.
Wid a fiddle an' bow across his knee.   Uh-huh! Uh-huh!

De nex' dat come wus Khyernel Wren.   Uh-huh! Uh-huh!
De nex' dat come wus Khyernel Wren,
An' he dance a reel wid de Turkey Hen.   Uh-huh! Uh-huh!

De nex' dat come wus Mistah Snake.   Uh-huh! Uh-huh!
De nex' dat come wus Mistah Snake,
He swallowed de whole weddin' cake!   Uh-huh! Uh-huh!

De nex' come in wus Cap'n Flea.   Uh-huh! Uh-huh!
De nex' come in wus Cap'n Flea,
An' he dance a jig fer de Bumblebee.   Uh-huh! Uh-huh!

An' now come in ole Giner'l Louse.   Uh-huh! Uh-huh!
An' now come in ole Giner'l Louse.
He dance a breakdown 'round de house.   Uh-huh! Uh-huh!

De nex' to come was Major Tick.   Uh-huh! Uh-huh!
De nex' to come wus Major Tick,
An' he e't so much it make 'im sick.   Uh-huh! Uh-huh!

Dey sent fer Mistah Doctah Fly.   Uh-huh! Uh-huh!
Dey sent fer Mistah Doctah Fly.
Says he: "Major Tick, you's boun' to die."   Uh-huh! Uh-huh!

Oh, den crep' in ole Mistah Cat.   Uh-huh! Uh-huh!
Oh, den crep' in ole Mistah Cat,
An' chilluns, dey all hollered, "Scat!!"   Uh-huh!!! Uh-huh!!!

It give dat frog a turble fright.   Uh-huh! Uh-huh!
It give dat frog a turble fright.
An' he up an' say to dem, "Good-night!"   Uh-huh! Uh-huh!

Dat frog, he swum de lake aroun'.   Uh-huh! Uh-huh!
Dat frog, he swum de lake aroun',
An' a big black duck come gobble 'im down.   Uh-huh! Uh-huh!

"What d'you say 'us Miss Mousie's lot?"   Uh-huh! Uh-huh!
"What d'you say 'us Miss Mousie's lot?"—
"W'y—, she got swallered on de spot!"   Uh-huh! Uh-huh!

Now, I don't know no mō' 'an dat.   Uh-huh! Uh-huh!
Now, I don't know no mō' 'an dat.
If you gits mō' you can take my hat.   Uh-huh! Uh-huh!

An' if you thinks dat hat won't do.   Uh-huh! Uh-huh!
An' if you thinks dat hat won't do,
Den you mought take my head 'long, too.   Uh-huh!!! Uh-huh!!!

302   Shoo! Shoo!

Shoo! Shoo!
What'll I do?
Run three mile an' buckle my shoe?

No! No!
I'se gwineter go,
An' kill dat chicken on my flō'.

Oh! My!
Chicken pie!
Sen' fer de Doctah, I mought die.

Christmus here,
Once a year.
Pass dat cider an' 'simmon beer

303   Flap-Jacks

The first couplet is quite common in early country music and in square
dance calls of the South; see White (136).

I loves my wife, an' I loves my baby:
An' I loves dem flap-jacks a-floatin' in gravy.
You play dem chyards, an' make two passes:
While I eats dem flap-jacks a-floatin' in 'lasses.

Now: in come a Nigger an' in come a bear,
In come a Nigger dat hain't got no hair.
Good-by, Nigger, go right on back,
Fer I hain't gwineter give you no flap-jack.

304   Teaching Table Manners

Now whilst we's here 'round de table,
All you young ones git right still.
I wants to l'arn you some good manners,
So's you'll think o' Uncle Bill.

Cose we's gwineter 'scuse Merlindy,
Caze she's jes a baby yit.
But it's time you udder young ones
Wus a-l'arnin' a liddle bit.

I can 'member as a youngster,
Lak you youngsters is to-day;
How my mammy l'arnt me manners
In a 'culiar kind o' way.

One o' mammy's ole time 'quaintance.
(Ole Aunt Donie wus her name)
Come one night to see my mammy.
Mammy co'se 'pared fer de same.

Mammy got de sifter, Honey;
An' she tuck an' make up dough,
Which she tu'n into hot biscuits.
Den we all git smart, you know.

'Zerves an' biscuits on de table!
Honey, noways could I wait.
Ole Aunt Donie wus a good ole 'oman,
An' I jes had to pass my plate.

I soon swallered down dem biscuit,
E't 'em faster dan a shoat.
Dey wus a liddle tough an' knotty,
But I chawed 'em lak a goat.

"Pass de biscuits, please, Mam!
Please, Mam, fer I wants some mō'."
Lawd! You'd oughter seed my mammy
Frownin' up, jes "sorter so."

"Won't you pass de biscuit, please, Mam?"
I said wid a liddle fear.
Dere wus not but one mō' lef', Sir.
Mammy riz up out'n her chear.

W'en Aunt Donie lef' our house, Suh,
Mammy come lak bees an' ants,
Put my head down 'twixt her knees, Suh,
Almos' roll me out'n my pants.

She had a great big tough hick'ry,
An' it help till it convince.
Frum dat day clean down to dis one,
I'se had manners ev'r since.

305   Miss Blodger

De rats an' de mice, dey rund up stairs,
Fer to hear Miss Blodger say her prayers.
Now here I stan's 'fore Miss Blodger.
She 'spects to hit me, but I'se gwineter dodge her.

306   The Little Negro Fly

Dere's a liddle Nigger fly
Got a pretty liddle eye;
But he don't know 'is A, B, C's.
He up an' crawl de book,
An' he eben 'pears to look;
But he don't know 'is A, B, C's.

307   Destinies of Good and Bad Children

"Segashurate means to associate with. Read the first stanza of 'Sheep Shell Corn' [No. 79, above] to know of old man Joe" (Talley). This common counting-out rhyme is still in circulation, with "old black Joe" replacing "ole man Joe" in some versions. See annotations and texts in Roger Abrahams, *Jump-Rope Rhymes: A Dictionary* (151–52).

One, two, three, fō', five, six, seben;
All de good chilluns goes to Heaben.
All de bad chilluns goes below,
To segashuate wid ole man Joe.

One, two, three, fō', five, six, seben, eight;
All de good chilluns goes in de Pearly Gate.
But all de bad chilluns goes the Broad Road below,
To segashuate wid ole man Joe.

308　Black-Eyed Peas for Luck

"The last stanza embodies one of the old superstitions" (Talley).

> One time I went a-huntin',
> I heared dat 'possum sneeze.
> I hollered back to Susan Ann:
> Put on a pot o' peas."
>
> Dat good ole 'lasses candy,
> What makes de eyeballs shine,
> Wid 'possum peas an' taters,
> Is my dish all de time.
>
> Dem black-eyed peas is lucky;
> When e't on New Year's day,
> You always has sweet taters,
> An' 'possum come your way.

309　Periwinkle

"The Periwinkle seems to have been used as an oracle by some Negroes in the days of their enslavement" (Talley). The periwinkle is a salt-water snail. Variations on this rhyme are reported in J. Mason Brewer's *American Negro Folklore* (305).

> Pennywinkle, pennywinkle, poke out yō' ho'n;
> An' I'll give you five dollahs an' a bar'l o' co'n.
> Pennywinkle! Pennywinkle! Dat gal love me?
> Jes stick out yō' ho'n all pinted to a tree.

310   Training the Boy

W'en I wus a liddle boy,
Jes thirteen inches high,
I useter climb de table legs,
An' steal off cake an' pie.

Altho' I wus a liddle boy,
An' tho' I wusn't high,
My mammy took dat keen switch down,
An' whupped me till I cry.

Now I is a great big boy,
An' Mammy, she cain't do it;
My daddy gits a great big stick,
An' pulls me right down to it.

Dey say: "No breakin' dishes now;
No stealin' an' no lies."
An' since I is a great big boy,
Dey 'spects me to act wise.

311   Bat! Bat!

"A superstition that it is good luck to catch a bat in one's hat if he doesn't
get bedbugs by doing so" (Talley).

Bat! Bat! Come un'er my hat,
An' I'll give you a slish o' bacon.
But don't bring none yō' ole bedbugs,
If you don't want to git fersaken.

312   Randsome Tantsome

Randsome Tantsome! — Gwine to de Fair?
Randsome Tantsome! — W'at you gwineter wear?
Dem shoes an' stockin's I'se bound to wear!"
Randsome Tantsome a-gwine to de Fair.

313 Are You Careful?

Is you keerful; w'en you goes down de street,
To see dat yō' cloze looks nice an' neat?
Does you watch yō' liddle step 'long de way,
An' think 'bout dem words dat you say?

314 Rabbit Hash

A widely known piece that appears in print in Odum and Johnson, *The Negro and His Songs* (215); Brown (3:211–13; and Langston Hughes and Anna Bontemps, *The Book of Negro Folklore* (39–40). It was popularized on the vaudeville stage as early as 1885 by blackface comic Billy Golden and was recorded by Golden some ten times on various cylinders and commercial recordings from 1898 to 1921. (See Robert G. Cogswell, "Jokes in Blackface: A Discographic Folklore Study," 161, 203, 204, 870–73.)

Dere wus a big ole rabbit
Dat had a mighty habit
A-settin' in my gyardin,
An' eatin' all by cabbitch.
I hit 'im wid a mallet,
I tapped 'im wid a maul.
Sich anudder rabbit hash,
You's never tasted 'tall.

315 Why the Woodpecker's Head Is Red

Bill Dillix say to dat woodpecker bird:
"W'at makes yō' topknot red?"
Says he: "I'se picked in de red-hot sun,
Till it's done burnt my head."

316   Blessings

"The chivalry of the Old South rather demanded that all friends should be invited to partake of the meal, if they chanced to come calling bout the time of the meal hour. This ideal also pervaded the lowly slave Negro's cabin. In order that this hospitality might not be abused, the Negroes had a little deterrent story which they told their children. Below are the fancied Blessings asked by the fictitious Negro family, in the story, whose hospitality had been abused" (Talley).

A

Blessing with Company Present

Oh Lawd now bless an' bīn' us,
An' put ole Satan 'hīn' us.
Oh let yō' Sperit mīn' us.
Don't let none hongry fīn' us.

B

Blessing without Company

Oh Lawd have mussy now upon us,
An' keep 'way some our neighbors from us.
For w'en dey all comes down upon us,
Dey eats mōs' all our victuals from us.

317   Animal Persecutors

I went up on de mountain,
To git a bog o' co'n.
Dat coon, he sicked 'is dog on me,
Dat 'possum blowed 'is ho'n.

Dat gobbler up an' laugh at me.
Dat pattridge giggled out.
Dat peacock squall to bust 'is sides,
To see me runnin' 'bout.

318   Four Runaway Negroes —
Whence They Came

For other references to "Guinea Gall," see No. 271 (above).

Once fō' runaway Niggers,
Dey met in de road.
An' dey ax one nudder:
Whar dey come from.
Den one up an' say:
    I'se jes come down from Chapel Hill
    Whar de Niggers hain't wuked an' never will."

Den anudder up an' say:
    "I'se jes come here from Guinea Gall
    Whar dey eats de cow up, skin an' all."

Den de nex' Nigger say
Whar he done come from:
    "Dey wuked you night an' day as dey could;
    Dey never had stopped an' dey never would."

De las' Nigger say
Whar he come from:
    "De Niggers all went out to de Ball;
    De thick, de thin, de short, de tall."

But dey'd all please set up,
Jes lak ole Br'er Rabbit
W'en he look fer a dog.
An' keep it in mind,
Whilst dey boasts 'bout deir gals
An' dem t'other things:
    "Dat none deir gals wus lak Sallie Jane,
    Fer dat gal wus sweeter dan sugar cane."

Wise Saying Section

319 Learn to Count

See White (383).

> Naught's a naught,
> Five's a figger.
> All fer de white man,
> None fer de Nigger.
>
> Ten's a ten,
> But it's mighty funny;
> When you cain't count good,
> You hain't got no money.

320 The War Is On

> De boll-weevil's in de cotton,
> De cut-worm's in de corn,
> De Devil's in de white man;
> An' de wah's a-gwine on.
> Poor Nigger hain't got no home!
> Poor Nigger hain't got no home!

321 How to Plant and Cultivate Seeds

> Plant: One fer de blackbird
>   Two fer de crow,

Three fer de jaybird
An' fō' fer to grow.

Den: When you goes to wuk,
    Don't never stand still;
    When you pull de grass,
    Pull it out'n de hill.

322   A Man of Words

A recitation which appears in a number of collections of nursery rhymes
and games from England from the 1840s to 1901; an American version collected in 1914 from Burke County, N.C., appears in Brown (1:202), along with
references to other sources. Talley's appears to be the first text collected from
a black informant.

A man o' words an' not o' deeds,
Is lak a gyarden full o' weeds.
    De weeds 'gin to grow
    Lak a gyarden full o' snow.
    De snow 'gin to fly
    Lak a eagle in de sky.
    De sky 'gin to roar
    Lak a hammer on yō' door.
    De door 'gin to crack
    Lak a hick'ry on yō' back.

    Yō' back 'gin to smart
    Lak a knife in yō' heart.
    Yō' heart 'gin to fail
    Lak a boat widout a sail.
    De boat 'gin to sink
    Lak a bottle full o' ink.
    Dat ink, it won't write
    Neider black nor white.
Dat man 'o words an' not o' deeds,
Is lak a gyarden full o' weeds.

323   Independent

I'se jes as innerpenunt as a pig on ice.
Gwineter git up ag'in if I slips down twice.
If I cain't git up, I can jes lie down.
I don't want no Niggers to be he'pin' me 'roun'.

324   Temperance Rhyme

Music from "Leading Themes" notebook, #7.

Whisky nor brandy hain't no friend to my kind.
Dey killed my pō' daddy, an' dey troubled my mind.
Sometime he drunk whisky, sometime he drunk ale;
Sometime he kotch de rawhide, an' sometime de flail.

On yon'er high mountain, I'll set up dar high;
An' de wild geese can cheer me while passin' on by.
Go 'way, young ladies, an' let me alone;
For you know I'se a poor boy, an' a long ways from home.

Go put up de hosses an' give 'em some hay;
But don't give me no whisky, so long as I stay.
For whisky nor brandy hain't friend to my kind;
Dey killed my pō' daddy, an' dey troubled my mind.

331   Self-Control

Talley noted in regard to the use of the word "donkey" in stanza 2: "The somewhat less dignified term was more commonly used."

> Befo' you says dat ugly word,
> You stop an' count ten.
> Den if you wants to say dat word,
> Begin an' count again.
>
> Don't have a tongue tied in de middle,
> An' loose frum en' to en'.
> You mus' think twice, den speak once;
> Dat donkey cain't count ten.

332   Speak Softly

The last three lines of the rhyme was a superstition current among antebellum Negroes" (Talley).

> "Wus dat you spoke,
> Or a fence rail broke?"
> Br'er Rabbit say to de Jay
> W'en you don't speak sof',
> Yō' baits comes off;
> An' de fish jes swim away.

333   Still Water Runs Deep

The general proverb has been collected in both England and America; see Brown (1:493, 483) for references.

> Dat still water, it run deep.
> Dat shaller water prattle.
> Dat tongue, hung in a holler head,
> Jes roll 'round an' rattle.

334   Don't Tell All You Know

Keep dis in min', an' all 'll go right;
As on yō' way you goes;
Be shore you knows 'bout all you tells,
But don't tell all you knows.

335   Jack and Dinah Want Freedom

"The writer wishes to give explanation as to why the rhyme 'Jack and Dinah want Freedom' appears under the Section of Psycho-Composite Rhymes as set forth in 'The Study— —' of our volume. The Negroes repeating this rhyme did not always give the names Jack, Dinah, and Billy, as we here record them, but at their pleasure put in the individual name of the Negro in their surroundings whom the stanza being repeated might represent. Thus this little rhyme was the scientific dividing, on the part of the Negroes themselves, of the members of their race into three general classes with respect to the matter of Freedom" (Talley). The "river" (stanza 2) Talley suggests is the Ohio; "Patterollers" were "white guards who caught and kept slaves at the master's home."

Music taken from "Leading Themes" notebook, item #4.

Ole Aunt Dinah, she's jes lak me.
She wuk so hard dat she want to be free.
But, you know, Aunt Dinah's gittin' sorter ole;
An' she's feared to go to Canada, caze it's so cōl'.

Dar wus ole Uncle Jack, he want to git free.
He find de way Norf by de moss on de tree.
He cross dat river a-floatin' in a tub.
Dem Patterollers give 'im a mighty close rub.

Dar is ole Uncle Billy, he's a mighty good Nigger.
He tote all de news to Mosser a little bigger.
When you tells Uncle Billy, you wants free fer a fac';
De nex' day de hide drap off'n yō' back.

Foreign Section

AFRICAN RHYMES

336 Tuba Blay OR An Evening Song

"The rhymes 'Tuba Blay,' 'Near Waldo Tee-do O mah nah mejai,' 'Sai Boddeoh Sumpun Komo,' and 'Byanswahn-Byanswahn' were kindly contributed by Mr. John H. Zeigler, Monrovia, Liberia and Mr. C. T. Wardoh of the Bassa Tribe, Liberia. They are natives and are now in America for collegiate study and training" (Talley).

1. Seah o, Tuba blay.
   Tuba blay, Tuba blay.
2. O blay wulna nahn blay.
   Tuba blay, Tuba blay.

Translation

1. Oh please Tuba sing.
   Tuba sing, Tuba sing.
2. Oh sing that song.
   Tuba sing, Tuba sing.

337 Near-Waldo-Tee-do O Mah Nah Mejai OR Near-Waldo-Tee-do Is My Sweetheart

1. A yehn me doddoc Near Waldo Tee-do.
   Yehn me doddoc o-o seoh-o-o.
   Omah nahn mejai Near Waldo Tee-do.
   Omah nahn mejai Near Waldo Tee-do.

Translation

1. Near Waldo Tee-do gave me a suit.
   He gave me a suit.
   Near Waldo Tee-do is my sweetheart.
   Near Waldo Tee-do is my sweetheart.

338 Sai Boddeoh Sumpun Komo OR I Am Not Going to Marry Sumpun

1. Sai Sumpun komo.
   De Sumpun nenah?
   Sumpun se jello jeppo
   Boddeoh Sumpun.

2. Sai Sumpun komo.
   De Sumpun nenah?
   Sumpun auch nahn jehn deddoc.
   Boddeoh Sumpun.

Translation

1. I am not going to marry Sumpun.
   What has Sumpun done?
   Sumpun doesn't live a seafaring life
   Boddeoh Sumpun.

2. I am not going to marry Sumpun.
   What has Sumpun done?
   Sumpun does not support me.
   Boddeoh Sumpun.

339 Byanswahn-Byanswahn OR A Boat Song

O-O Byanswahn blay Tanner tee-o-o.
O Byanswahn jekah jubha.
De jo Byanswahn se kah jujah dai.
O Byanswahn blay dai Tanner tee-o-o.

Translation

Oh boat, come back to me.
Since you carried my child away,
I have not seen that child.
Oh boat come back to me.

340   The Owl

"We are indebted for this Baluba rhyme to Dr. and Mrs. William H. Sheppard, pioneer missionaries under the Southern Presbyterian Church. The little production comes from Congo, Africa" (Talley).

> Sala wa měn těnge, Cimpungelu.
> Sala wa měn těnge, Cimpungelu.
> Meme taya wewe, Cimpungelu.
> Sala wa měn těnge, Cimpungelu.

Translation

> The dancing owl waves his spread tail feathers. I'm the owl.
> The dancing owl waves his spread tail feathers. I'm the owl.
> I now tell you by my dancing, I'm the owl.
> The dancing owl waves his spread tail feathers.
> I'm the owl.

341   The Turkey Buzzard

"Dr. C. C. Fuller: a missionary at Chikore Melsetter, Rhodesia, Africa, was good enough to secure for the compiler this rhyme, written in Chindau, from the Rev. John E. Hatch, also a missionary in South Africa" (Talley).

> Riti, riti, mwana wa rashika.
> Ndizo, ndizo kurgya ku wande.
> Riti, riti, mwana wa oneka.
> Ndizo, ndizo ti wande issu.

Translation

Turkey, buzzard, turkey buzzard, your child is lost.
That is all right, the food will be more plentiful.
Turkey buzzard, turkey buzzard, your child is found.
That is all right, we will increase in number.

342 The Frogs

"The following child's play rhyme in Baluba with its translation was contributed by Mrs. L. G. Shepard, who was for many years a missionary in Congo, Africa" (Talley).

Cula, Cula, Kuya kudi Kunyi?
Tuyiya ku cisila wa Baluba.
Tun kuata tua kuesa cinyi?
Tua kudimuka kua musode.

Translation

Frogs, frogs, where are you going?
We are going to the market of the Baluba.
If they catch you, what will they do?
They will turn us all into lizards.

JAMAICA RHYME

343 Buscher Garden

"This Negro rhyme from rural Jamaica was contributed by Dr. Cecil B. Roddock, a native of that country. The word *Buscher* means an overseer or master of a plantation" (Talley).

All a night, me da watch a brother Wayrum;
Wayrum ina me Buscher garden.
Oh, Brother Wayrum! Wha' a you da do,

To make a me Buscher a catch a you?
Oh a me Buscher, in a me Buscher garden;
Me a beg a me Buscher a pardon!

VENEZUELAN NEGRO RHYMES

344   A "Would Be" Immigrant

"These Venezuelan rhymes: 'A "Would be" Immigrant' and 'Game Contestant's Song,' came to us through the kindness of Mr. J. C. Williams, Caracas, Venezuela, S.A. He is a native of Venezuela" (Talley).

Conjo Celestine! Oh
He was going to Panama.
Reavay Trinidad!
Celestine Revay, la Grenada!
What d'you think bring Celestine back?
What d'you think bring Celestine back?
What d'you think bring Celestine to me?
Twenty cents for a cup of tea.

345   Game Contestant's song

Talley explains that "cici" (line 5) is a kind of game.

We're going to dig!
We're going to dig a sepulcher to bury those regiments.
White Rose Union!
Get yourself in readiness to bury those regiments.
Oh Grentville! Cici! Cici!
Beat them forever.

Sa your de vrai!
We'll send them a challenge,
To mardi carnival.
Sa your de vrai!!

TRINIDAD NEGRO RHYMES

347   Un Belle Marie Coolie OR Beautiful Marie, The East Indian

"We are very grateful to Mr. L. A. Brown for his kindness in giving to us the two Venezuelan rhymes which follow. His home is in Princess Town, Trinidad, B.W.I." (Talley).

> Un belle Marie Coolie!
> Un belle Marie Coolie!
> Un belle Marie Coolie!
> Vous belle dame, vous belle pour moi.
> Papa est un African.
> Mamma est un belle Coolie.
> Un belle Marie Coolie!
> Vous belle dame, vous belle pour moi.

Translation

> Beautiful Marie, the East Indian!
> Beautiful Marie, the East Indian!
>
> Beautiful Marie, the East Indian!
> You beautiful woman, you're good enough for me.
> Papa is an African.
> Mamma is a beautiful East Indian!
> Beautiful Marie, the East Indian!
> You beautiful woman, you're good enough for me.

348   A Tom Cat

> My father had a big Tom cat,
> That tried to play a fiddle.
> He struck it here, and he struck it there,
> And he struck it in the middle.

349   Philippine Island Rhyme

"The following rhyme came to me through the kindness of Mr. C. W. Ransom, Grand Chain, Ill., U.S.A. Mr. Ransom served three years with the United States Army in the Philippine Islands" (Talley).

> See that Monkey up the cocoanut tree,
> A-jumpin' an' a-throwin' nuts at me?
> El hombre no savoy,
> No like such play.
> All same to Americano,
> No hay diqué.

Additional Songs from Manuscript

350 Plant Flowers on My Grave

This text was found in the Talley papers, apparently sent to him by unknown informant. A sentimental favorite of early country and gospel singers, the song is rarely found in black tradition; Talley might have rejected it for *Negro Folk Rhymes* because of its excessive sentimentality. A popular commercial recording of it was made by the Alabama group McClendon Brothers and Georgia Dell in 1938 (Bluebird B-8922) and by Jimmie Davis, the famed singing governor of Louisiana, in 1940 (Decca 6065).

> Darling, soon I shall be sleeping,
> In the churchyard over there,
> Where the grass and vines are creeping,
> And the birds singing everywhere.
>
> *Refrain*
> When the green grass grows above me,
> And the springtime blossoms peep,
> Promise you will, if you love me,
> Plant sweet flowers on my grave.
>
> When the golden threads are broken,
> And you lay me down to sleep,
> This shall be my only token,
> Of my lover I wish to keep.
>
> (*Refrain*)

351   Buy Flowers of Me

Found in manuscript in Talley papers, from an unnamed informant.

When but a small lad, I had a bad dad,
Bad in his name and his ways,
Every dollar and cent, for liquor he spent,
Til death came and carried him away.

Refrain
Flowers, bouquets, flowers hear me cry,
Every dollar and cent for liquor she [*sic*] spent,
I am struggling for mother and I.

Will you buy, will you buy,
Will you buy these flowers of me?

Flowers, bouquets, flowers hear me cry,
Every dollar and cent for liquor he spent,
Til death came and carried him away.

352   You Shall Be Free

A nigger will be a nigger, don't care what you do,
Tie a bow of ribbon on de toe of his shoe,
Hang his hat upon de wall,
Eat dem flapjacks, butter an' all.

Refrain
Ain't he eatin' some, you shall be free,
Ain't he eatin' some, you shall be free,
Ain't he eatin' some, you shall be free,
When de good Lord set you free.

Why down yonder where I come from,
Fed dem niggers on hard parched corn,
Ate so much, got so fat,
Head busted open and couldn't wear [a] hat.

(*Refrain*)

My gal works in de white folks yard,
Make dem biscuits wid de baker's lard,
Kill der chicken, save me de wing,
Think I'm working when I ain't doing a thing.

Ain't I gittin dare, you shall be free,
Ain't I gittin dare, you shall be free,
Ain't I gittin dare, you shall be free,
When de good Lord set you free.

Me an' my wife had a falling out,
I'll just tell you what 'twas all about,
She told me to go to town and hurry back,
She wanted me to work on the railroad track.

Couldn't do dat, you shall be free,
Too delicate, you shall be free,
Might hurt me, you shall be free,
When de good Lord sat me free.

My gal works in white folks yard,
Made dem buscuits wid de baker lard,
Tell you chillen, 'twas awful hard,
Great God the tempter fur to go in de yard.

Bad biting dog, you shall be free,
Might snag me, you shall be free,
Might nag me, you shall be free,
When de good Lord sat you free.

353 Needle and Thread

This quatrain was sent to Talley by Joe H. Bishop from Belfast, Tennessee, in August 1920. It did not appear in the original edition. For a similar stanza, see Brown (3:143).

I had a needle and thread,
As fine as I could sew,
I'd sew my true-love to my side,
And fly to the Eastern shore.

354   Rock the Cradle Lucy

Sent to Talley by Joe H. Bishop on August 9, 1920, but not used in the original edition of *Negro Folk Rhymes*. Scarborough (153–55) prints a close variant from Arkansas, and the general association of "Old Joe" and "rocking" is seen in Brown's versions of "Old Joe Clark" (3:121–24). The tune was apparently popular with black fiddlers as well, and two Georgia bands, The Cofer Brothers and The Skillet Lickers, made commercial recordings of it as a fiddle tune in the 1920s (cf. the Skillet Lickers version on Columbia 15538, 1929, and the Cofer version [Okeh, rec. 1929, unissued until 1978]).

Joe he cut off his two big toes,
He hung them up to dry,
The girls and boys came riding by,
Ole Joe began to cry.

When Joe was a little boy,
Living by himself,
All the bread and cheese he had,
He laid them on the shelf.

Rock the cradle, Lucy,
Rock the cradle Joe,
I will not rock, I will not rock,
For the body does not know.

355   The Raccoon

Words only, found in an undated and unsigned holograph in papers with the "Leading Themes" notebook, presumably sent to Talley from a correspondent, ca. 1920. Variants of each stanza appear elsewhere in the collection; stanza 1 is similar to "Tails" (No. 7); stanza 2 resembles "Shake the Persimmons Down" (No. 48); stanza 3 resembles "Captain Coon" (No. 270). A

similar grouping of the verse appears both in Brown (3:207–209) and White
(234–35).

> The raccoon has a bushy tail,
> Possum tail, she bear,
> The rabbit has no tail at all,
> But a little bunch of hair.
>
> The possum up the simmon tree,
> The raccoon on the ground,
> The raccoon said to the possum,
> Shake them 'simmons down.
>
> The raccoon is a cunning thing,
> He rambles in the dark,
> He never thinks to curl his tail,
> Till old Ringo bark.

356   When I had But Fifty Cents

From an unsigned, undated holograph found with the "Leading Themes"
notebook and apparently sent to Talley by a correspondent around 1920.
White (*American Negro Folk Songs*) prints a similar version of the song dating
from a "Negro minstrel" show in Alabama at about the same time and suggests it "was originally a white man's song" (212–13); he also provides numerous nineteenth-century songster citations. Small differences between this text
and those in White and Randolph (3:250–251) suggest some degree of oral
circulation. The song was also a favorite of old-time country recording artists, being done commercially by Middle Tennessee singer Jack Jackson (Victor 40129, 1928), Georgia singers Riley Puckett (Columbia 15015, 1924) and
Bill Chitwood (Okeh 45131, 1927), and southwestern singers Ped Moreland
(Victor 40209, 1929) and Otto Gray (Vocalion 5256, 1927).

> I took my gal to a fancy ball,
> It was a social hop,
> Stayed until the folks went out,
> The music it did stop.
> Took her to a resturant,
> The best one on the street,
> She said she was not hungry,

And did not care to eat,
I have money in my old clothes,
You bet she can't be beat.

She took in the courses all,
One dozen raw, a plate of slaw,
Chicken and some roast,
Apple sass, some sparrow grass,
Soft shell crabs on toast,
Big buck stew, crackers, too,
Appetite was immense,
When she called for pie,
I thought I would die,
For I only had fifty cents.

She had an awful tank,
She said she was not thirsty,
But this is what she drank:
Whiskey skimmed, a glass of gin,
Made me shake with fear,
Ginger pop with a room on top,
A schooner of beer,
A glass of ale, a gin cocktail,
She ought to have more sense,
When she called for more,
I fell on the floor,
I only had fifty cents.

She said she'd bring her family around,
Someday and we would have fun,
I paid the man the fifty cents,
But this is what he done,
Banged my nose, tore my clothes,
Hit me in the jaw,
Give me a prize of two black eyes,
And with me swept the floor,
Took me where my clothes hung loose,
Threw me over the fence,
Take my advice and don't try twice,
When you only got fifty cents.

357 Kitty with a Lonely Eye

Words and music found only in the "Leading Themes" manuscript, #18. For possible analogues, see Brown (3:149), White (175). The final couplet, of course, is often found as a conclusion to "Frog Went A-Courtin'," though Talley's version (above) does not use it.

He went down to this cabin do',
Johnny make a kitty ki o,
He asked for bread, he'd asked befo',
Kitty wid de lonely eye,
Dere am a piece o' bread is dere on de shelf,
If you wants to eat mo' you can get it yo'self,
Johnny make kitty ki o.

358 Johnny Keep Pickin' on the Banjo

This short piece is found only in the "Leading Themes" notebook, #32. The first part of the piece apears in "Other Side of Jordan," recorded and popularized by early Grand Ole Opry star Uncle Dave Macon. (See his "Jordan Is a Hard Road to Travel," Vocalion 5153 [1927], and a transcription of the song in the *New Lost City Ramblers Songbook*, 204.) See also Talley's own version of "The Other Side of Jordan," No. 380.

Rain forty days and rain forty nights,
Rain forty days and rain forty nights,
Rain forty days and rain forty nights,
Johnny keep a-pickin' on the banjo.

359   She Said I Couldn't Come Anymore

Found in manuscript only; compare "A Short Letter" from original edition, No. 165 above. Music from "Leading Themes" notebook, #37.

In about six months more,
She sent me the hard word,
She said by the hard word,
I can't come no mo',
Oh, I can't come no mo'.

360   Solid as a Hole in the Wall

Words and music found only in "Leading Themes" notebook, item #44. Portions of the second stanza appear to be crossed through.

I'm as solid as a hole in the wall,
I'm as solid as a hole in the wall,
I'm as solid as a hole in the wall,
And I don't know what makes me dis a way.

Oh me lubin' gal she tol' me so,
Oh my lubin' gal she tol' me so,
Oh my lubin gal she tol' me so,
Dat I must not take [?] it any more.

361   Little Sweetheart Downtown

Words and music found only in "Leading Themes" notebook, #46.

I had a little sweetheart, she lived downtown,
I gave her a dress for a morning gown.

Goodbye, little sweetheart, jes' stay downtown,
Dar's plenty good gals in the country 'round.

She beat me and she begged me and run me from town,
She make me wish I never seed a morning gown.
I hope she never seed dat morning gown.

362   Sister Mary Wears a Pretty Green Shawl

Found only in manuscript notebook, #47.

Sister Mary wears a pretty green shawl,
A pretty green shawl,
A pretty green shawl,
Sister Mary wears a pretty green shawl,
Early in the morning.

363   How Old Are You?

Words and music found only in manuscript in "Leading Themes" notebook,
#49. The quatrain is well known in Anglo-American tradition; for similar
text, see Ruth Crawford Seeger *American Folk Songs for Children* (56–57). In
the 1930s the popular country radio duo of Lulu Belle and Scotty (Wiseman)
popularized the song over WLS Chicago.

How old are you my pretty little miss,
How old are you my honey?
Every time she answered,
I'll be sixteen next Sunday,
I'll be sixteen next Sunday.

364   Rule, Rule, Rule Over

A game song, with words and music found only in the "Leading Themes" notebook, #51.

Rule, rule, rule over,
Draw wine but drink water,
Rule, rule, rule over,
Draw wine but drink water.

Who is the ruler, sometimes, oh,
Who is the ruler, sometimes, oh,

Who is the ruler, sometimes, oh,
Who is the ruler, sometimes?

John is the ruler, sometimes, oh, etc.
Mary is the ruler, sometimes, oh, etc.

365   Old Louisiana Gal

Words and music not in original edition but found only in the "Leading
Themes" notebook, #52.

Come, honey come, come go wid me,
Come, honey come, come go wid me.

Come go wid me to Tennessee, Ole Louisiana Gal,
Come go wid me, I'll get you free, Ole Louisiana Gal.
Come go wid me to Tennessee, Ole Louisiana Gal,
Come go wid me, I'll set you free, Ole Louisiana Gal.

Come, honey come, come go wid me,
Come, honey come, come go wid me.

Hawk and buzzard went to lunch, Ole Louisiana Gal,
Hawk and buzzard went to lunch, Ole Louisiana Gal.

366   A Partridge in a Pear Tree

This fragment of the familiar Christmas song is found only in the "Leading Themes" notebook, #53.

De second day of Christmas, my true love gave for me,
Partridge in a pear tree,
Six hens a laying,
Seben ducks a swimming,
Come now sing round my sweet love,
My color'd girl, my turtle dove,
Partridge in a pear tree.

367   Follow That Gent'men wi'd a Hat on His Head

Omitted from the original edition, the words and music are both found in the "Leading Themes" notebook, #59.

Follow that gent'man with a hat on his head,
Green grows the willow tree,
Follow that gent'man with a hat on his head,
Green grows the willow tree.
Oh young laides, oh young gent'men,
Don't you think its hard,
You've all got a true love and I hain't got one,
Green grows the willow tree.

368   The Only Love I Know

Words and music found only in "Leading Themes" notebook, #60. In the manuscript, Talley originally titled this "The Only Girl I Know." Probably an old play-party game or ring game.

Johnny had a little girl and she walk'd around,
Oh boys, don't you know,
Johnny had a little girl and she walk'd around,
The only love I know.
    Come in the ring and kiss her hand,
    Come in the ring and kiss her hand.

Mary had a little beau and he walk'd all around,
Oh boys don't you know.
Mary had a little beau and he walk'd around,
The only love I know.
  Come in the ring and bow to him low,
  Come in the ring and bow to him low.

369   Poor Little Lamb Said "Mammy"

Found in "Leading Themes" notebook without music or title, this song is almost identical to "Lullaby" in John W. Work's *American Negro Songs and Spirituals* (250), which includes music. Since Work and Talley were colleagues at Fisk, there is almost certainly some connection. The song is also reported in numerous other collections, such as Brown (3:152–53), Scarborough (147–49), and Randolph (2:345–46). It seems to have been widespread in both white and black traditions; there was even an early country recording of it by the Three Georgia Crackers (Columbia 15653, 1931).

  Old Molly Glascow, where is your lamb?
  I left him down in the meadow,
  Birds and flies picking out his eyes,
  Poor little lamb said "Mammy."

370   Go to Sleep, Little Baby

Found only in the "Leading Themes" notebook, where it is listed as #81; an arrangement was apparently also made for Sonoma Talley.

  Hush-a-bye and don't you cry,
  Go to sleep, little baby!
  When you wake, you shall have,
  A coach and six little ponies.

371 Bye-o

A lullaby fragment found only in the "Leading Themes" notebook, #82. It, like
the following one, was collected from Mrs. John W. Work (see "Introduction").

Bye oh, bye oh.
Bye oh, bye oh.
Bye oh, bye oh,
Bye oh, bye oh, my darling.

(Repeat)

372 Papa Loves His Little Baby

Talley collected this lullaby fragment from Mrs. John W. Work. It appears
only in the "Leading Themes" notebook, #83.

Papa loves his little baby, bye-o,
Papa loves his little baby, bye-o,
Papa loves his little baby, bye-o,
Hush, hush a by.

(*Repeat*)

373   Rag Man's Songs

Talley was years ahead of his time in his perception that some of the roots
of black traditional music lay in the "proto-music" of the field holler, the
work chant, or the street cry. In his "Study of Negro Folk Rhymes" (below)
he discusses the importance of the call-response pattern, and transcribes
several field calls. In the "Leading Themes" notebook are two examples of
street calls which he apparently heard in Nashville sometime between 1900
and 1915. A similar street cry from a ragman is found in the collection by
Talley's colleague John W. Work, *American Negro Songs,* (244). See also a similar cry published in Natalie Curtis Burlin, *Hampton Series Negro Folk Songs*
(4:39–40).

I

This entry is listed as #80 in the notebook.

Any rags or any bones or any bottles today?
Any rags, any bones, any bottles today?

A big black man standin' out in the street a cryin'
Any rags, bones, bottles today,
Any rags or any bones or any bottles today?

II

This entry is listed, without title, as #84 in the notebook.

Rag man, rag man, bottles today,
Rag man, rag man, bottles today.
And a big black man standing out in the street,
Cryin' rags, old bones, and bottles today.

374   The Old Man's Song

Talley did not include this naming song in his original edition, and it is
found only in the manuscript (#87); apparently he thought highly enough
of it, however, as he apparently made an arrangement of it for his daughter
Sonoma Talley.

1. Old man, old man, and what's your sons' names?
    Oh come now, old man, just tell me the same,
    Won't you call them off whilst I whittle with my knife,
    I haven't never seed such a fine gang in my life.

    Refrain
    Well, there's my son Willie, my son Billie,
    My son Jimmy, my son Timmy,
    My son John, Jake, and Jipton
    My son Henry and my son Tipton.

2. Old man, old man, is yo' sons hard to feed?
    Old man, old man, does you ever get in need?
    "Oh, dey feeds all day in de watermelon field,
    And catchin' dem possum dey's Charlie at de wheel.

    (*Refrain*)

375   The Old Gray Goose Is Dead

This familiar nursery rhyme song has been widely collected for years. For a sampling of references and variants, see Brown (3:177–78). Talley's version is found only in the "Leading Themes" notebook, #89. This version has some curious variations; the song has not often been collected from Middle Tennessee, nor from black sources and the melody is slightly different from the one commonly found with the song.

Go and tell Aunt Betsie,
Go and tell Aunt Betsie,
Go and tell Aunt Betsie,
Dat de ole gray goose is dead.

One dat she's been savin,'
One dat she's been savin,'
One dat she's been savin,'
For to make dat fedder bed.

Dat ole fox has done come,
Dat ole fox has done come,
Dat ole fox has done come,
And he have bit off her head.

376   The Old Gray Horse Came Tearin' through the Wilderness

Found in the "Leading Themes" notebook only, #90. Similar versions are found in Brown (3:216–17). It has been labeled, variously, as a Negro spiritual, a play-party song (Botkin, 268), a Civil War song (FSV 260–261), and a lullaby. It was popular with white fiddlers in the 1920s; commercial phonograph records were made by north Georgian Earl Johnson (Okeh 45183, 1927) and by Ted Sharp (Champion 16751, late 1920s); a Middle Tennessee native, Obed Pickard, also made a version featuring a Jew's harp for Columbia records in 1926 (Col. 15246).

The ole gray horse came tearing through the wilderness,
Tearin' through the wilderness,
Tearin' through the wilderness,
The ole gray horse came tearing through the wilderness,
Making for de road.

    Ho, Dinah, ho,
    Ho, Dinah, ho, my gal,
    Ho, Dinah, ho!
    Oh, don't you hear him blow.

(*For* 2): Ho, Dinah, ho,
          Ho, Dinah, ho, my gal,
          Ho, Dinah, ho!
          His bridle do rattle so!

(*For* 3): Ho, Dinah, ho
          Ho, Dinah, ho, my gal!
          Ho, Dinah, do!
          Say, don't you want to go?

377   Shoo Fly! (I Would Not Marry a Black Girl)

Three verses of the song appear earlier in the collection under the title "I Would Not Marry a Black Girl" (No. 76). The "Shoo Fly" part seems derived from the 1869 "walk around" credited to Billy Reeves and Frank Campbell and referred to by Ewen (47) as a "blackface Reconstruction classic." It has been collected widely by folklorists; see Scarborough (200–201) and Randolph (3:352) for representative versions and further annotation. This version is from the "Leading Themes" notebook (#91), where a notation by Talley reads: "The repeat is used only at the beginning and end of the piece."

Refrain
Shoo fly! Don't bother me,
Shoo fly! Don't bother me,
Shoo fly! Don't bother me,
I belong to the upper three.

I wouldn' marry a black gal,
I'll tell you de reason why:
When she goes to comb dat head
De naps'll 'gin to fly.

378   Go to Sleep, I Do Love My Lamb

Found only in the "Leading Themes" notebook (#92); handwritten annotations suggest "slowly" and explain that the song should begin with the refrain.

Refrain
Yes, I do love my lamb, yes I do love my lamb.
Yes, I do love my lamb, yes I do love my lamb.

(1) Go to sleep little baby, I do love my lamb,
Go to sleep little baby, I do love my lamb.

(2) Shut yo' eyes little baby, I do love my lamb,
Shut yo' eyes little baby, I do love my lamb.

(3) The morning comes, I do love my lamb.
   The morning comes, I do love my lamb.

379 Mammy, Is Massa Gwine to Sell Me Tomorrow?

Text, as well as music, found only in the "Leading Themes" notebook, #98. Like many of the unused songs, this features a heavily repetitive text, which either Talley or his editors may have thought "unliterary" or less interesting as poetry.

Mammy, is Masser gwine to sell me tomorrow?
Yes, Yes, yes.
Mammy, is Masser gwinte to sell me tomorrow?
Yes, yes, yes.
Mammy, is Masser gwine to sell me tomorrow?
Yes, yes, yes.
Then water and pray.

Mammy, is Masser gwine to sell me down Georgia?
Yes, yes, yes.
Mammy, is Masser gwine to sell me down Georgia?
Yes, yes, yes.
Mammy, is Masser gwine to sell me down Georgia?
Yes, yes, yes.
Then water and pray.

Mammy, oh farewell, I will meet you in Heaben,
Yes, yes, yes.
Mammy, oh farewell, I will meet you in Heaben,
Yes, yes, yes.
Mammy, oh farewell, I will meet you in Heaben,
Yes, yes, yes.
Oh, water and pray.

380   The Other Side of Jordan

Talley preserved both words and music to this in his *Negro Traditions* manuscript, where it appears in the story "The Devil's Daughter." The song possibly has roots in the minstrel tradition and is related to "Jordan Am a Hard Road to Travel," published as early as 1853, with music attributed to noted minstrel composer Dan Emmett and words credited to T.F. Briggs; Randolph (*Ozark Folksongs*) prints a version from white tradition that allegedly dates back to the 1940s. Uncle Dave Macon recorded a version of the song in 1927 (reissued on RBF RF 51), but it shares only the refrain with this version. Another recording from the same period, by Georgia singer Riley Puckett, offers different but related verses (cf. County LP reissue 411).

Oh, de Devil an' black Jack, dey wus a playin' seben-up,
Dat 'ar game up dar call fer a half a dollar,
Chile, de Devil kick'd de Jack from de bottom of de pack,
An' de Imps 'cross Jurdon heard 'im holler!

Refrain
Pull off you' coat boys, roll up yo' sleeves,
Jurdon's a hard road to travel!
Pull off yo' coat boys, roll up yo' sleeves,
Jurdon's a hard road to travel!

Oh, I wush I wus de Devil, wid his hawns an' hoofs an' shovel,
Den I'd han' down to de Imps a liddle burden.
Put de Niggers in a hiddle, lak de ducks all in a puddle;
An' den lan' 'em on de tother side of Jurdon.

Oh, ole Missus an' ole Mosser wus got heaps of kinds of meat,
It wus sheep an' ham an' lam' an' hog an' mutton.
Black Jack step'd up to de house, stuffed a ham down in his mouf,
Den he brung awau de balunce jes' a struttin.'

381   Throwin' San' on Me

This is another song that appears in the "Leading Themes" notebook (#16) but not in the original edition of *Negro Folk Rhymes*. It was apparently taken out to be used in the "Negro Traditions" manuscript, in the story called "Why the Jaybird Goes to See the 'Bad Man' on Friday." In a footnote to the song in that manuscript, Talley writes: "I have written this note as G# through this song because that is the best of which the Caucasian scale will admit. In the Melody as sung by the antebellum Negro, the technically scientific G♭ was the note used—a note lower in pitch and giving an impression of sorrow. The other Negro intervals were also just a little different but it cannot be shown on our musical scale."

Refrain
Car' de news! Car'd de news to Mary!
Car' de news! Dey's throwin' san' on me!

De Jaybird jump from lim' to lim'.
Throwin' san' on me!
An' he tell Brer Rabbit to do lak him,
Throwin' san' on me!
Brer Rabbit say to de cunnin elf,
Throwin' san' on me!
You wants me to fall an' kill myself,
Throwin' san' on me!

   (*Refrain*)

Dat Jaybird sittin on a swingin' lim',
Throwin' san' on me!

He wink at me an' I wink at him,
Throwin' san' on me!
He laugh at me when my gun "crack,"
Throwin' san' on me!
It kick me down on de flat o' my back,
Throwin' san' on me!

(*Refrain*)

De nex' day de Jaybird dance dat lim',
Throwin' san' on me!
I grabs my gun fer to shoot at him,
Throwin' san' on me!
When I crack down it split my chin,
Throwin' san' on me!
Ole Ag-gie — Con-jer fly lak sin,
Throwin' san' on me!

(*Refrain*)

A-way down yoner at de ris-in sun,
Throwin' san' on me!
Dat Jay-bird talkin wid a forked tongue;
Throwin' san' on me!
He's been down dar whar de Bad Men's dwell,
Throwin' san' on me!
"Ole Fri-day Devil" far' you well!
Throwin' san' on me!

382   Gum Tree Canoe

Found only in the "Leading Themes" notebook (#100), this is part of the familiar nineteenth-century parlor song by S. S. Steele, widely reprinted in various song anthologies of the day, and collected from traditional sources by people like Randolph (4:302), Ira Ford (288–289), and Brown (3:318). It was recorded commercially by several early country singers in the 1930s but is rarely found in black collections. Talley omits most of the first stanza in his MS.

On the Tombigbee River so bright, I was born,
. . . .
One night like a tiger I bounded far away,
I could not get back and I thought I would stay,
One hand on my banjo and toe on my oar,
At night I sail round in my gum tree canoe,
Rowing the water so blue,
Like a feather I float in my gum tree canoe.

383 My Heart's Gone A-Weeping

Music and partial words appear in "Leading Themes" notebook (#55); fuller
text appears in "The Devil's Daughter" in "Negro Traditions" manuscript.

Come un'er! Come un'er! My Honey, my Love, my Heart's-above!
Case my heart's gone a weepin, 'way down below de trees.

Come eat den! Come eat den! My Honey, my Love, my Heart's-above!
Case my heart's gone a weepin, 'way down below de trees.

He's cotch you fer his pris'ner! My Honey, my Love, my Heart's-above!
Case my heart's gone a weepin, 'way down below de trees.

384   Hard Times in Shelbyville Rock Jail

Many folksong collections contain versions of a "Hard Times" song which
uses the "hard times" refrain to satirize merchants, preachers, women, and
lawyers; see Brown (3:385) and Emrich, *American Folk Poetry* (767), for examples
of these. Possibly related to the older song is a "jailhouse" "Hard Times,"
of which this seems a version. Alan Lomax prints one of these in his *The
Folk Songs of North America* (438–39), but much closer to Talley's is one dating
from 1890 in North Carolina and printed in Brown (3:419) as "Durham Jail."
The melody Talley uses here is close to that used on an early country music
"Hard Times" song recorded by Uncle Dave Macon, "All in Down and Out
Blues" (Bluebird 7350, 1937).

Shelbyville is the Middle Tennessee town where Talley was born in 1870.

Refrain
Hard times in Shelbyville rock jail,
Oh dere's hard times, poor boy!
Hard times in Shelbyville rock jail,
Oh dere's hard times, poor boy!

I tells you my boy to keep 'way from town,
For de police will grab you and take you on down, to

(Refrain)

Old Jake the Jailer, wid the keys in his hand,
Says, Come on in here you black nigger man, to:

(Refrain)

As hard as rock and as heavy as lead,
Jake pitches you in an old lump of corn bread, for

(Refrain)

De place is so cold, yo water's all ice,
But you always keep warm cause dere's so many lice,

(Refrain)

An den dat old judge, he sit up dar on high,
And he sends you to the devil for blinkin' [?] your eye.

(Refrain)

The lawyer he lies and says you're to blame,
And he call you by everything cept its your name, oh.

(Refrain)

385   Arguing a Bargain

Text and music found only in "Leading Themes" notebook (#93).

Refrain:
Ise a arg'in de bargain, my honey love,
Ise a arg'in de bargain, my honey love.

1 Don't you remember, a liddle while ago,
   You told me dat you lov'd me, it may be so.

2 My heart is all love, an' dat love it seem to grow,
   If you just love me darling, it can be so.

3 If you don't love me, I'll sorrow 'way always,
   I'll die and go to glory, it will be so.

386   The Hammer That Killed John Henry

Scholars are not sure of the relationship between this song and the more familiar "John Henry" (No. 146, above); some see it as a "hammer song"—a work song—unrelated to the ballad, while others think it might be the source of the ballad. Good discussions of the problem are found in Norm Cohen's *Long Steel Rail: The Railroad in American Folksong* (571–82) and Archie Green's *Only a Miner: Studies in Recorded Coal-Mining Songs* (329–54). A stanza similar to this one was published by Howard Odum in 1911 (see "Folk-Song and Folk Poetry," 386); White prints a version very similar to this (261–62) as well as a melody (409). Scarborough offers two variants of the piece (219–20). None of these printed sources, though, contain Talley's "Working on the railroad/ Dollar 'in quarter day" stanza. Two famous black singers from the 1920s and 1930s made influential commercial records of the song: Mississippi John Hurt, "Spike Driver Blues" (Okeh 8692, 1928); and Huddie Ledbetter (Lead-belly), "Take Dis Hammer" (Asch 101, 1942).

This is the hammer   (bam!)
That killed John Henry   (bam!)
It won't kill me   (bam!)
It won't kill me   (bam!)
This is the hammer   (bam!)
That killed John Henry   (bam!)
It won't kill me   (bam!)
It won't kill me   (bam!)
    Workin' on de railraod   (bam!)
    Doller 'in quarter day   (bam!)
    Dollar for my baby   (bam!)
    Quarter throw'd away   (bam!)

Take my hammer   (bam!)
To the walkin' boss   (bam!)
Tell him I've gone   (bam!)
Take this hammer   (bam!)
Down to the walkin' boss   (bam!)
Tell him I've gone   (bam!)
Tell him I've gone   (bam!)

387 Big Ball Down Town

Talley's appears to be the first collection from traditional sources of a song
that has been customarily associated with vaudeville and country music performers. There are few printed variants; one in *The New Lost City Ramblers
Songbook* (216–17) is derived from a 1940s commercial recording. The recorded
history of the song extends as far back as 1898, when blackface vaudeville
singer Billy Golden recorded it for Edison (Edison cylinder 4002). In the
later 1920s, it became a favorite of country string bands, with recordings by
The Skillet Lickers (Columbia 15204, 1927) and The Georgia Yellow Ham-
mers (Victor 40138, 1927), two north Georgia bands, and an East Tennessee
band, Warren Caplinger's Cumberland Mountain Entertainers (Brunswick

241, 1928). Vance Randolph collected several obscene versions of the song in the Ozarks in the 1930s, versions not as yet published. In 1966, the song was rewritten by Texas musician Hoyle Nix, and made into a hit record by western swing star Bob Wills, (Kapp K11506).

Talley's musical theme, #97 in the "Leading Theme" notebook, is unusual in that it suggests a vocal arrangement, possibly for a quartet.

Big ball down town,
Big ball down town,
Big ball down town,
So turn 'em all aroun'.

(*Solo*)
Once da hawk and da buzzard,
Went to law . . . chom (turn'em all aroun'),
And da hawk came back wid a broken jaw . . . chom (turn 'em
all around).

388 Bolly-o

Text and music found only in "Leading Themes" notebook, #99.

Way down in de hills an' a "bolly-o,"
Way down in de hills an' a "bolly-o,"
Way down in de hills an' a "bolly-o,"
Come my love and kiss 'er sweet,
An' tell 'er "bolly-o."

Oh, who will you have an' a "bolly-o,"
Oh, who will you have an' a "bolly-o,"
Oh, who will you have an' a "bolly-o,"
Come my love and kiss 'er sweet,
An' tell 'er "bolly-o."

389   Old Joe, What Is the Matter?

Found only in the "Leading Themes" notebook (#103), the melody resembles
the popular schoolroom song "Oh Dear What Can the Matter Be?"

Old Joe, what is the matter?
Old Joe, what is the matter?
Ah, old Joe,
What is the matter?
My horses go lookin' up hill.

Baby, he must get fatter,
Oh, baby, he must get fatter,
Oh Baby,
He must get fatter,
My horses go lookin' up hill.

390   Oh Go to Sleep, My Baby

Words and music found only in "Leading Themes" notebook, #105. Scarborough (145–47) prints some lullabies somewhat, although not exactly, like this.

Oh go to sleep, de night's done come,
Oh go to sleep my baby,
You'se in my arms, you need not fear,
Oh go to sleep my baby.
Oh sweet baby, oh sweet baby,
Oh go to sleep my baby.

The birds is restin' in the trees,
Oh go to sleep my baby,
Dere hain't no workin' by de bees,
Oh go to sleep my baby.
Oh sweet baby, oh sweet baby,
Oh go to sleep my baby.

391   Liza Jane

Most of the stanzas here are found, though separately, in White (172–74), and the chorus is similar to that found in early country music recordings by The Tenneva Ramblers and The Hill Billies (cf. annotations for "Rejected by Eliza Jane," a related song, No. 199, above).

Words and music found only in "Leading Themes" notebook, #103A. Melody similar to that used on commercial recordings cited with No. 199.

Chorus
Whooper Liza a pretty liddle gal,
Whooper Liza Jane,
Whooper Liza a pretty liddle gal,
She died on da train.

Last time I seed Liza,
Standing in the door,
Shoes and stockings in her hand,
Feet all over the floor.

(Chorus)

Liza was a beauty,
Everybody knows,
Coal black eyes a sparklin',
An' her hair hang down befo'.

(*Chorus*)

Fare well, fare well, Liza,
Farewell Liza Jane,
I'se a gwine away to leave you,
But I'se comin' back 'gain.

392   A Little More Water

A work song that Talley used in the story "The Devil's Daughter," a Jack
tale, in his "Negro Traditions" manuscript. Music from "Leading Themes"
notebook, #30.

Fetch a liddle mo' water, buddie,
I need a liddle mo' water on de wheel,
Fetch a liddle mo' water, buddie,
Way down in de old wheat field.

393 Bound to Put on Airs

Probably of minstrel origin, this song is found only in Talley's "Leading Themes" notebook, #54. The manuscript omits lines for music measures 4-9.

I love dat gal dat dey call Suze Ann,
. . . .
No use a talkin',
No use a talkin',
Just go everywhere,
Dey do lak de people of de fashion do,
And dey are bound to put on airs.

Instrumental Tunes from Manuscript

394 Long Summer Day

Found in "Leading Themes" notebook, #45.

395 Negro Fiddle Tune

Found in "Leading Themes" notebook, item #56. The high part (or first strain) resembles a tune known to some Middle Tennessee fiddlers as "Ladies in the Ballroom"; the low part (or second strain) resembles in some ways the low part of "Eighth of January," found in the repertoire of many black fiddlers from Middle Tennessee, including Frank Patterson and John Lusk, both recorded in the 1940s by the Library of Congress.

396 Oh Rock My Baby

Found in "Leading Themes" notebook, #57.

397 Chinquapin a-Huntin'

Found in "Leading Themes" notebook, #71. "Chinquapins" are edible chestnuts. A tune by this name, and with this same general melody, is popular with Appalachian banjo players and has been recorded by several young traditional white musicians.

398   Times Are Mighty Hard

Found in "Leading Themes" notebook, #86.

399   Nickels and Dimes

Found in "Leading Themes" notebook, #8.

400 Hop Light Ladies

From "Leading Themes" notebook (#39), this is a familiar fiddle tune. See Ira Ford (31), as well as Marion Thede's *The Fiddle Book* (99).

401 Father's Old Song

One of the last entries in the "Leading Themes" notebook, #105. Talley penciled in under the title: "Words forgotten." Presumably, he was recalling a tune heard from his own father, Civil War Union veteran Charles Washington Talley.

402 Old Uncle Ben

"Leading Themes" notebook, #12.

403   Get Away Julie

"Leading Themes" notebook, #19.

404   You Can Come Back

"Leading Themes" notebook, #24.

405   Little Frog

"Leading Themes" notebook, #29.

406 In Some Lady's Garden

"Leading Themes" notebook, #31. Scarborough prints two melodies similar to this; the first, with the same title as Talley's, has words and the notation that it is an "old song, the dance to which it was sung being like a Virginia reel" (114); the second, "Do, Do, Pity My Case" (140) is taken from Newell's 1883 *Games and Songs of American Children.*

407 Oh, Fare You Well

"Leading Themes" notebook, #35.

408   Tell Ten Thousand Lies

"Leading Themes" notebook, #14.

409   Young Ladies Go A-Courting

"Leading Themes" notebook, #22.

410   [Untitled]

This tune was found in the "Leading Themes" notebook (#96), but without title, lyric, or identifying annotation of any kind. It is one of the longer scores, however, and shows signs that Talley had taken pains to edit it and include it. Its intervals suggest an instrumental tune, possibly a fiddle tune, which the compiler had collected but not been able to name. It resembles no common fiddle tune. We include it here for completeness, and because it was obviously thought worthwhile by Talley.

411–416

Note: six additional songs or tunes are included in the body of the following essay, "A Study in Negro Folk Rhymes." These include 411, Alabama Field Call and Response; 412, Tennessee Field Call and Response; 413, Holly Dink; 414, 'Tain't Gwineter Rain No Mo'; 415, Tune Played on a Little Set of Quills; and 416, Tune Played on a Big Set of Quills.

A Study in Negro Folk Rhymes

Thomas W. Talley

The lore of the American Negro is rich in story, in song, and in Folk rhymes. These stories and songs have been partially recorded, but so far as I know there is no collection of the American Negro Folk Rhymes. The collection in Part I is a compilation of American Negro Folk Rhymes, and this study primarily concerns them; but it was necessary to have a Foreign Section of Rhymes in order to make our study complete. I have therefore inserted a little Foreign Section of African, Venezuelan, Jamaican, Trinidad, and Philippine Negro Rhymes; and along with them have placed the names of the contributors to whom we are under great obligations, as well as to the many others who have given valuable assistance and suggestions in the matter of the American Negro Rhymes recorded.

When critically measured by the laws and usages governing the best English poetry, Negro Folk Rhymes will probably remind readers of the story of the good brother, who arose solemnly in a Christian praise meeting, and thanked God that he had broken all the Commandments, but had kept his religion.

Though decent rhyme is often wanting, and in the case of the "Song to the Runaway Slave," there is no rhyme at all, the rhythm is found almost perfect in all of them.

A few of the Rhymes bear the mark of a somewhat recent date in composition. The majority of them, however, were sung by Negro fathers and mothers in the dark days of American slavery to their children who listened with eyes as large as saucers and drank them down with mouths wide open. The little songs were similar in structure to the Jubilee Songs, also of Negro Folk origin.

If one will but examine the recorded Jubilee songs, he will find that it is common for stanzas, which are apparently most distantly related in structure, to sing along in perfect rhythm in the same tune that carefully counts from measure to measure one, two; or one, two, three, four. Here is an example of two stanzas taken from the Jubilee song, "Wasn't That a Wide River?"

> 1. "Old Satan's just like a snake in the grass,
>   He's a-watching for to bite you as you pass.
> 2. Shout! Shout! Satan's about.
>   Just shut your door, and keep him out."

An examination of stanzas in various Jubilee songs will show in the same song large variations in poetic feet, etc., not only from stanza to stanza; but very often from line to line, and even from phrase to phrase. Notwithstanding all this variation, a well trained band of singers will render the songs with such perfect rhythm that one scarcely realizes that the structure of any one stanza differs materially from that of another.

A stanza, as it appears in Negro Folk Rhymes, is of the same construction as that found in the Jubilee Songs. A perfect rhythm is there. If while reading them you miss it, read yet once again; you will find it in due season if you "faint not" too early.

As a rule, Negro Folk verse is so written that it fits into measures of music written 4/4 or 2/4 time. You can therefore read Negro Folk Rhymes silently counting: one, two; or, one, two, three, four; and the stanzas fit directly into the imaginary music measures if you are reading in harmony with the intended rhythm. I know of only three Jubilee Songs whose stanzas are transcribed as exceptions. They are — (1) "I'm Going to Live with Jesus," 6/8 time, (2) "Gabriel's Trumpet's Going to Blow," 3/4 time, and (3) "Lord Make Me More Patient," 6/8 time. It is interesting to note along with these that the "Song of the Great Owl," the "Negro Soldier's Civil War Chant," and "Destitute Former Slave Owners," are seemingly the only ones in our Folk Rhyme collection which would call for a 3/4 or 6/8 measure. Such a measure is rare in all literary Negro Folk productions.

The Negro, then, repeated or sang his Folk Rhymes, and danced them to 4/4 and 2/4 measures. Thus Negro Folk Rhymes, with very few exceptions, are poetry where a music measure is the unit of measurement for the words rather than the poetic foot. This is true whether the Rhyme is, or is not, sung. *Imaginary measures either of two or four beats, with a given number of words to a beat, a number that can be varied limitedly at will, seems to be the philosophy underlying all Negro slave rhyme construction.*

As has just been casually mentioned, the Negro Folk Rhyme was used for the dance. There are Negro Folk Rhyme Dance Songs and Negro Folk Dance Rhymes. An example of the former is found in "The Banjo Picking," and of the latter, "Juba," both found in this collection. The reader may wonder how a Rhyme simply repeated was used in the dance. The procedure was as follows: Usually one or two individuals "star" danced at time. The others of the crowd (which was usually large) formed a circle about this one or two who were to take their prominent turn at dancing. I use the terms "star" danced and "prominent turn" because in the latter part of our study we shall find that all those present engaged sometimes at intervals in the dance. But those forming the circle, for most of the time, repeated the Rhyme, clapping their hands together, and patting their feet in rhythmic time with the words of the Rhyme being repeated. It was the task of the dancers in the middle of the circle to execute some graceful dance in such a manner that their feet would beat a tattoo upon the ground answering to every word, and sometimes to every syllable of the Rhyme being repeated by those in the circle. There were many such Rhymes. "'Possum Up the Gum Stump," and "Jawbone" are good examples. The stanzas to these Rhymes were not usually limited to two or three, as is generally the case with those recorded in our collection. Each selection usually had many stanzas. Thus as there came variation in the words from stanza to stanza, the skill of the dancers was taxed to its utmost, in order to keep up the graceful dance and to beat a changed tattoo upon the ground corresponding to the changed words. If any find fault with the limited number of stanzas recorded in our treatise, I can in apology only sing the words of a certain little encore song each of whose two little stanzas ends with the words, "Please don't call us back, because we don't know any more."

There is a variety of Dance Rhyme to which it is fitting to call attention. This variety is illustrated in our collection by "Jump Jim Crow," and "Juba." In such dances as these, the dancers were required to give such movements of body as would act the sentiment expressed by the words while keeping up the common requirements of beating

these same words in a tattoo upon the ground with the feet and ex-
ecuting simultaneously a graceful dance.

It is of interest also to note that the antebellum Negro while repeating his Rhymes which had no connection with the dance usually accompanied the repeating with the patting of his foot upon the ground.
Among other things he was counting off the invisible measures and
bars of his Rhymes, things largely unseen by the world but very real
to him. Every one who has listened to a well sung Negro Jubilee Song
knows that it is almost impossible to hear one sung and not pat the
foot. I have seen the feet of the coldest blooded Caucasians pat right
along while Jubilee melodies were being sung.

All Negro Folk productions, including the Negro Folk Rhymes,
seem to call for this patting of the foot. The explanation which follows
is offered for consideration. The orchestras of the Native African were
made up largely of crudely constructed drums of one sort or another.
Their war songs and so forth were sung to the accompaniment of
these drum orchestras. When the Negroes were transported to America, and began to sing songs and to chant words in another tongue,
they still sang strains calling, through inheritance, for the accompaniment of their ancestral drum. The Negro's drum having fallen from
him as he entered civilization, he unwittingly called into service his
foot to take its place. This substitution finds a parallelism in the highly
cultivatd La France rose, which being without stamens and pistils
must be propagated by cuttings or graftings instead of by seeds. The
rose, purposeless, emits its sweet perfume to the breezes and thus it
attracts insects for cross fertilization simply because its staminate and
pistillate ancestors thus called the insect world for that purpose. The
rattle of the crude drum of the Native African was loud by inheritance
in the hearts of his early American descendants and its unseen ghost
walks in the midst of all their poetry.

Many Negro Folk Rhymes were used as banjo and fiddle (violin)
songs. It ought to be borne in mind, however, that even these were
quite often repeated without singing or playing. It was common in
the early days of the public schools of the South to hear Negro children use them as declamations. The connection, however, of Negro
Folk Rhymes with their secualr music productions is well worthy of
notice.

I have often heard those who liked to think and discuss things musical, wonder why little or no music of a secular kind worth while seemed to be found among Negroes while their religious music, the Jubilee Songs, have challenged the admiration of the world. The songs of most native peoples seem to strike "high water mark" in the secular form. Probably numbers of us have heard the explanation: "You see, the Negro is deeply emotional; religion appealed to him as did nothing else. The Negro therefore spent his time singing and shouting praises to God, who alone could whisper in his heart and stir up these emotions." There is perhaps much truth in this explanation. It is also such a delicate and high compliment to the Negro race, that I hestiate to touch it. One of the very few gratifying things that has come to Negroes is the unreserved recognition of their highly religious character. There is a truth, however, about the relation between the Negro Folk Rhyme and the Negro's banjo and fiddle music which ought to be told even though some older, nicer viewpoints might be a little shifted.

There were quite a few Rhymes sung where the banjo and fiddle formed what is termed in music a simple accompaniment. Examples of these are found in "Run, Nigger, Run," and "I'll Wear Me a Cotton Dress." In such cases the music consisted of simple short tunes unquestionably "born to die."

There was another class of Rhymes like "Devilish Pigs," that were used with the banjo and fiddle in quite another way. It was the banjo and fiddle productions of this kind of Rhyme that made the "old time" Negro banjo picker and fiddler famous. It has caused quite a few, who heard them, to declare that, saint or sinner, it was impossible to keep your feet still while they played. The compositions were comparatively long. From one to four lines of a Negro Folk Rhyme were sung to the opening measures of the instrumental composition; then followed the larger and remaining part of the composition, instruments alone. In the Rhyme "Devilish Pigs" four lines were used at a time. Each time that the music theme of the composition was repeated, another set of Rhyme lines was repeated; and the variations in the music theme were played in each repeat which recalled the newly repeated words of the Rhyme. The ideal in composition from an instrumental viewpoint might quite well remind one of the ideal in piano compositions, which consists of a theme with variations. The first movement of Beethoven's Sonata, Opus 26, illustrates the music ideal in composition to which I refer.

So far as I know no Caucasian instrumental music composer has ever ordered the performers under his direction to sing a few of the first measures of his composition while the string division of the orchestra played its opening chords. Only the ignorant Negro composer has done this. Some white composers have made little approaches to it. A fair sample of an approach is found in the Idylls of Edward McDowell, for piano, where every exquisite little tone picture is headed by some gem in verse, reading which the less musically gifted may gain a deeper insight into the philosophical tone discourse set forth in the notes and chords of the composition.

The Negro Folk Rhyme, then, furnished the ideas about which the "old time" Negro banjo picker and fiddler clustered his best instrumental music thoughts. It is too bad that this music passed away unrecorded save by the hearts of men. Paul Laurence Dunbar depicts its telling effects upon the hearer in his poem "The Party":

> "Cripple Joe, de ole rheumatic, danced dat flo' frum side to middle.
> Throwed away his crutch an' hopped it, what's rheumatics 'gainst a fiddle?
> Eldah Thompson got so tickled dat he lak to los' his grace,
> Had to take bofe feet an' hold 'em, so's to keep 'em in deir place.
> An' de Christuns an' de sinnahs got so mixed up on dat flo',
> Dat I don't see how dey's pahted ef de trump had chonced to blow."

Perhaps a new school of orchestral music might be built on the Negro idea that some of the performers sing a sentence or so here and there, both to assist the hearers to a clearer musical understanding and to heighten the general artistic finish. The old Negro performers generally sang lines of the Folk Rhymes at the opening but occasionally in the midst of their instrumental compositions. I do not recall any case where lines were sung to the closing measures of the compositions.

It might seem odd to some that the grotesque Folk Rhyme should have given rise to comparatively long instrumental music compositions. I think the explanation is probably very simple. The African on his native heath had his crude ancestral drum as his leading musical instrument. He sang or shouted his war songs consisting of a few words, and of a few notes, then followed them up with the beating

of his drum, perhaps for many minutes, or even for hours. In civilization, the banjo, fiddle, "quills," and "triangle" largely took the place
of his drum. Thus the singing of opening strains and following them
with the main body of the instrumental composition, is in keeping
with the Negro's inherited law for instrumental compositions from his
days of savagery. The rattling, distinct tones of the banjo, recalling
unconsciously his inherited love for the rattle of the African ancestral
drum, is probably the thing which caused that instrument to become
a favorite among Negro slaves.

I would next consider the relation of the Folk Rhymes to Negro
child life. They were instilled into children as warnings. In the years
closely following our Civil War, it was common for a young Negro
child, about to engage in a doutful venture, to hear his mother call
out to him the Negro Rhyme recorded by Joel Chandler Harris, in
the Negro story, "The End of Mr. Bear":

> "Tree stan' high, but honey mighty sweet—
> Watch dem bees wid stingers on der feet."

These lines commonly served to recall the whole story, it being the
Rabbit's song in that story, and the child stopped whatever he was
doing. Other and better examples of such Rhymes are "Young Master
and Old Master," "The Alabama Way," and "You Had Better Mind
Master," found in our collection.

The warnings were commonly such as would help the slave to escape more successfully the lash, and to live more comfortably under
slave conditions. I would not for once intimate that I entertain the
thought that the ignorant slave carefully and philosophically studied
his surroundings, reasoned it to be a fine method to warn children
through poetry, composed verse, and like a wise man proceeded to
use it. Of course thinking preceded the making of the Rhyme, but
a conscious system of making verses for the purpose did not exist.
I have often watched with interest a chicken hen lead forth her brood
of young for the first time. While the scratching and feeding are going
on, all of a sudden the hen utters a loud shriek, and flaps her wings.
The little chicks, although they have never seen a hawk, scurry hither
and thither, and so prostrate their little brown and ashen bodies upon
the ground as almost to conceal themselves. The Negro Folk Rhymes

of warning must be looked upon a little in this same light. They are but the strains of terror given by the promptings of a mother instinct full enough to love to give up life itself for its defenseless own.

Many Rhymes were used to convey to children the common sense truths of life, hidden beneath their comic, crudely cut coats. Good examples are "Old Man Know-All," "Learn to Count," and "Shake the Persimmons Down." All through the Rhymes will be found here and there many stanzas full of common uncommon sense, worthwhile for children.

Many Negro Folk Rhymes repeated or sung to children on their parents' knees were enlarged and told to them as stories, when they became older. The Rhyme in our collection on "Judge Buzzard" is one of this kind. In the Negro version of the race between the hare and the tortoise ("rabbit and terrapin"), the tortoise wins not through the hare's going to sleep, but through a gross deception of all concerned, including even the buzzard who acted as Judge. The Rhyme is a laugh on "Jedge Buzzard." It was commonly repeated to Negro children in olden days when they passed erroneous judgments. "Buckeyed rabbit! Whoopee!" in our volume belongs with the Negro story recorded by Joel Chandler Harris under the title, "How Mr. Rabbit Lost His Fine Bushy Tail," though for some reason Mr. Harris failed to weave it into the story as was the Negro custom. "The Turtle's Song," in our collection, is another, which belongs with the story, "Mr. Terrapin Shows His Strength"; a Negro story given to the world by the same author, though the Rhyme was not recorded by him. It might be of interest to know that the Negroes, when themselves telling the Folk stories, usually sang the Folk Rhyme portions to little "catchy" Negro tunes. I would not under any circumstances intimate that Mr. Harris carelessly left them out. He recorded many little stanzas in the midst of the stories. Examples are:

> (a) "We'll stay at home when you're away
>   'Cause no gold won't pay toll."
> (b) "Big bird catch, little bird sing.
>   Bug bee zoom, little bee sting.
>   Little man lead, and the big horse follow,
>   Can you tell what's good for a head in a hollow?"

These and many others are fragmentarily recorded among Mr. Harris' Negro stories in "Nights With Uncle Remus."

Folk Rhymes also formed in many cases the words of Negro Play Songs. "Susie Girl," and "Peep Squirrel," found in our collection, are good illustrations of the Rhymes used in this way. The words and the music of such Rhymes were usually of poor quality. When, however, they were sung by children with the proper accompanying body movements, they might quite well remind one of the "Folk Dances" used in the present best up-to-date Primary Schools. They were the little rays of sunshine in the dark dreary monotonous lives of black slave children.

Possibly the thing which will impress the reader most in reading Negro Folk Rhymes is their good-natured drollery and sparkling nonsense. I believe this is very important. Many have recounted in our hearing, the descriptions of "backwoods" Negro picnics. I have witnessed some of them where the good-natured vender of lemonade and cakes cried out:

> "Here's yō' cōl' ice lemonade,
> It's made in de shade,
> It's stirred wid a spade.
> Come buy my cōl' ice lemonade.
> It's made in de shade
> An' sōl' in de sun.
> Ef you hain't got no money,
> You cain't git none.
> One glass fer a nickel,
> An' two fer a dime,
> Ef you hain't got de chink,
> You cain't git mine.
> Come right dis way,
> Fer it sho' will pay
> To git candy fer de ladies
> An' cakes fer de babies."

"Did these venders sell?" Well, all agree that they did. The same principle applied, with much of the nonsense eliminated, will probably make of the Negro a great merchant, as caste gives way enough to allow him a common man's business chance. Of all the races of men, the Negro alone has demonstrated his ability to come into contact with the white man and neither move on nor be annihilated. I believe this is largely due to his power to muster wit and humor on all occasions, and even to laugh in the face of adversity. He refused during the days of slavery to take the advice of Job's wife, and to "Curse God and die." He repeated and sang his comic Folk Rhymes, danced, lived, and came out of the Night of Bondage comparatively strong.

The compiler of the Rhymes was quite interested to find that as a rule the country-reared Negro had a larger acquaintance with Folk Rhymes than one brought up in the city. The human mind craves occasional recreation, entertainment, and amusement. In cities where there is an almost continuous passing along the crowded thoroughfares of much that contributes to these ends, the slave Negro needed only to keep his eyes open, his ears attentive and laugh. He directed his life accordingly. But, in the country districts there was only the monotony of quiet woods and waving fields of cotton. The rural scenes, though beautiful in themselves, refuse to amuse or entertain those who will not hold communion with them. The country Negro longing for amusement communed in his crude way, and Nature gave him Folk Rhymes for entertainment. Among those found to be clearly of this kind may be mentioned "The Great Owl's Song," "Tails," "Redhead Woodpecker," "The Snail's Reply," "Bobwhite's Song," "Chuck Will's Widow Song," and many others.

The Folk Rhymes were not often repeated as such or as whole compositions by the "grown-ups" among Negroes apart from the Play and the Dance. If, however, you had had an argument with an antebellum Negro, had gotten the better of the argument, and he still felt confident that he was right, you probably would have heard him close his side of the debate with the words: "Well, 'Ole Man Know-All is Dead.'" This is only a short prosaic version of his rhyme "Old Man Know-All," found in our collection. Many of the characteristic sayings of "Uncle Remus" woven into story by Joel Chandler Harris had their origin in these Folk Rhymes. "Dem dat know too much sleep under de ash-hopper" (Uncle Remus) clearly intimates to all who know about the old-fashioned ash-hopper that such an individual lies. This saying is a part of another stanza of "Old Man Know-All," but I cannot recall it from my dim memory of the past, and others whom I have asked seem equally unable to do so, though they have once known it.

As is the case will all things of Folk origin, there is usually more than one version of each Negro Folk Rhyme. In many cases the exercising of a choice between many versions was difficult. I can only express the hope that my choices have been wise.

There are two American Negro Folk Rhymes in our collection: "Frog in a Mill" and "Tree Frogs," which are oddities in "language." They are rhymes of a rare type of Negro, which has long since disappeared. They were called "Ebo" Negroes and "Guinea" Negroes. The so-called "Ebo" Negro used the word "la" very largely for the word "the." This and some other things have caused me to think that the "Ebo" Negro was probably one who was first a slave among the French, Spanish, or Portuguese, and was afterwards sold to an English-speaking owner. Thus his language was a mixture of African, English, and one of these languages. The so-called "Guinea" Negro was simply one who had not been long from Africa; his language being a mixture of his African tongue and English. These rhymes are to the ordinary Negro rhymes what "Jutta Cord la" in "Nights with Uncle Remus," by Joel Chandler Harris, is to the ordinary Negro stories found there. They are probably representative, in language, of the most primitive Negro Folk productions.

Some of the rhymes are very old indeed. If one will but read "Master Is Six Feet One Way," found in our collection, he will find in it a description of a slave owner attired in Colonial garb. It clearly belongs, as to date of composition, either to Colonial days, or to the very earliest years of the American Republic. When we consider it as a slave rhyme, it is far from crudest, notwithstanding the early period of its production.

If one carefully studies our collection of rhymes, he will probably get a new and interesting picture of the Negro's mental attitude and reactions during the days of his enslavement. One of these mental reactions is calculated to give one a surprise. One would naturally expect the Negro under hard, trying, bitter slave conditions, to long to be white. There is a remarkable Negro Folk rhyme which shows that this was not the case. This rhyme is: "I'd Rather Be a Negro Than a Poor White Man." We must bear in mind that a Folk Rhyme from its very nature carries in it the crystallized thought of the masses. This rhyme, though a little acidic and though we have recorded the milder version, leaves the unquestioned conclusion that, though the Negro masses may have wished for the exalted station of the rich Southern white man and possibly would have willingly had a white color as a passport to position, there never was a time when the Negro masses desired to be white for the sake of being white. Of course there is the Negro rhyme, "I Wouldn't Marry a Black Girl," but along with it is another Negro rhyme, "I Wouldn't Marry a White or a Yellow Negro Girl." The two rhymes simply point out together a division of Negro opinion as to the ideal standard of beauty in personal complexion. One part of the Negroes thought white or yellow the more beautiful standard and the other part of the Negroes thought black the more beautiful standard.

The body of the Rhymes, here and there, carries many facts between the lines, well worth knowing.

This collection also will shed some light on how the Negro managed to go through so many generations "in slavery and still come out" with a bright, capable mind. There were no colleges or schools for them, but there were Folk Rhymes, stories, Jubilee songs, and Nature; they used these and kept mentally fit.

I now approach the more difficult and probably the most important portion of my discussion in the Study of Negro Folk Rhymes. It is a discussion that I would have willingly omitted, had I not thought that some one owed it to the world. Seeing a debt, as I thought, and not seeing another to pay it, I have reluctantly undertaken to discharge the obligation.

If I were so fortunate as to possess a large flower garden with many new and rare genera and species, and wished to acquaint my friends with them, I should first take these friends for a walk through the garden, that they might see the odd tints and hues, might inhale a little of the new fragrance, and might get some idea as to the prospects for the utilization of these new plants in the world. Then, taking these friends back to my study room, I should consider in a friendly manner along with them, the Families and Species, and the varieties. Finally, I should endeavor to lay before them from whence these new and strange flowers came. I have endeavored to pursue this method in my discussion of the Negro Folk Rhymes. In the foregoing I have endeavored to take the friendly reader for a walk through this new and strange garden of Rhymes, and I now extend an invitation to him to come into the Study Room for a more critical view of them.

When one enters upon the slightest contemplation of Negro Folk Rhyme classification, and is kind-hearted enough to dignify them with a claim to kinship to real poetry, the word *Ballad* rolls out without the slightest effort, as a term that takes them all in. Yes, this is very true, but they are of a strange type indeed. They are Nature Ballads, many of them, in the sense as ordinarily used. In quite another sense, however, from that in which Nature Ballad is ordinarily used, about all Folk Rhymes are Nature Ballads.

I do not have reference to the thought content, but have reference to what I term Nature Ballads in form. Permit me to explain by analogy just what I would convey by the term Nature Ballad in form.

All Nature is one. Though we arbitrarily divide Nature's objects for study, they are indissolubly bound together and every part carries in some part of its constitution some well defined marks which characterize the other parts with which it has no immediate connection. To illustrate: the absolutely pure sapphire, pure aluminic oxide, crystallized, is commonly colorless, but we know that Nature's most beautiful sapphires are not colorless, but are blue, and of other beautiful tints. These color tints are due to minutest traces of other substances, not at all of general common sapphire composition. We call them all sapphires, however, regardless of their little impurities which are present to enhance their charm and beauty. Likewise, all animal life begins with one cell, and though the one cell in one case develops into a vertebrate, and in another case into an invertebrate the cells persist and so all animal life has cellular structure in common. Yet, each animal branch has predominant traits that distinguish it from all other branches. This same thing is true of plants.

Nature's method, then, of making things seems to be to put in a large enough amount of one thing to brand the article, and then to mix in, in small amounts, enough of other things to lend charm and beauty without taking the article out of its general class.

This is that which goes to make Negro Folk Rhymes Nature Ballads in form. They are ballads, but all in the midst of even a Dance Song, by Nature an ordinary ballad, there may be interwoven comedy, tragedy, and nearly every kind of imaginable thing which goes rather with other general forms of poetry than with the ballad. As an example, in the Dance Song, "Promises of Freedom," we have mustered before our eyes the comic drawing of a deceptive ugly old Mistress and then follows the intimation of the tragic death of a poisoned slave owner, and as we are tempted to dance along in thought with the rhymer, we cannot escape getting the subtle impression that this slave had at least some "vague" personal knowledge of how the Master got that poison. It is a common easy-going ballad, but it is tinted with tragedy and comedy. This general principle will be found to run very largely through the highest types of Negro Folk Rhymes. It is the Nature method of construction, and thus we call them Nature Ballads in structure, or form.

Other good examples of rhymes, Nature Ballads in structure, are "Frog Went a-Courting," "Sheep Shell Corn," "Jack and Dinah Want Freedom."

I now direct attention further to the classification of Negro Rhymes as Ballads. My earnest desire was to classify Negro Rhymes under ordinary headings such as are used by literary men and women everywhere in their general classification of Ballads. I considered this very important because it would enable students of comparative Literature to compare easily the Negro Folk Rhymes with the Folk Rhymes of all peoples. I was much disappointed when I found that the Negro Folk Rhymes, when invited, refused to take their places whole-heartedly in the ordinary classification. As an example of many may be mentioned the little Rhyme "Jaybird." It is a Dance Song, and thus comes under the Dance Song Division, commonly used for Ballads. But, it also belongs under Nature Lore heading, because the Negroes many years ago often told a story, in conjunction with song, of the great misfortunes which overtook a Negro who tried to get his living by hunting Jaybirds. Finally it also belongs under the heading Superstitions, for its last stanza very plainly alludes to the old Negro superstition of slavery days which declared that it was almost impossible to find Jaybirds on Friday because they went to Hades on that day to carry sand to the Devil.

But so important do I think of comparative study that I have taken the ordinary headings used for Ballads and, after adding that omnibus heading "Miscellaneous," have done my best. The majority of the Rhymes can be placed under headings ordinarily used. This was to be expected. It is in obedience to Natural Law. We see it in the Music World. The Caucasian music has eight fundamental tones, the Japanese music has five, while, according to some authorities, Negro Jubilee-music has nine; yet all these music scales have five tones in common. In the Periodic System of Elements there are two periods; a short period and a long period, but both periods embrace, in common, elements belonging to the same family. So with the Ballads, certain classification headings will very well take in both the Negro and all others. The Negro Ballad, however, does not entirely properly fit in. I have therefore resorted to the following expedient: I have taken the headings ordinarily used, and have listed under each heading the Negro Rhymes which belong with it, as nearly as possible. I have placed this classified list at the end of the book, under the title "Comparative Study Index." By using this Index one can locate and compare Negro Folk productions with the corresponding Folk productions of other peoples.

The headings found in this Comparative Study Index are as follows:

1. Love Songs.
2. Dance Songs.
3. Animal and Nature Lore.
4. Nursery Rhymes.
5. Charms and Superstitions.
6. Hunting Songs.
7. Drinking Songs.
8. Wise and Gnomic Sayings.
9. Harvest Songs.
10. Biblical and Religious Themes.
11. Play Songs.
12. Miscellaneous.

With the way paved for others to make such comparative study as they would like, I now feel free to use a classification which lends itself more easily to a discussion of the origin and evolution of Negro Rhyme. The basic principle used in this classification is Origin and under each source of origin is placed the various classes of Rhymes produced. It has seemed to the writer, who is himself a Negro, and has spent his early years in the midst of the Rhymes and witnessed their making, that there are three great divisions derived from three great mainsprings or sources.

The Divisions are as follows:

I. Rhymes derived from the Social Instinct.

II. Rhymes derived from the Homing Instinct.

III. Rhymes of Psycho-composite origin.

The terms Social and Homing Instincts are familiar to every one, but the term Psycho-composite was coined by the writer after much hesitation and with much regret beacause he seemed unable to find a word which would express what he had in mind.

To make clear: the classes of Rhymes falling under Divisions I and II owe their crudest initial beginnings to instinct, while those under Division III owe their crudest beginnings partly to instinct, but partly also to intelligent thinking processes. To illustrate — Courtship Rhymes come under Division II, because courtship primarily arises from the homing instinct, but when we come to "quasi" wise sayings — directly largely to criticism or toward improvement, there is very much more than instinct concerned. In Division III the Rhymes are directed largely to improvement. In explanation of why they are in Division III, I would say, the desire to better one's condition is instinctive, but the slightest attainment of the desire comes through thought pure and simple. I have invented the term Psycho-composite to include all this.

In reading the Rhymes under Division III, one finds comparatively large, abstract, general conclusions, such as — General loquaciousness is unwise: Assuming to know everything is foolish: Self-control is a great virtue. Proper preparation must be made before presuming to give instruction, etc. Such generalizations involve something not necessarily present in the crudest initiations of such Rhymes as those found under Divisions I and II. Below is a tabular view of my proposed classification of Negro Folk Rhymes:

DIVISION	CLASS
I. Social Instinct Rhymes	1. Dance Rhymes
	2. Dance Rhyme Songs
	3. Play Songs
	4. Pastime Rhymes

II. Homing Instinct Rhymes   1. Love Rhymes
                                    2. Courtship Rhymes
                                    3. Marriage Rhymes
                                    4. Married Life Rhymes

III. Psycho-composite Rhymes   1. Criticism and Improvement
                                    Rhymes

Under this tabulation, let us now proceed to discuss the Origin and Evolution of Negro Folk Rhymes.

Early in my discussion the reader will recall that I explained in considerable detail how the Dance Rhyme words were used in the dance. I am now ready to announce that the Dance Rhyme was derived from the dance, and to explain how the Dance Rhyme became an evolved product of the dance.

I witnessed in my early childhood the making of a few Dance Rhymes. I have forgotten the words of most of those whose individual making I witnessed but the "Jonah's Band Party" found in our collection is one whose making I distinctly recall. I shall tell in some detail of its origin because it serves in a measure to illustrate how the Dance Rhymes probably had their beginnings. First of all be it known that there was a "step" in dancing, originated by some Negro somewhere, called "Jonah's Band" step. There is no need that I should try to describe that step which, though of the plain dance type, was accompanied from the beginning to the end by indescribable "frills" of foot motion. I can't describe it, but if one will take a stick and cause it to tap so as to knock the words: "Setch a kickin' up san'! Jonah's band," while he repeats the words in the time of 2/4 music measure, the taps will reproduce the tattoo beaten upon the ground by the feet of the dancers, when they danced the "Jonah's Band" step. The dancers formed a circle placing two or more of their skilled dancers in the middle of it. Now when I first witnessed this dance, there were no words said at all. There was simply patting with the hands and dancing, making a tattoo which might be well represented by the words supplied later on in its existence. Later, I witnessed the same dance, where the patting and dancing were as usual, but one man, apparently the leader, was simply crying out the words, "Setch a kickin' up san'!" and the crowd answered with the words, "Jonah's Band!"—the words all being repeated in rhythmic harmony with the patting and dancing. Thus was born the line, "Setch a kickin' up san'! Jonah's Band!" In some places it was the custom to call on the dancers to join with those of the circle, at intervals in the midst of the dance, in dancing other steps than the Jonah's Band step. Some dance leaders, for example, simply called in plain prose—"Dance the Mobile Buck," others calling for another step would rhyme their call. Thus arose the last lines to each stanza, such as—

> "Raise yō' right foot, kick it up high!
> Knock dat 'Mobile Buck' in de eye!"

This is the genesis of the "Jonah's Band Party," found in our collection. The complete rhyme becomes a fine description of an old-time Negro party. It is probable that much Dance Rhyme making originated in this or a similar way.

Let us assume that Negro customs in Slavery days were what they were in my childhood days, then it would come about that such an occasional Rhyme making in a crowd would naturally stimulate individual Rhyme makers, and from these individuals would naturally grow up "crops" of Dance Rhymes. Of course I cannot absolutely know, but I think when I witnessed the making of the "Jonah's Band Party," that I witnessed the stimulus which had produced the Dance Rhyme through the decades of preceding years. I realize, however, that this does not account for the finished Rhyme products. It simply gives one source of origin. How the Rhyme grew to its complex structure will be discussed later, because that discussion belongs not to the Dance Rhyme alone, but to all the Rhymes.

There was a final phase of development of "Jonah's Band Party" witnessed by the writer; namely, the singing of the lines, "Setch a kickin' up san'! Jonah's Band!" The last lines of the stanzas, the lines calling for another step on the part of both the circle and the dancers, were never sung to my knowledge. The little tune to the first lines consisted of only four notes, and is inserted below.

Setch a kick-in' up   san'! Jon - ah's band!

Setch a kick-in' up san'! Jon-ah's band!

I give this as of interest because it marks a partial transition from a Dance Rhyme to a Dance Rhyme Song. In days of long ago I occasionally saw a Dance Rhyme Song "patted and danced" instead of sung or played and danced. This coupled with the transition stage of the "Jonah's Band Dance" just given has caused me to believe that Dance Rhyme Songs were probably evolved from Dance Rhymes pure and simple, through individuals putting melodies to these Dance Rhymes.

As Dance Rhymes came from the dance, so likewise Play Rhymes came from plays. I shall now discuss the one found in our collection under the caption — "Goosie-gander." Since the Play has probably passed from the memory of most persons, I shall tell how it was played. The children (and sometimes those in their teens) sat in a circle. One individual, the leader, walked inside the circle, from child to child, and said to each in turn, "Goosie-gander." If the child answered "Goose," the leader said, "I turn your ears loose," and went on to the next child. If he answered "Gander," the leader said, "I pull yō' years 'way yander." Then ensued a scuffle between the two children; each trying to pull the other's ears. The fun for the circle came from watching the scuffle. Finally the child who got his ears pulled took his place in the circle, leaving the victor as master of ceremonies to call out the challenge "Goosie-gander!" The whole idea of the play is borrowed from the fighting of the ganders of a flock of geese for their mates. Many other plays were likewise borrowed from Nature. Examples are found in "Hawk and Chickens Play," and "Fox and Geese Play." "Caught by a Witch Play" is borrowed from superstition. But to return to "Goosie-gander" — most children of our childhood days played it, using common prose in the calls, and answers just as we have here described it. A few children here and there so gave their calls and responses as to rhyme them into a kind of a little poem as it is recorded in our collection. Without further argument, I think it can hardly be doubted that the whole thing began as a simple prose call, and response, and that some child inclined to rhyming things, started "to do the rest," and was assisted in accomplishing the task by other children equally or more gifted. This reasonably accounts for the origin of the Play Rhyme.

Now what of the Play Rhyme Songs? There were many more Play Rhyme Songs than Play Rhymes. There were some of the Play Rhyme Songs sung in prose version by some children and the same Play Song would be sung in rhymed version by other children. Likewise the identical Play Song would not be sung at all by other children; they would simply repeat the words as in the case of the Rhyme "Goosie-gander," just discussed. The little Play Song found in our collection under the caption, "Did You Feed My Cow?" is one which was current in my childhood in the many versions as just indicated. The general thought in the story of the Rhyme was the same in all versions whether prose or rhyme, or song. In cases where children repeated it instead of singing it, it was generally in prose and the questions were so framed by the leader that all the general responses by the crowd were "Yes, Ma'am!" Where it was sung, it was invariably rhymed; and the version found in this collection was about the usual one.

The main point in the discussion at this juncture is—that there were large numbers of Play Songs like this one found in the transition stage from plain prose to repeated rhyme, and to sung rhyme. Such a status leaves little doubt that the Play Song travelled this general road in its process of evolution.

I might take up the Courtship Rhymes, and show that they are derivatives of Courtship, and so on to the end of all the classes given in my outline, but since the evidences and arguments in all the cases are essentially the same I deem it unnecessary.

I now turn attention to a peculiar general ideal in Form found in Negro Folk Rhymes. It probably is not generally known that the Negroes, who emerged from the House of Bondage in the 60's of the last century, had themselves given a name to their own peculiar form of verse. If it be known I am rather confident that it has never been written. They named the parts of their verse "Call," and (Re) "Sponse." After explaining what is meant by "call" and "sponse," I shall submit an evidence on the matter. In its simplest form "call" and "sponse" were what we would call in Caucasian music, solo and chorus. As an example, in the little Play Song used in our illustration of Play Songs, "Did You Feed My Cow?" was sung as a solo and was known as the "Call," while the chorus that answered "Yes, Ma'am" was known as the "Sponse."

I now beg to offer testimony in corroboration of my assertion that Negroes had named their Rhyme parts "Call" and "Sponse." So well were these established parts of a Negro Rhyme recognized among Negroes that the whole turning point of one of their best stories was based upon it. I have reference to the Negro story recorded by Mr. Joel Chandler Harris in his "Nights with Uncle Remus," under the caption, "Brother Fox, Brother Rabbit, and King Deer's Daughter." Those who would enjoy the story, as the writer did in his childhood days, as it fell from the lips of his dear little friends and dusky playmates, will read the story in Mr. Harris' book. The gist of the story is as follows: The fox and the rabbit fall in love with King Deer's daughter. The fox has just about become the successful suitor, when the rabbit goes through King Deer's lot and kills some of King Deer's goats. He then goes to King Deer, and tells him that the fox killed the goats, and offers to make the fox admit the deed in King Deer's hearing. This being agreed to, the rabbit goes to find the fox, and proposes that they serenade the King Deer family. The fox agreed. Then the rabbit proposes that he sing the "Call" and that the fox sing the "Sponse" (or, as Mr. Harris records the story, the "answer"), and this too was agreed upon. We now quote from Mr. Harris:

Ole Br'er Rabbit, he make up de song he own se'f en' he fix it so that he sing de *Call* lak de Captain er de co'n-pile, en ole Br'er Fox, he hatter sing de answer . . . Ole Br'er Rabbit, he got de call en he open up lak dis:

Some folks pile up mo'n dey kin tote,
En dat w'at de matter wid King Deer's goat.

en den Br'er Fox, he make *answer*, 'Dat's so, dat's so, en I'm glad dat it's so.' Den de quills, and de tr'angle, dey come in, en den Br'er Rabbit pursue on wid de call—

Some kill sheep, en some kill shote,
But Br'er Fox kill King Deer goat,

en den Br'er Fox, he jine in wid de answer, 'I did, I did, en I'm glad dat I did.

The writer would add that the story ends with a statement that King Deer came out with his walking cane, and beat the fox, and then invited the rabbit in to eat chicken pie.

From the foregoing one will recognize the naming, by the Negroes themselves, of the parts of their rhymed song, as "call," and "answer." Now just a word concerning the term "answer," instead of "sponse," as used by the writer. You will notice that Mr. Harris records incidentally, of Br'er Rabbit "dat he sing de *call*, lak de Captain er de co'n pile." This has reference to the singing of the Negroes at corn huskings where the leaders sings a kind of solo part, and the others by way of response, sing a kind of chorus. At corn huskings, at plays, and elsewhere, when Negroes sang secular songs, some one was chosen to lead. As a little boy, I witnessed secular singing in all these places. When a leader was chosen, the invariable words of his commission were: "You sing the 'call' and we'll sing the '*sponse*.'" Of course the sentence was not quite so well constructed grammatically, but "call" and "sponse" were the terms always used. This being true, I have felt that I ought to use these terms, though I recognize the probability of there being communities where the word *answer* would be used. All folk terms and writings have different versions.

The "sponses" in most of the Negro Folk Rhymes in our collection are wanting, and the Rhymes themselves, in most cases, consist of calls only. As examples of those with "sponses" left, may be mentioned "Juba" with its sponse "Juba"; "Frog Went A-courting," with its sponse "Uh-huh!"; "Did You Feed My Cow?" with its sponse, "Yes, Ma'am," etc., and "The Old Black Gnats," where the sponses are "I cain't git out'n here, etc."

I shall now endeavor to show why the Negro Folk Rhymes consist in most cases of "calls" only, and how and why the "sponses" have disappeared from the finished product. I record here the notes of two common Negro Play Songs along with sample stanzas used in the singing of them. I hope through a little study of these, to make clear the matter of Folk Rhyme development, to the point of dropping the "sponse."

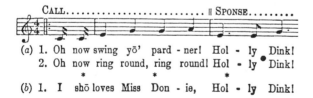

CALL. . . . . ‖ SPONSE. . . . .

(*a*) 1. Oh now swing yō' pard - ner! Hol - ly Dink!
     2. Oh now ring round, ring round! Hol - ly Dink!

(*b*) 1. I shō loves Miss Don - ie, Hol - ly Dink!

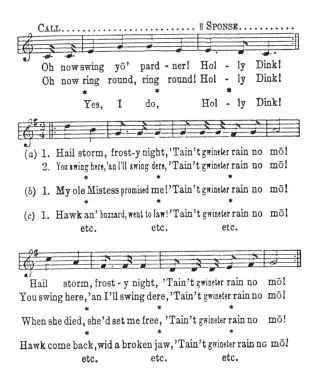

CALL........................... ‖ SPONSE...........

Oh now swing yō' pard - ner! Hol - ly Dink!
Oh now ring round, ring round! Hol - ly Dink!
Yes, I do, Hol - ly Dink!

(a) 1. Hail storm, frost-y night, 'Tain't gwineter rain no mō!
    2. You swing here,'an I'll swing dere, 'Tain't gwineter rain no mō!

(b) 1. My ole Mistess promised me!'Tain't gwineter rain no mō!

(c) 1. Hawk an' buzzard, went to law!'Tain't gwineter rain no mō!
        etc.   etc.   etc.

Hail   storm, frost - y night, 'Tain't gwineter rain no   mō!
You swing here,'an I'll swing dere,'Tain't gwineter rain no mō!
When she died, she'd set me free, 'Tain't gwineter rain no   mō!
Hawk come back,wid a broken jaw,'Tain't gwineter rain no mō!
        etc.   etc.   etc.

These simple little songs, — the first made up of five notes, and the
second of seven, — are typical Negro Play songs. I shall not describe
the simple play which accompanied them because that description
would not add to the knowledge of the evolution under consideration.

At a Negro Evening Entertainment several such songs would be sung
and played, and some individual would be chosen to lead or sing the
"calls" of each of the songs. The 'sponses in some cases were meaningless
utterances, like "Holly Dink," given in the first song recorded, while
others were made up of some sentence like "'Tain't Gwineter Rain No
Mō'!" found in the second song given. The "sponses" were not expected
to bear a special continuous relation in thought to the "calls." Indeed
no one ever thought of the 'sponses as conveyers of thought, whether
jumbled syllables or sentences. The songs went under the names of the
various sponses. Thus the first Play Song recorded was known as "Holly
Dink," and the second as "'Tain't Gwineter Rain No Mō'."

The playing and singing of each of these songs commonly went
on continuously for a quarter of an hour or more. This being the

case, we scarcely need add that the leader of the Play Song had both his memory and ingenuity taxed to their utmost, in devising enough "calls" to last through so long a period of time of continuous playing and singing. The reader will notice under both of the Play Songs recorded, that I have written under "(a)" two stanzas of prose "calls." I would convey the thought to the reader, by these illustrations, that the one singing the "calls" was at liberty to use, and did use any prose sentence that would fit in with the "call" measures of the song.

Of course these prose "calls" had to be rhythmic to fit into the measures, but much freedom was allowed in respacing the time allotted to notes, and in the redivision of the notes in the "fitting in" process. Even these prose stanzas bore the mark of Rhyme to the Negro fancy. The reader will notice that, where the "call" is in prose, it is always repeated, and thus the line in fancy rhymed with itself. Examples as found in our Second Play Song:

> "Hail storm, frosty night.
> Hail storm, frosty night."

Now, it was considered by Negroes, in the days gone by, something of an accomplishment for a leader to be able to sing "calls," for so long a time, when they bore some meaning, and still a greater accomplishment to sing the calls both in rhyme and with meaning. This led each individual to rhyme his calls as far as possible because leaders were invited to lead songs during an evening's entertainment, largely in accordance with their ability, and thus those desiring to lead were compelled to make attainment in both rhyme and meaning. Now, the reader will notice under "Holly Dink," heading "(b)," I shō' loves Miss Donie." This is a part of the opening line of our Negro Rhyme, "Likes and Dislikes." I would convey the thought to the reader that this whole Rhyme, and any other Negro Rhyme which would fit into a 2/4 music measure, could be, and was used by the Play Song leader in singing the calls of "Holly Dink." Thus a leader would lead such a song; and by using one whole Rhyme after another, succeed in rhyming the calls for a quarter of an hour. If his Rhymes "gave out," he used rhythmic prose calls; and since these did not need to have meaning, his store was unlimited. Just as any Rhyme which could be fitted into a 2/4 music measure would be used with "Holly Dink," so any Rhyme which could be fitted into a 4/4 measure would be used with the "'Tain't Gwineter Rain No Mō." Illustrations given under "(b)" and "(c)" under the last mentioned song are—"Promises of Freedom," and "Hawk and Buzzard."

Since all Negro Songs with a few exceptions were written in 4/4 measures and 2/4 measures, and Negro rhymed "calls" were also written in the same way, the rhymed "calls" which may have originated with one song were transferred to, and used with other songs. *Thus the rhymed "calls" becoming detached for use with any and all songs into which they could be fitted, gave rise to the multitude of Negro Folk Rhymes, a small fragment of which multitude is recorded in our collection.* Negro Dances and Dance Rhymes were both constructed in 2/4 and 4/4 measures, and the Rhymes were propagated for that same reason. Rhymes, once detached from their original song or dance, were learned, and often repeated for mere pastime, and thus they were transmitted to others as unit compositions.

We have now seen how detached rhymed "calls" made our Negro Folk Rhymes. Next let us consider how and why whole little "poems" arose in a Play Song. One will notice in reading Negro Folk Rhymes that the larger number of them tell a little story or give some little comic description, or some little striking thought. Since all the Rhymes had to be memorized to insure their continued existence, and since Memory works largely through Association; one readily sees that the putting of the Rhymes into a story, descriptive, or striking thought form, was the only thing that could cause their being kept alive. It was only through their being composed thus that Association was able to assist Memory in recalling them. Those carrying another form carried their death warrant.

Now let us look a little more intimately into how the Rhymes were probably composed. In collecting them, I often had the same Rhyme given to me over and over again by different individuals. Most of the Rhymes were given by different individuals in fragmentary form. In case of all the Rhymes thus received, there would always be a half stanza, or a whole stanza which all contributors' versions held in common. As examples: in "Promises of Freedom," all contributors gave the lines—

"My ole Mistiss promise me
W'en she died, she'd set me free."

In "She Hugged Me and Kissed Me," the second stanza was given
by all. In "Old Man Know-All," the first two lines of the last stanza
came from all who gave the Rhyme. The writer terms these parts of
the individual Rhymes, seemingly known to all who know the "poems,"
key verses. The very fact that the key verses, only, are known to all,
seems to me to warrant the conclusion that these were probably the
first verses made in each individual Rhyme. Now when an individual
made such a key verse, one can easily see that various singers of "call"
using it would attempt to associate other verses of their own making
with in in order to remember them all for their long "singing Bees."
The story, the description, and the striking thought furnished con-
venient vehicles for this association of verses, so as to make them easy
to keep in memory. This is why the verses of many singers of "Calls"
finally became blended into little poem-like Rhymes.

I have pointed out "call" and "sponse," in Rhymes, and have shown
how, through them, in song, the form of the Negro Rhyme came into
existence. But many of the Pastime Rhymes apparently had no connection with the Play or the Dance. I must now endeavor to account
for such Rhymes as these.

In order to do this, I must enter upon the task of trying to show
how "call" and "sponse" originated.

The origin of "call" and "sponse" is plainly written on the faces of
the rhymes of the Social Instinct type. Read once again the following
rhyme recorded in our collection under the caption of "Antebellum
Courtship Inquiry"—

(He) —"Is you a flyin' lark, or a settin' dove?"
(She)—"I'se a flyin' lark, my Honey Love."
(He) —"Is you a bird o' one fedder, or a bird o' two?"
(She)—"I'se a bird o' one fedder, w'en it comes to you."
(He) —"Den Mam:
    I has desire an' quick temptation
    To jine my fence to yō' plantation."

This is primitive courtship; direct, quick, conclusive. It is the crude
call of one heart, and the crude response of another heart. The two

answering and blending into one, in the primitive days, made a rhymed couplet — one. It is "call" and "sponse," born to vibrate in complementary unison with two hearts that beat as one. "Did all Negroes carry on courtship in this manner in olden days?" No, not by any means. Only the more primitive by custom, and otherwise used such forms of courtship. The more intelligent of those who came out of slavery had made the white man's customs their own, and laughed at such crudities, quite as much as we of the present day. The writer thinks his ability to recall from childhood days a clear remembrance of many of these crude things is due to the fact that he belonged to a Negro family that laughed much, early and late, at such things. But the simple forms of "call" and "sponse" were used much in courtship by the more primitive. This points out something of the general origin of "call" and "sponse" in Social Instinct Rhymes, but does not account for their origin in other types of Rhymes. I now turn attention to those.

About eighteen years ago I was making a Sociological investigation for Tuskegee Institute, which carried me into a remote rural district in the Black Belt of Alabama. In the afternoon, when the Negro laborers were going home from the fields and occasionally during the day, these laborers on one plantation would utter loud musical "calls" and the "calls" would be answered by musical responses from the laborers on other plantations. These calls and responses had no peculiar significance. They were only for whatever pleasure these Negroes found in the cries and apparently might be placed in a parallel column alongside of the call of a song bird in the woods being answered by another. Dr. William H. Sheppard, many years a missionary in Congo, Africa, upon inquiry, tells me that similar calls and responses obtain there, though not so musical. He also tells me that the calls have a meaning there. There are calls and responses for those lost in the forest, for fire, for the approach of enemies, etc. These Alabama Negro calls, however, had no meaning, and yet the calls and responses so fitted into each other as to make a little complete tune.

Now, I had heard "field" calls all during my early childhood in Tennessee, and these also were answered by men in adjoining fields. But the Tennessee calls and responses which I remembered had no kinship which would combine them into a kind of little completed song as was the case with the Alabama calls and responses.

Again, in Tennessee when a musical call was uttered by the laborers in one field, those in the other fields around would often use identically the same call as a response. The Alabama calls and responses were short, while those of Tennessee were long.

I am listing an Alabama "call" and "response." I regret that I cannot recall more of them. I am also recording three Tennessee calls or responses (for they may be called either). Then I am recording a fourth one from Tennessee, not exactly a call, but partly call and partly song. The reason for this will appear later. By a study of these I think we can pretty reasonably make a final interesting deduction as to the general origin of "call" and "sponse" in the form of the types of Rhyme not already discussed.

ALABAMA FIELD CALL AND RESPONSE

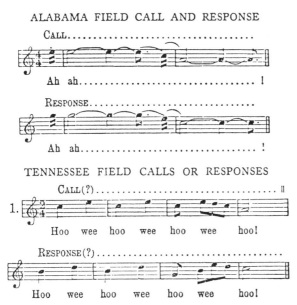

In the Alabama Field Call and response one cannot help seeing a counterpart in music of the "call" and "sponse" in the words of the types of Rhymes already discussed.

If one looks at Number 1 under the Tennessee calls or responses, there is nothing to indicate especially that it was ever other than the whole as it is here written. But when he looks at Number 2 under Tennessee calls or responses he is struck with the remarkable fact that it changes right in the midst from the rhythm of the 9/8 measure to that of the 6/8 measure. Now if there be any one characteristic which is constant in Negro music it is that the rhythm remains the same throughout a given production. In a very, very few long Negro productions I have known an occasional change in the time, but *never* in a musical production consisting of a few measures. The only reasonable explanation to be offered for the break in the time of Number 2, as a Negro production, is that it was originally a "call" and "response"; the "call" being in a 9/8 measure and the "response" being in a 6/8 measure. Here then we have "call" and "sponse." It would look as if the Negroes in Tennessee had combined the "calls" and "sponses" into one and had used them as a whole. When we accept this view all the differences, between the Alabama and Tennessee productions, before mentioned are accounted for. Then looking again at Number 1 under

Tennessee calls or responses, one sees that it would conveniently divide right in the middle to make a "call" and "sponse." Now look at Number 3 under Tennessee calls. It was usually cried off with the syllable *ah* and would easily divide in the middle. I remember this "call" very distinctly from my childhood because the men giving it placed the thumb upon the larynx and made it vibrate longitudinally while uttering the cry. The thumb thus used produced a peculiar screeching and rattling tone that hardly sounded human. But the words "I want a piece of hoecake, etc.," as recorded under the "call," were often rhymed off in song with it. Thus we trace the form of "call" and "sponse" from the friendly musical greeting between laborers at a distance to the place of the formation of a crude Rhyme to go with it. I would have the reader notice that these words finally supplied were in "call" and "sponse" form. The idea is that one individual says: "I want a piece of hoecake, I want a piece o' bread," and another chimes in by way of response: "Well, I'se so tired and hongry dat I'se almos' dead."

"Ole Billie Bawlie" found as Number 4 was a little song which was used to deride men who had little ability musically to intonate "calls" and "sponses." The name "Bawlie" was applied to emphasize that the individual bawled instead of sounding pleasant notes. It is of interest to us because it is a mixture of Rhyme and Field "call" and completes the connecting links along the line of Evolution between the "call" and "sponse" and the Rhyme.

Wherever one thing is derived from another by process of Evolution, there is the well known biological law that there ought to be every grade of connecting link between the original and the last evolved product. The law holds good here in our Rhymes. If this last statement holds good then the law must be universal. May we be permitted to digress enough to show that the law is universal because, though it is a law whose biological phase has been long recognized, not much attention has been paid to it in other fields.

It holds good in the world of inanimate matter. There are three general classes of chemical compounds: acids, bases, and salts. But along with these three general classes are found all kinds of connecting links: acid salts, basic salts, hydroxy acids, etc.

It holds good in the animal and plant worlds. Looking at the ancestors of the horse in geological history we find that the first kind of horse to appear upon the earth was the Œohippus. He had four toes on the hind foot and three on the front one. Through a long period of development, the present day one-toed horse descended from this many-toed primitive horse. There is certainty of the line of descent of the horse because all the connecting links have been discovered in fossil form, between the primitive horse and the present day horse. Plants in like manner show all kinds of connecting links.

The law holds sway in the world of language; and that is the world with which we are concerned here. The state of Louisiana once belonged to the French; now it belongs to an English-speaking people. If one goes among the Creoles in Louisiana he will find a very few who speak almost Parisian French and very poor English. Then he will find a very large number who speak a pure English and a very poor French. Between these classes he will find those speaking all grades of French and English. These last mentioned are the connecting links, and the connecting links bespeak a line of evolution where those of French descent are gradually passing over to a class which will finally speak the English language exclusively.

Now let us turn our attention again directly to the discussion of the evolution of Negro Folk Rhymes. One can judge whether or not he has discovered the correct line of descent of the Rhymes by seeing whether or not he has all the connecting links requiste to the line of evolution. I think it must be agreed that I have given every type of connecting link between common Field "calls" and "sponses," and incipient crude Negro Rhymes. They set the mold for the other general Negro Rhymes not hitherto discussed.

If the reader will be kind enough to apply the test of connecting links to the Play and other Rhymes already discussed, he will find that the reactions will indicate that we have traced their correct lines of origin and descent.

The spirit of "call" and "sponse" hovers ghost-like over the very thought of many Negro Rhymes. In "Jaybird," the first two lines of each stanza are a call in thought, while the last two lines are a "sponse" in thought to it. The same is true of "He Is My Horse," "Stand Back, Black Man," "Bob-White's Song," "Promises of Freedom," "The Town and Country Bird," and many others.

Then "call" and "sponse" looms up in the midst in thought between stanza and stanza in many Rhymes. Good examples are found in "The Great Owl's Song," "Sheep and Goat," "The Snail's Reply," "Let's

Marry—Courtship," "Shoo! Shoo!" "When I Go to Marry," and many others.

"Call" and "sponse" even runs, at least in one case, between whole Rhymes. "I Wouldn't Marry a Black Girl" as a "call" has for its "sponse": "I Wouldn't Marry a Yellow or a White Negro Girl." The Rhyme "I'd Rather Be a Negro Than a Poor White Man" is a "sponse" to an imaginary "call" that the Negro is inferior by nature.

After some consideration, as compiler of the Negro Rhymes, I thought I ought to say something of their rhyming system, but before doing this I want to consider for a little the general structure of a stanza in Negro Rhymes.

Of course there is no law, but the number of lines in a stanza of English poetry is commonly a multiple of two. The large majority of Negro Rhymes follows this same rule, but, even in case of these, the lines are so unsymmetrical that they make but the faintest approach to the commonly accepted standards. Then there are Rhymes with stanzas of three lines and there are those with five, six, and seven lines. This is because the imaginary music measure is the unit of measurement instead of feet, and the stanzas are all right so long as they run in consonance with the laws governing music measures and rhythm. In a tune like "Old Hundred" commonly used in churches as a Doxology, there are four divisions in the music corresponding with the four lines of the stanza. Each division is called, in music, a Phrase. Two of these Phrases make a Phrase Group and two Phrase Groups make a Period. Now when one moves musically through a Phrase Group his sense of rhythm is partially satisfied and when he has moved through a Period the sense of Rhythm is entirely satisfied.

When one reads the three line stanzas of Negro Folk Rhymes he passes through a music Period and thus the stanza satisfies in its rhythm. Example:

> "Bridle up er rat,
> Saddle up er cat,
> An' han' me down my big straw hat."

Here the first two lines are a Phrase each and constitute together a Phrase Group. The third line is made up of two Phrases, or a Phrase Group in itself. Thus this third line along with the first two makes a Music Period and the whole satisfies our rhythmic sense though the lines are apparently odd. In all Negro Rhymes, however odd in number and however ragged may seem the lines, the music Phrases and Periods are there in such symmetry as to satisfy our sense of rhythm.

I now turn attention to the rhyming of the lines in Negro verse. The ordinary systems of rhyming as set forth by our best authors will take in most Negro Rhymes. Most of them are Adjacent and Interwoven Rhymes. There are five systems of rhyming commonly used in the white man's poetry but the Negro Rhyme has nine systems. Here again we find a parallelism, as in case of music scales, etc. Five in each system are the same. The ordinary commonly accepted systems are:

> *a a a*—Where the adjacent lines rhyme by twos. We call it "Adjacent rhymes" or "a Couplet."

> *a b a b*—Where the alternating lines rhyme we call it "Alternate" or "Interwoven Rhythm."

> *a b b a*—Where lines 1 and 4, and 2 and 3, rhyme respectively with each other. This is called "Close Rhyme."

> *a b c b*—Where in a stanza of four lines, lines 2 and 4 only rhyme. This is sometimes also called "Alternate Rhyme."

> *a a b a*—Where in a stanza of four lines 1, 2 and 4 rhyme. This is called "Interrupted Rhyme."

I now beg to offer a system of classification in rhyming which will include all Negro Rhymes. I shall insert the ordinary names in parenthesis along with the new names wherever the system coincides with the ordinary system for white men's Rhymes. The only reason for not using the old names exclusively in these places is that nomenclature should be kept consistent in any proposed classification, so far as that is possible.

In classifying the rhyming of the lines or verses I have borrowed terms from the gem world, partly because the Negro hails from Africa, a land of gems; and partly because the verses bear whatever beauty there might have been in his crude crystalized thoughts in the dark days of his enslavement.

I present herewith the outline and follow it with explanations:

CLASS	SYSTEMS
I Rhythmic Solitaire.	*a.* Regular measured lines
II Rhymed Doublet	*a.* Regular (Adjacent Rhyme)
	b. Divided (Includes Close Rhyme)
	c. Supplemented.
III Rhyming Doublet	*a.* Regular (Includes Alternate Rhyme)
	b. Inverted (Close Rhyme)
IV Rhymed Cluster	*a.* Regular
	b. Divided (Interrupted Rhyme)
	c. Supplemented

I a. Rhythmic Solitaire, Rhythmic measured lines. In many Rhymes there is a rhythmic line dropped in here and there that doesn't rhyme with any other line. They are rhythmic like the other lines and serve equally to fill out the music Phrases and Periods. These are the Rhythmic Solitaires and because of their solitaire nature it follows that there is only one system. Examples are found in the first line of each stanza of "Likes and Dislikes"; in the second line of each stanza of "Old Aunt Kate;" in lines five and six of each stanza of "I'll Wear Me a Cotton Dress," in lines three and four of the "Sweet Pinks Kissing Song," etc. The Rhythmic Solitaires do not seem to have been largely used by Negroes for whole compositions. Only one whole Rhyme in our collection is written with Rhythmic Solitaires. That Rhyme is: "Song to the Runaway Slave." This Rhyme is made up of blank verse as measured by the white man's standard.

II a. The Regular Rhymed Doublet. This is the same as our common Adjacent Rhyme. There are large numbers of Negro Rhymes which belong to this system. The "Jaybird" is a good example.

II b. The Divided Rhymed Doublet. It includes Close Rhyme and there are many of this system. In ordinary Close Rhyme one set of rhyming lines (two in number) is separated by two intervening lines, but this "Rhyming Couplet" in Negro Rhymes may be separated by three lines as in "Bought Me a Wife," where the divided doublet consists of lines 3 and 7. Then the Divided Rhymed Doublet may be separated by only one line, as in "Good-by, Wife," where the Doublet is found in lines 5 and 7.

II c. The Supplemented Rhymed Doublet. It is illustrated by "Juba" found in our collection. The words "Juba! Juba!" found following the second line of each stanza, are the supplement. I shall take up the explanation of Supplemented Rhyme later, since the explanation goes with all Supplemented Rhyme and not with the Doublet only. I consider the Supplement one of the things peculiarly characteristic of Negro Rhyme. The following stanza illustrates such a Supplemented Doublet:

"Juba jump! Juba sing!

Juba cut dat Pidgeon's Wing! Juba! Juba"

Representing such a rhyming by letters we have a a $\bar{n}$ x.

III. The Rhyming Doublet. It is generally made up of two consecutive lines not rhyming with each other but so constructed that one of the lines will rhyme with one line of another Doublet similarly constructed and found in the same stanza.

III a. The Regular Rhyming Doublet. It is the same as our common interwoven rhyme and is very common among Negro Rhymes. There is one peculiar Interwoven Rhyme found in our collection; it is "Watermelon Preferred." In it the second Rhyming Doublet is divided by a kind of parenthetic Rhythmic Solitaire.

III b. The Inverted Rhyming Doublet. It is the same as our ordinary Close Rhyme.

The writer had expected to find the Supplemented Rhyming Doublet among Negro Rhymes but peculiarly enough it does not seem to exist.

IV a. The Regular Rhymed Cluster. It consists of three consecutive lines in the same stanza which rhyme. An example is found in "Bridle Up a Rat," one of whose stanzas we have already quoted. It is represented by the lettering a a a.

IV b. The Divided Rhymed Cluster. It includes ordinary Interrupted Rhyme—with the lettering a a b a. (An example is found in the Ebo or Guinea Rhyme "Tree Frogs.") But in Negro Folk Rhymes two lines may divide the Rhymed Cluster instead of one. An example of this is found in "Animal Fair," whose rhyming may be represented by the lettering *a a b b a.*

IVc. The Supplemented Rhymed Clusters. They are well represented by Negro Rhymes. Some have a single supplement as in "Negroes Never Die," whose rhyming is lettered *a a a n̄ x.* Some have double supplements as in "Frog Went a-Courting" whose rhyming is lettered *a x̄ a a x̄.*

Now Negroes did not retain, permanently, meaningless words in their Rhymes. The Rhymes themselves were "calls" and had meaning. The "sponses," such as "Holly Dink," "Jing-Jang," "Oh, fare you well," "'Tain't gwineter rain no more,'" etc., that had no meaning, died year after year and new "sponses" and songs came into existence.

Let us see what these permanently retained seemingly senseless Supplements mean.

In "Frog Went a-Courting" we see the Supplement "uh-huh! uh-huh!" It is placed in the midst to keep vividly before the mind of the listener the ardent singing of the frog in Spring during his courtship season, while we hear a recounting of his adventures. It is to this Simple Rhyme what stage scenery is to the Shakespearian play or the Wagnerian opera. It seems to me (however crude his verse) that the Negro has here suggested something new to the field of poetry. He suggests that, while one recounts a story or what not, he could to advantage use words at the same time having no bearing on the story to depict the surroundings or settings of the production. The gifted Negro poet, Paul Laurence Dunbar, has used the supplement in this way in one of his poems. The poem is called "A Negro Love Song." The little sentence, "Jump back, Honey, jump back," is thrown in, in the midst and at the end of each stanza. Explaining it, the following is written by a friend, at the heading of this poem:

"During the World's Fair he (Mr. Dunbar) served for a short time as a hotel waiter. When the Negroes were not busy they had a custom of congregating and talking about their sweethearts. Then a man with a tray would come along and, as the dining-room was frequently crowded, he would say when in need of passing room, 'Jump back, Honey, jump back.' Out of the commonplace confidences, he wove the musical little composition—'A Negro Love Song.'"

Now, this line, "Jump back, Honey, jump back," was used by Mr. Dunbar to recall and picture before the mind the scurrying hotel waiter as he bragged to his fellows of his sweetheart and told his tales of adventure. It is the "stage scenery" method used by the slave Negro verse maker. Mr. Dunbar uses this style also in "A Lullaby," "Discovered," "Lil' Gal" and "A Plea." Whether he used it knowingly in all cases, or whether he instinctively sang in the measured strains of his benighted ancestors, I do not know.

The Supplement was used in another way in Negro Folk Dance Rhymes. I have already explained how the Rhymes were used in a general way in the Dance. Let us glance at the Dance Rhyme "Juba" with its Supplement, "Juba! Juba!" to illustrate this special use of the Supplement. "Juba" itself was a kind of dance step. Now let us imagine two dancers in a circle of men to be dancing while the following lines are being patted and repeated:

> "Juba Circle, raise de latch,
> Juba dance dat Long Dog Scratch, Juba! Juba!"

While this was being patted and repeated, the dancers within the circle described a circle with raised foot and ended doing a dance step called "Dog Scratch." Then when the Supplement "Juba! Juba!" was said the whole circle of men joined in the dance step "Juba" for a few moments. Then the next stanza would be repeated and patted with the same general order of procedure.

The Supplement, then, in the Dance Rhyme was used as the signal for all to join in the dance for a while at intervals after they had witnessed the finished foot movements of their most skilled dancers.

The Supplement was used in a third way in Negro Rhymes. This is illustrated by the Rhyme, "Anchor Line" where the Supplement is "Dinah." This was a Play Song and was commonly used as such, but the Negro boy often sang such a song to his sweetheart, the Negro father to his child, etc. When such songs were sung on other occasions than the Play, the name of the person to whom it was being sung was often substituted for the name Dinah. Thus it would be sung

> "I'se gwine out on de Anchor Line — Mary," etc.

The Supplement then seems to have been used in some cases to broaden the scope of direct application of the Rhyme.

The last use of the Supplement to be mentioned is closely related in its nature to the "stage scenery" use already mentioned. This kind of Supplement is used to depict the mental condition or attitude of an individual passing through the experiences being related. Good examples are found in "My First and My Second Wife" where we have the Supplements, "Now wusn't I sorrowful in mind," etc.; and in "Stinky Slave Owners" with its Supplements "Eh-Eh!" "Shoo-shoo!" etc.

The Negro Rhymes here and there also have some kind of little introductory word or line to each stanza. I consider this also something peculiar to Negro Rhyme. I have named these little introductory words or sentences the "Verse Crown." They are receivers into which verses are set and serve as dividing lines in the production. As the reader knows, the portion of the ring which receives the gems and sets them into a harmonious whole is called the "Crown." Having borrowed the terms Solitaire, Doublet, etc. for the verses, the name for these introductory words and lines automatically became "Verse Crown."

Just as I have figuratively termed the Supplements in one place "stage scenery," so I may with equal propriety term the "Verse Crown" the "rise" or the "fall" of the stage curtain. They separate the little Acts of the Rhymes into scenes. As an example read the comic little Rhyme "I Walked the Roads." The word "Well" to the first stanza marks the raising of the curtain and we see the ardent Negro boy lover nonsensically prattling to the one of his fancy about everything in creation until he is so tired that he can scarcely stand erect. The curtain drops and rises with the word "Den." In this, the second scene, he finally gets around to the point where he makes all manner of awkward protestations of love. The hearer of the Rhyme is left laughing, with a sort of satisfactory feeling that possibly he succeeded in his suit and possibly he didn't. Among the many examples of Rhymes where verse crowns serve as curtains to divide the Acts into scenes may be mentioned "I Wish I Was an Apple," "Rejected by Eliza Jane," "Courtship," "Plaster," "The Newly Weds," and "Four Runaway Negroes."

Though the stanzas in Negro Rhymes commonly have just one kind of rhyming, in some cases as many as three of the systems of rhyming are found in one stanza. I venture to suggest the calling of those with one system "Simple Rhymed Stanzas;" those with two, "Complex Rhymed Stanzas;" those with more than two "Complicated Complex Rhymed Stanzas."

I next call attention to the seeming parodies found occasionally among Negro Rhymes. The words of most Negro parodies are such that they are not fit for print. We have recorded three: "He Paid Me Seven," Parody on "Now I Lay Me Down to Sleep," and Parody on "Reign, Master Jesus, Reign." We can best explain the nature of the Negro Parody by taking that beautiful and touching well-known Jubilee song, "Steal Away to Jesus" and briefly recounting the story of its origin. Its history is well known. We hope the reader will not be disappointed when we say that this song is a parody in the sense in which Negroes composed and used parodies.

The words around which the whole song ranges itself are "Steal away to Jesus, I hain't got long to stay here." Now the slave Negroes on the far away plantations of the South occasionally met in the dead of night in some secluded lonely spot for a religious meeting even when they had been forbidden to do so by their master. So they made up this song, "Steal away to Jesus, I hain't got long to stay here." Late in the afternoons when the slaves on any plantation sang it, it served as a notice to slaves on other plantations that a secret religious meeting was to be held that night at the place formerly mutually agreed upon for meetings.

Now here is where the parody comes in under the Negro standard: To the slave master the words meant that his good, obedient slaves were only studying how to be good and to get along peaceably, because they considered, after all, that their time upon earth was short and not of much consequence; but to the listening Negro it meant both a notification of a meeting and slaves disobedient enough to go where they wanted to go. To the listening master it meant that the Negro was thinking of what a short time it would be before he would die and leave the earth, but to the listening slaves it meant that he was thinking of how short a time it would be before he left the cotton field for a pleasant religious meeting. All these meanings were truly literally present but the meaning apparent depended upon the viewpoint of the listener. It was composed thus, so that if the master suspected the viewpoint of the slave hearers, the other viewpoint, intended for him, might be held out in strong relief.

Now let us consider the parodies recorded in our Collection. The Parody on the beautiful little child prayer, "Now I lay me down to sleep" is but the bitter protest from the heart of the woman who, after putting the little white children piously repeating this child prayer, "Now I lay me down to sleep," in their immaculate beds, herself retired to a vermin infested cabin with no time left for cleaning it. It was a tirade against the oppressor but the comic, good-natured "It means nothing" was there to be held up to those calling the one repeating it to task. The parody on "Reign, Master Jesus, Reign!" when heard by the Master meant only a good natured jocular appeal to him for plenty of meat and bread, but with the Negro it was a scathing indictment of a Christian earthly master who muzzled those who produced the food. "He Paid Me Seven" is a mock at the white man for failing to practice his own religion but the clown mask is there to be held up for safety to any who may see the *real* side and take offense.

Slave parodies, then, are little Rhymes capable of two distinct interpretations, both of which are true. They were so composed that if a slave were accused through one interpretation, he could and would truthfully point out the other meaning to the accuser and thus escape serious trouble.

Under all the classes of Negro Rhymes, with the exception of the one Marriage Ceremony Rhyme, there were those which were sung and played on instruments. Since instrumental music called into existence some of the very best among Negro Rhymes it seems as if a little ought to be said concerning the Negro's instruments. Banjos and fiddles (violins) were owned only limitedly by antebellum Negroes. Those who owned them mastered them to such a degree that the memory of their skill will long linger. These instruments are familiar and need no discussion.

Probably the Negro's most primitive instrument, which he could call his very own, was "Quills." It is mentioned in the story, "Brother Fox, Brother Rabbit, and King Deer's Daughter" which I have already quoted at some length. If the reader will notice in this story he will see, after the singing of the first stanza by the rabbit and fox, a description in these words, "Den de quills and de tr'angle, dey come in, an' den Br'er Rabbit pursue on wid de call." Here we have described in the Negro's own way the long form of instrumental music composition which we have hitherto discussed, and "quills" and "tr'angles" are given as the instruments.

In my early childhood I saw many sets of "Quills." They were short reed pipes, closed at one end, made from cane found in our Southern cane-brakes. The reed pipes were made closed at one end by being so cut that the bottom of each was a node of the cane. These pipes were "whittled" square with a jack knife and were then wedged into a wooden frame, and the player blew them with his mouth. The "quills," or reed pipes, were cut of such graduated lengths that they constituted the Negro's peculiar music Scale. The music intervals though approximating those of the Caucasian scale were not the same. At times, when in a reminiscent humor, I hum to myself some little songs of my childhood. On occasions, afterwards, I have "picked out" some of the same tunes on the piano. When I have done this I have always felt like giving its production on the piano the same greeting that I gave a friend who had once worn a full beard but had shaved. My greeting was "Hello, friend A; I came near not knowing you."

"Quills" were made in two sets. They were known as a "Little Set of Quills" and a "Big Set of Quills." There were five reeds in the Little Set but I do not know how many there were in a Big Set. I think there were more than twice as many as in a Little Set. I have inserted a cut of a Little Set of "Quills." (Figure I.) The fact that I was in the

A LITTLE SET OF QUILLS

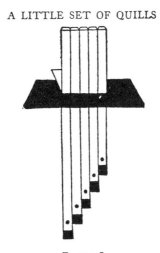

FIGURE I

class of "The Little Boy Who Couldn't Count Seven" when I saw and handled quills makes it necessary to explain how it comes that I am sure of the number of "Quills" in a "Little Set." I recall the intricate tune that could be played only by the performers's putting in the lowest pitched note with his voice. I am herewith presenting that tune,

and "blocking out" the voice note there are only five notes left, thus
I know there were five "Quills" in the set. I thought a tune played on
a "Big Set" might be of interest and so I am giving one of those also.
If there be those who would laugh at the crudity of "Quills" it might
not be amiss to remember in justice to the inventors that "Quills" constitute a pipe organ in its most rudimentary form.

TUNE PLAYED ON A LITTLE SET OF QUILLS

TUNE PLAYED ON A BIG SET OF QUILLS

The "tr'angle" or triangle mentioned as the other primitive instrument used by the rabbit and fox in serenading King Deer's family was only the U-shaped iron clives which with its pin was used for hitching horses to a plow. The ante-bellum Negro often suspended this U-shaped clives by a string and beat it with its pin along with the playing on "Quills" much after the order that a drum is beaten. These crude instruments produced music not of unpleasant strain and inspired the production of some of the best Negro Rhymes.

I would next consider for a little the origin of the subject matter found in Negro Rhymes. When the Negro sings "Master Is Six Feet One Way" or "The Alabama Way" there is no question where the subject matter came from. But when he sings of animals, calling them all "Brother" or "Sister," and "Bought Me a Wife," etc., the origin of the conception and subject matter is not so clear. I now come to the question: From whence came such subject matter?

First of all, Mr. Joel Chandler Harris, in his introduction to "Nights with Uncle Remus," has shown that the Negro stories of our country have counterparts in the Kaffir Tales of Africa. He therefore leaves strong grounds for inference that the American Negroes probably brought the dim outlines of their Br'er Rabbit stories along with them when they came from Africa. I have already ponited out that some of the Folk Rhymes belong to these Br'er Rabbit stories. Since the origin of the subject matter of one is the origin of the subject matter of the other, it follows that we are reasonably sure of the origin of such Folk Rhymes because of the "counterpart" data presented by Mr. Harris. But I have been fortunate enough recently to secure direct evidence that one of the American Negro stories recorded by Mr. Harris came from Africa.

While collecting our Rhymes, I asked Dr. C. C. Fuller of the South African Mission, at Chikore, Melsetter, Rhodesia, Africa, for an African Rhyme in Chindau. I might add parenthetically: I have never seen pictures of a cruder or more primitive people than these people who speak Chindau. He obtained and sent me the Rhyme "The Tur-

key Buzzard" found in our Foreign Section. It was given to him by
the Reverend J. E. Hatch of the South African General Mission. Along
with this rhyme came the following in his kind and obliging letter:

"We thought the story of how the Crocodile got its scaly skin might be
of interest also":

"Why the Crocodile Has a Hard, Scaly Skin."

"Long ago the Crocodile had a soft skin like that of the other animals.
He used to go far from the rivers and catch animals and children and
by so doing annoyed the people very much. So one day when he was far
away from water, they surrounded him and set the grass on fire on every
side, so that he could not escape to the river without passing through the
fire. The fire overtook him and scorched and seared his back, so that from
that day his skin has been hard and scaly, and he no longer goes far from
the rivers."

This is about as literal an outline of the American Negro story
"Why the Alligator's Back is Rough" as one could have. The slight
difference is that the direct African version mixes people in with the
plot. This along with Mr. Harris's evidences practically establishes the
fact that the Negro animal story outlines came with the Negroes themselves from Africa and would also render it practically certain that
many animal rhymes came in the same way since these Rhymes in
many cases accompany the stories.

Then there are Rhymes, not animal Rhymes, which seem to carry
plainly in their thought content a probable African origin. In the
Rhyme, "Bought Me a Wife," there is not only the mentioning of buy-
ing a wife, but there is the setting forth of feeding her along with
guineas, chickens, etc., out under a tree. Such a conception does not
fit in with American slave life but does fit into widely prevailing conditions found in Africa.

Read the last stanza of "Ration Day," where the slave sings of going
after death to a land where there are trees that bear fritters and where
there are ponds of honey. Surely there is nothing in America to suggest such thoughts, but such thoughts might have come from Africa
where natives gather their fruit from the bread tree and dip it into
honey gathered from the forests.

Read "When My Wife Dies." This is a Dance Rhyme Song. When

the Rhymer chants in seemingly light vein in our hearing that he will simply get another wife when his wife dies, we turn away our faces in disgust, but we turn back almost amazed when he announces in the immediately succeeding lines that his heart will sorrow when she is gone because none better has been created among women. The dance goes on and we almost see grim Death himself smile as the Rhymer closes his Dance Song with directions not to bury him deep, and to put bread in his hand and molasses at his feet that he may eat on the way to the "Promised Land."

If you had asked a Negro boy in the days gone by what this Dance Rhyme Song meant, he would have told you that he didn't know, that it was simply an old song he had picked up from somewhere. Thus he would go right along thoughtlessly singing or repeating and passing the Rhyme to others. The dancing over the dead and the song which accompanied it certainly had no place in American life. But do you ask where there was such a place? Get Dr. William H. Sheppard's *Presbyterian Pioneers in Congo* and read on page 136 the author's description of the behavior of the Africans in Lukenga's Land on the day following the death of one of their fellow tribesmen. It reads in part as follows: "The next day friends from neighboring villages joined with these and in their best clothes danced all day. These dances are to cheer up the bereaved family and to run away evil spirits." Dr. Sheppard also tells us that in one of the tribes in Africa where he labored, a kind of funnel was pushed down into the grave and down this funnel food was dropped for the deceased to feed upon. I have heard from other missionaries to other parts of Africa similar accounts. The minute you suppose the Rhyme "When My Wife Dies" to have had its origin in Africa, the whole thought content is explained. Of course the stanza concerning the pickling of the bones in alcohol is probably of American origin but I doubt not that the thought of the "key verses" came from Africa.

These Rhymes whose thought content I have just discussed I consider only illustrative of the many Rhymes whose thought drift came from Africa.

Many of the Folk Rhymes fall under the heading commonly denominated "Nature Rhymes." By actual count more than a hundred and fifty recorded by the writer have something in their stanzas concerning some animal. I do not think the makers of these Rhymes were makers of Nature Rhymes in the ordinary sense of the term. It would really be more to the point to call them "Animal Rhymes" instead of "Nature Rhymes." With the exception of about a half dozen Rhymes which mention some kind of tree or plant, all the other Rhymes with Nature allusions pertain to animals. The Uncle Remus stories recorded by Joel Chandler Harris are practically all animal stories. I have said in my foregoing discussion that the Negro communed with Nature and she gave him Rhymes for amusement. This is true, but when we say "communed" we simply express a vague intangible something the existence of which lives somewhere in a kind of mental fiction.

Though I was brought up with the Rhymes I make no pretensions that I really know why so many of them were made concerning the animal world. I have heard no Negro tradition on this point. I have thought much on it and I now beg the reader to walk with me over the peculiar paths along which my mind has swept in its search for the truth of this mystery of Animal Rhyme.

Before the great American Civil War the Negro slave preachers could not, as a class, read and they were taught their Bible text by white men, commonly their owners. The texts taught them embraced most of the central truths of our Bible. The subjects upon which the ante-bellum Negro preached, however, were comparatively few. Of course a very few ante-bellum Negro preachers could read. In case of these individuals their texts and subjects were scarcely limited by the "lids" of the Bible. I heard scores of these men preach in my childhood days.

The following subjects embrace about all those known to the average of these slave preachers. 1. Joshua. 2. Samson. 3. The Ark. 4. Jacob. 5. Pharoah and Moses. 6. Daniel. 7. Ezekiel—vision of the valley of dry bones. 8. Judgment Day. 9. Paul and Silas in jail. 10. Peter. 11. John's vision on the Isle of Patmos. 12. Jesus Christ—his love and his miracles. 13. "Servants, obey your Masters."

Now it is strange enough that the ignorant slave, while adopting his Master's religious topics, refused to adopt his hymns and proceeded to make his own songs and to cluster all these songs in thought around the Bible subjects with which he was acquainted. If the reader will get nearly any copy of Jubilee Songs he will find that the larger number group themselves about Jesus Christ and the others cluster about Moses, Daniel, Judgment Day, etc., subjects partially known and handled by the preachers in their sermons. There is just one exception. There is no Jubilee Song on "Servants, obey your Masters." We shall leave for the "feeble" imagination of the reader the reason why. The Negroes practically left out of their Jubilee Songs, Jeremiah, Job, Abraham, Isaac, Solomon, Samuel, Ezra, Mark, Luke, John, James, The Psalms, The Proverbs, etc., simply because these subjects did not fall among those taught them as preaching subjects.

Now let us consider for a while the Negro's religion in Africa. Turning to Bettanny's "The World's Religions" we learn the following facts about aboriginal African worship.

The Bushmen worshipped a Caddis worm and an antelope (a species of deer). The Damaras believed that they and all living creatures descended from a kind of tree and they worshiped that tree. The Mulungu worshiped alligators and lion-shaped idols. The Fantis considered snakes and many other animals messengers of spirits. The Dahomans worshiped snakes, a silk tree, a poison tree and a kind of ocean god whom they called Hu.

Now turning our attention to Negro Folk Rhymes we find them clustering around the animals of aboriginal African Folk worship. The Negro stories recorded by Mr. Harris center around these animals also. In the Folk Rhyme "Walk Tom Wilson" our hero steps on an alligator. In "The Ark" the lion almost breaks out of his enclosure of palings. In one rhyme the snake is described as descended from the Devil and then the Devil figures prominently in many Rhymes. Then we have "Green Oak Tree Rocky-o" answering to the tree worship.

I have placed in our collection of Rhymes a small foreign section including African Rhymes. I have recorded precious few but those few are enough to show two things. (1) That the Negro of savage Africa has the rhyme-making habit and probably has always had it, and thus the American Negro brought this habit with him to America. (2) That a small handful from darkest Africa contains stanzas on the owl, the frog, and the turkey buzzard just like the American rhymes.

Knowing that the Negro made rhymes in Africa, and knowing that he centered his Jubilee Song words around his American Christian religion, is it not reasonable to suppose that he centered his secular or African Rhymes around his African religion? He must have done so unless he changed all his rhyme-making habits after coming to America, for he certainly clustered his American verse largely around his religion. Assuming this to be true the large amount of animal lore in Negro rhyme and story is at once explained.

Possibly the greatest hindrance to one's coming to this conclusion is the fact that the Rabbit and some other animals found in Negro rhyme and story do not appear in the records among those worshiped by aboriginal Africans. The known record of the Africans' early religion covers only a very few pages. Christians have not been willing to spend any time to speak of in investigating the religions of the primitive and the lowly. Thus if these animals were widely worshiped it could not be strange if we should never have heard of it. Let us consider what is known, however.

Taking up the matter of the rabbit Mr. John McBride, Jr., had a very fine and lengthy discussion on "Br'er Rabbit in the Folk Tales of the Negro and other Races" in *The Sewanee Review*, April 1911. On page 201 of that journal's issue we find these words: "Among the Hottentots, for example, there is a story in which the hare appears in the moon and of which several versions are extant. The story goes that the moon sent the hare to the earth to inform men that, as she died away and rose again, so should all men die and again come to life," etc. I drop the story here because so much of it suffices my purpose. It brings out the fact that the African here had probably truly considered the Rabbit as a messenger of the moon. Now the fact that the Hottentots were thus talking in lore of receiving messages concerning immortality from the moon means there must have been at least a time in their history when they considered the Moon a kind of superbeing, a kind of god.

I quote again from Dr. Sheppard's "Presbyterian Pioneers in Congo," page 113. "King Lukenga offers up a sacrifice of a goat or lamb on every new moon. The blood is sprinkled on a large idol in his own fetich house, in the presence of all his counselors. This sacrifice is for the heatlhfulness of all the King's country, for the crops," etc.

I think after considering the foregoing one will see that there are those of Africa who connect their worship with the moon. We learn also that there are those who claim the rabbit to be the moon's messenger. From this, if we should accept the theory for Animal Rhymes advanced, we would easily see why the rabbit as a messenger of a god or gods would figure so largely in Rhyme and in story. We also would easily see how and why as a messenger of a god he would become "Brother Rabbit." If one will read the little Rhyme "Jaybird" he will notice that the rhymer places the intelligence of the rabbit above his own. Our theory accounts for this.

I would next consider the frog, but I imagine I hear the reader saying: "That is not a beginning. How about your bear, terrapin, wolf, squirrel, etc.?"

Seeing that I am faced by so large an array of animals, I beg the reader to walk with me through just one more little path of thought and with his consent I shall leave the matter there.

We see, in two of our African Rhymes, lines on a buzzard and an owl; yet these African natives do not worship these birds. The American Negro children of my childhood repeated Folk Rhymes concerning the rabbit, the fox, etc., without any thought whatever of worshiping them. These American children had received the whole through dim traditional rhymes and stories and engaged in passing them on to others without any special thought. The uncivilized and the unlettered hand down everything by word of mouth. Religion, trades, superstition, medicine, sense, and nonsense all flow in the same stream and from this stream all is drunk down without question. If therefore the Negro's rhyme-clustering habit in America was the same as it had ever been and the centering of rhymes about animals is due to a former worship of them in Africa, the verses would include not only the animals worshiped in modern Africa but in ancient Africa. The verses would take in animals included in any accepted African religion antedating the comparatively recent religions found there.

The Bakuba tribe have a tradition of their origin. Quoting from Dr. Sheppard's book again, page 114, we have the following: "From all the information I can gather, they (the Bakuba) migrated from the far North, crossed rivers and settled on the high table land." Here is one tradition, standing as a guide post, with its hand pointing toward Egypt. A one fact premise practically never forms a safe basis for a conclusion, but when we couple this tradition with the fact that, so far as we know, men originated in Southwest Asia and therefore probably came into Africa by way of the Isthmus of Suez, I think the case of the Bakuba hand pointing toward a near Egyptian residence a strong one. Now turn to your *Encyclopedia Britannica,* Vol. X, ninth edition, with American revisions and additions, to the article on "Glass," page 647. Near the bottom of the second column on that page we read: "The Phoenicians probably derived this knowledge of the art (of glass making) from Egypt. . . . It seems probable that the earliest products of the industry of Phoenicia in the art of glass making are the colored beads which have been found in almost all parts of Europe, in India, and other parts of Asia, and in *Africa*. The "aggry" beads so much valued by the *Ashantees and other natives* of that part of Africa which lies near the Gold Coast, have *probably* the same origin. . . . Their wide dispersion may be referred with much probability to their having been objects of barter between the Phoenician merchants and the barbarous inhabitants of the various countries with which they traded." Here are evidences, then, that the African in his prehistoric days traded with somebody who bartered in beads of Phoenician or Egyptian make. I say Egyptian or Phoenician because if the Phoenicians got this art from the Egyptians I think it would be very difficult for those who lived thousands of years afterward to be sure in which country a specific bead was made, the art as practiced by one country being a kind of copy of the art as practiced in the other country. With the historic record that the Phoenicians were the great traders of the Ancient World our writers attributed the carrying of the beads into Africa, among the natives, to the Phoenicians. Without questioning these time-honored conclusions, we do know that Egyptian caravans still make journeys into the interior of Africa for the purpose of trade. Shall we think this trading practice on the part of Egypt in Africa one of recent origin or probably one that runs back through the centuries? I see no reason for believing this trading custom to be other than an ancient one. If the ancient Egyptians traded with the surrounding Africans and these Africans gradually migrated South, as is stated in the Bakuba tradition, the whole matter of how all kinds of animals got mixed into Negro Folk Rhymes by custom becomes clear. It also will explain how animal worship got scattered throughout Africa, for it is the unbroken history of the world that traders of a race superior in attainment always somehow manage to carry along their religion to the race inferior in attainment. The religious emissaries generally follow along in the wake of the traders. If we make the assumption, on the foregoing grounds, that the very ancient African Negro got in touch with the religion of Ancient Egypt, then the appearance of the frog, birds, etc., in Negro Rhymes is explained, for if we read the lists of animal gods of Ancient Egypt and the animal states through which spirits were supposed to pass, we have no trouble finding the list of animals extolled in Negro rhyme and story.

If Negro Rhyme has always centered about Negro religion, then when the Negro was brought to America and began changing his religion, he should have had some songs or rhymes on the dividing line between the old and the new. In other words, there ought to be connecting links between "secular" Folk Rhymes and Jubilee Songs, songs that by nature partake of both types. This must happen in order to be in accord with the law of the presence of connecting links where evolution produces a new type from an old one. By using the procedure under Mendel's law of mating like descendants from a cross between two and by eliminating those who do not reproduce constant to the type which we are trying to produce, we can produce a new and constant type in the third succeeding generation of descendants.

Now the Negro slave turned quickly in America from heathenism to Christianity. This was accomplished through white Christians correcting and eliminating all thoughts and productions which hovered on the border line between heathen ideals and Christianity. They used the Mendelian procedure of eliminating all crosses that did not give a product with Christian characterisitcs and thus necessarily eliminated Rhymes or songs of the connecting link type. They did a good thorough job but the writer believes he sees two connecting links that escaped their sensitive ears and sharp eyes. They are Jubilee songs; one is "Keep inching along like a poor inch worm, Jesus will come by-and-by," the other is "Go chain the lion down before the Heaven doors close."

The reader will recall that I have already shown that the worm and the lion were connected with native African worship. Of course we all know quite well that a "Caddis worm" is not an "Inch worm," but for a man trying to turn from the old to the new, from idolatry to Christianity, a closer relation than this might not be very comfortable neutral ground.

The following Folk Rhymes found in our collection might also pass for connecting links: "Jawbone," "Outrunning the Devil," "How to Get to Glory Land," "The Ark," "Destinies of Good and Bad Children," "How to Keep or Kill the Devil," "Ration Day," and "When My Wife Dies." The superstitions of the Negro Rhymes are possibly only fossils left in one way or another by ancient native African worship.

In a few Rhymes the vice of stealing is either laughed at, or apparently laughed at. Such Rhymes carry on their face a strictly American slave origin. An example is found in "Christmas Turkey." If one asks how I know its origin to be American, the answer is that the native African had no such thing as Christmas and turkeys are indigenous to America. In explanation of the origin of these "stealing" Rhymes I would say that it was never the Negro slave's viewpoint that his hard-earned productions righteously belonged to another. His whole viewpoint in all such cases, where he sang in this kind of verse, is well summed up in the last two lines of this little Rhyme itself:

> "I tuck mysef to my tucky roos',
> An' I brung *my* tucky home."

To the Negro it was his turkey. This was the Negro slave view and accounts for the origin and evolution of such verse. We leave to others a fair discussion of the ethics and a righteous conclusion; only asking them in fairness to conduct the discussion in the light of slave conditions and slave surroundings.

In a few of the Folk Rhymes one stanza will be found to be longer than any of the others. Now as to the origin of this, in the case of those sung whose tunes I happen to know, the long stanza was used as a kind of chorus, while the other stanzas were used as song "verses." I therefore think this is probably true in all cases. The reader will note that the long stanza is written first in many cases. This is because the Negro habitually begins his song with the Chorus, which is just the opposite to the custom of the Caucasian who begins his ordinary songs with the verse. This appears then to be the possible genesis of stanzas of unequal length.

I have written this little treatise on the use, origin, and evolution of the Negro Rhyme with much hesitation. I finally decided to do it only because I thought a truthful statement of fact concerning Negro

Folk Rhymes might prove a help to those who are expert investigators in the field of literature and who are in search of the origin of all Folk literature and finally of all literature. The Negro being the last to come to the bright light of civilization has given or probably will give the last crop of Folk Rhymes. Human processes being largely the same, I hope that my little personal knowledge of the Negro Rhymes may help others in the other larger literary fields.

I am hoping that it may help and I am penning the last strokes to record my sincere desire that it may in no way hinder.

Bibliography

Note: references in headnotes to commercial phonograph recordings begin with the record company's original catalogue release number, and then cite the date of the release. Many of these vintage recordings are available on LP album or compact disc reissue, and tapes of others are available from a number of taping services and archives.

Abrahams, Roger D., ed. *Jump-Rope Rhymes: A Dictionary*. Austin: University of Texas Press, 1969.

Arnold, Byron. *Folksongs of Alabama*. University: University of Alabama Press, 1950.

Bastin, Bruce. *Red River Blues: The Blues Tradition in the Southeast*. Champaign-Urbana: University of Illinois Press, 1986.

Bayard, Samuel Preston. *Hill Country Tunes: Instrumental Folk Music of Southwestern Pennsylvania*. Philadelphia: American Folklore Society, 1944.

Botkin, B. A. *The American Play-Party Song*. Lincoln: University Studies of the University of Nebraska, 1937.

Brewer, J. Mason. *American Negro Folklore*. Chicago: Quadrangle Books, 1968.

The Frank C. Brown Collection of North Carolina Folklore. 6 vols. Ed. Henry M. Belden, Arthur Palmer Hudson, Jan Philip Schinhan. Durham, N.C.: Duke University Press, 1952–62.

Browne, Ray B. *The Alabama Folk Lyric*. Bowling Green, Ohio: Bowling Green State University Popular Press, 1979.

Burlin, Natalie Curtis. *Hampton Series, Negro Folk Songs*. 4 vols. New York: Schirmer, 1918–19.

Christy's Nigga Songster. N.p., 1855.

Cogswell, Robert G. "Jokes in Blackface: A Discographic Folklore Study." Ph.D. diss. Indiana University, 1984.

Cohen, John, and Mike Seeger, eds. *The New Lost City Ramblers Songbook*. New York: Oak Publications, 1964.

Cohen, Norm. *Long Steel Rail: The Railroad in American Folksong.* Champaign-Urbana: University of Illinois Press, 1981.

Courlander, Harold. *Negro Folk Music, U.S.A.* New York: Columbia University Press, 1963.

Cox, John Harrington. *Folk-Songs of the South.* 1925. Rpt., Hatboro, Pa: Folklore Associates, 1963.

Dunbar, Paul Lawrence. *Complete Poems.* New York: Dodd, Mead, 1980.

Emrich, Duncan, ed. *American Folk Poetry: An Anthology.* Boston: Little, Brown, 1974.

Epstein, Dena. *Sinful Tunes and Spirituals: Black Folk Music to the Civil War.* Champaign-Urbana: University of Illinois Press, 1977.

Ewen, David. *All the Years of American Popular Music.* Englewood Cliffs, N.J.: Prentice-Hall, 1977.

Ford, Ira W. *Traditional Music of America.* 1940. Rpt., Hatboro, Pa: Folklore Associates, 1965; and New York: Da Capo Press, 1978.

Godrich, John, and H. Dixon. *Blues and Gospel Records, 1902–1942.* London: Storyville Publications, 1969.

Green, Archie. *Only a Miner: Studies in Recorded Coal-Mining Songs.* Champaign-Urbana: University of Illinois Press, 1972.

Harris, Joel Chandler. *Uncle Remus and His Friends: Old Plantation Stories, Songs, and Ballads, with Sketches of Negro Character.* Boston: Houghton Mifflin, 1892.

Hughes, Langston, and Anna Bontemp. *The Book of Negro Folklore.* New York: Dodd, Mead, 1958.

Jabbour, Alan. Brochure notes, *North American Fiddle Tunes.* Washington: The Library of Congress, LP record, LCLP AFS 62.

Jones, Bessie, and Bess Lomax Hawes. *Step It Down: Games, Plays, Songs & Stories from the Afro-American Heritage.* 1972. Rpt., Athens: University of Georgia Press, 1987.

Jones, Loyal. *Radio's Kentucky Mountain Boy, Bradley Kincaid.* Berea, Ky.: Appalachian Center, 1980.

Kirkland, Edwin C. "A Check List of the Titles of Tennessee Folksongs." *Journal of American Folklore* (October–December 1946), 423–76.

Lomax, Alan. *The Folk Songs of North America.* Garden City, N.Y.: Doubleday, 1960.

Lomax, John, and Alan Lomax. *American Ballads and Folk Songs.* New York: Macmillan, 1934.

———. *Folk Song U.S.A.* New York: Duell, Sloan and Pierce, 1947.

Miles, Emma Bell. *The Spirit of the Mountains.* 1905. Rpt., Knoxville: University of Tennessee Press, 1975.

Nathan, Hans. *Dan Emmett and the Rise of Early Negro Minstrelsy.* Norman, Okla.: University of Oklahoma Press, 1962.

Negro Forget-Me-Not Songster. 2 vols. N.p., 1847.

Negro Minstrel. Glasgow: n.p., 1850.

Negro Singer's Own Book, Containing Every Negro Song That Has Ever Been Sung or Printed. Philadelphia: Turner and Fisher, 1846.

Newell, William Wells. *Games and Songs of American Children.* New York: Harper and Brothers, 1883.

Odum, Howard W. "Folk-Song and Folk Poetry as Found in the Secular Songs of the Southern Negroes." *Journal of American Folklore* 24 (1911), 255–94 and 351–96.

Odum, Howard W., and Guy B. Johnson. *The Negro and His Songs.* 1925. Rpt., Hatboro: Folklore Associates, 1964.

————. *Negro Workaday Songs.* Chapel Hill: University of North Carolina Press, 1926.

Oliver, Paul. *The Meaning of the Blues.* 1960. Rpt., New York: Collier Books, 1963.

————. *Screening the Blues: Aspects of the Blues Tradition.* London: Cassell, 1968.

————. *Songsters and Saints: Vocal Traditions on Race Records.* London: Cambridge University Press, 1984.

Parsons, Elsie Crews. *Folk-Lore of the Sea Islands, South Carolina.* New York: G. E. Stechert, 1923.

Perrow, E. C. "Songs and Rhymes from the South." *Journal of American Folklore,* 25 (1912), 137–55; 26 (1913), 123–73; 28 (1915), 129–190.

Popular National Songster. Philadelphia: n.p., 1848.

Randolph, Vance. *Ozark Folksongs.* 4 vols. Columbia: State Historical Society of Missouri, 1946–50.

————. *Ozark Folksongs.* Edited and Abridged by Norm Cohen. Champaign-Urbana: University of Illinois Press, 1982.

Richardson, Ethel Park. *American Mountain Songs.* New York: Greenburg, 1927.

Russell, Irwin. *Christmas-Night in the Quarters and Other Poems.* New York: The Century Company, 1917.

Scarborough, Dorothy. *On the Trail of Negro Folk-Songs.* Cambridge: Harvard University Press, 1925.

Seeger, Ruth Crawford. *American Folk Songs for Children.* Garden City, N.Y.: Doubleday, 1948.

Sharp, Cecil J. *Nursery Songs from the Appalachian Mountains.* 2 vols. London: Novello, 1921–23.

Talley, Thomas. "Leading Themes Used in Singing Negro Folk Rhymes." Manuscript, ca. 1921. Talley papers, Fisk University.

————. "Negro Traditions." Manuscript, ca. 1923. Talley papers of Thomasina Greene, Jefferson City, Missouri.

————. "The Origin of Negro Traditions." *Phylon* (4th quarter, 1942), 371–77, and (1st quarter, 1943), 30–38.

Thede, Marion. *The Fiddle Book*. New York: Oak Publications, 1967.

White. *Serenader's Song Book*. N.p., 1851.

White, Newman Ivey. *American Negro Folk-Songs*. 1928. Rpt., Hatboro: Folklore Associates, 1965.

Wiggins, Gene. *Fiddlin' Georgia Crazy: Fiddlin' John Carson, His Real World and the World of His Songs*. Champaign-Urbana: University of Illinois Press, 1987.

Wilgus, D. K. *Anglo-American Folksong Scholarship Since 1898*. Brunswick, N.J.: Rutgers University Press, 1959.

Work, John, II. *Folk Songs of the American Negro*. Nashville: Fisk University Press, 1915.

Work, John, III. *American Negro Songs and Spirituals*. New York: Crown Publishers, 1940.

Talley's Original Comparative Study Index

First-Line Index

Title Index

Index to Essays

Negro Folk Rhymes was designed by Dariel Mayer, composed by Lithocraft, Inc., and printed and bound by BookCrafters, Inc. The book is set in Baskerville and printed on 50-lb Glatfelter Natural, B-16.